MIST, a sorceress from beyond the sea, drawn to the walled city of Drinn by the smell of magic gone sour.

JAREN, a mercenary, mountain-bred and battle-trained, believing he is a match for anything in the backwater town of Drinn. He is wrong.

ARELNATH, soldier and sorceress, hiding her sex beneath chain mail and leather, for in Drinn the women walk veiled, little better than slaves.

SHANDY, a street urchin, living in the back alleys of Drinn, carefully avoiding the Eyes of the Temple. His luck is running out.

RANIRA, a bond servant, watching her parents burn in the town square, sentenced to cruel death on mere *suspicion* of sorcery. She will not, cannot, admit that she is the daughter of witches.

Also by Patricia C. Wrede from Orbit:

SHADOW MAGIC
CAUGHT IN CRYSTAL

PATRICIA C. WREDE

Daughter of Witches

ORBIT

An Orbit Book

ISBN 0 7088 4784 6

Reproduced, printed and bound in Great Britain by
BPCC Hazell Books
Aylesbury, Bucks, England
Member of BPCC Ltd.

Orbit Books
A Division of
Macdonald & Co (Publishers) Ltd
Orbit House
1 New Fetter Lane
London EC4A 1AR

A member of Maxwell Macmillan Pergamon Publishing Corporation

DAUGHTER OF WITCHES

Donna
Fraser's
x x

CHAPTER ONE

The sun was already high in the sky as Ranira hurried across the bridge toward the Temple of Chaldon, cursing the innkeeper Lykken to whom she was bonded. How like him to send her on a long errand just before her half-holiday! Bond servants were only entitled to half a day of free time every three weeks; she would be lucky to have an hour to herself by the time she finished at the Temple.

Muttering behind the veil that covered her face from the eyes down, Ranira wove expertly through the narrow, crowded streets of Drinn. Why did the fat fool have to wait until the day before Festival to make this week's offering? It was going to take her twice as long as usual. And all because Lykken couldn't bear to part with a copper until he was forced into it.

At last she reached the heavy, wrought-iron gates of the Temple courtyard. Eyes lowered, she waited her turn to step up to the two armored Watchmen at the gate. Then she bowed her head and said ritually, "I come to the great Temple to give thanks and offerings from the Inn of Nine Doors and to receive humbly the words of the god."

"Enter-for-what-the-god-gives," a guard responded in a bored monotone. Ranira bowed again and passed through the gate. Inside the courtyard it was less crowded, and the girl quickened her step. She hated the gloom of the Temple, and spent as little time there as she could without arousing suspicion. Still, some attendance in addition to the mandatory rituals was a good idea; she had no wish to be accused of heresy or witchcraft.

Her first stop was the offering booth, halfway around the courtyard. The line was long; Lykken was not the only shopkeeper in Drinn who paid the required offerings at the last possible moment. After twenty minutes of standing, her legs began to ache, and she tried to shift her weight unobtrusively from one foot to the other to ease her muscles. The only noticeable result was a disapproving stare from one of the Templemen. When she realized that she had been seen, she abandoned her efforts to make herself more comfortable and concentrated on an appropriately pious demeanor instead. The guard turned in another direction, and Ranira breathed an inward sigh of relief.

After another half hour of waiting, she reached the dour-faced priest who had charge of the large iron coinbox and the black ledger in which the offering was recorded. Ranira handed him the little bag of copper and silver pieces that represented one out of every five earned by the Inn of Nine Doors. The priest raised an eyebrow when he saw the iron bracelets that marked Ranira as a bondwoman, but he made no comment as he noted the offering and made out a receipt. When he handed the paper to her, she bowed with careful respect.

As she turned away from the offering booth, Ranira sighed. Half the business was done, but nearly an hour and a half of her precious afternoon was gone as well. She turned toward the booth where the business of the Midwinter Festival was being conducted, and shuddered. The line there was twice the length of the one she had just gone through. Muttering curses once more, she made her way across the courtyard to the end of the line.

At least this part of her errand would be as unwelcome to Lykken as giving up one of his precious silver pieces, she thought. The Temple required all merchants and innkeepers in the city to provide a certain amount of free food and housing for the pilgrims to the Midwinter Festival. Theoretically, this was to furnish a place for the poorer folk from outside the city, but, in truth, most of the free goods went to friends of Temple personnel. She hoped vindictively that Lykken's list of required services would be a long one.

It was another hour and a half before Ranira finally finished her business with the priests. With a sigh of relief, she turned toward the gates once more. If she hurried, she could reach the inn in time to deliver the list and still get a little of her time off. Once she was free to do as she pleased, Ranira vowed silently, she wouldn't go back until midnight, even if it meant a beating. It would serve Lykken right if he had to clean the kitchen himself!

As she walked toward the gate, she noticed one of the priests staring in her direction. He was older than most of the others, and the greying of his black hair around his temples lent an air of intensity to the angular planes of his face. Ranira shivered and ducked her head quickly, hoping she had not accidentally broken one of the many Temple rules. No guard accosted her, however, and she reached the street without incident.

The crowded streets were difficult to negotiate with any speed. The pilgrims, come to Drinn for the Midwinter Festival of Chaldon, were depressingly alike in their black and brown robes. Occasionally Ranira saw the bright flash of a Trader's cloak among the drab gowns, but such glimpses were few. No one from outside the Empire of Chaldreth was allowed inside Drinn during the seven days of the Midwinter Festival, and most of the visitors had already left the city. The few foreigners that remained would be gone by evening.

The main bridge across the river Annylith was even more crowded than the streets, though it was more than three times as wide. Ranira frowned. For a moment she was tempted to try one of the smaller bridges, but walking down to another bridge would take almost as much time as waiting at this one. Resignedly, she joined the crowd inching its way across the river.

By the time she reached the inn, it was late afternoon. She found Lykken in the large room that served as meeting place and dining hall for the inn's patrons. She stood waiting until he noticed her and came puffing over.

"And where have you been so long?" he demanded as

soon as he was within earshot. "With Festival tomorrow there's work to be done! Let's see the receipt; you'd rob me to ruin if you could."

Silently, Ranira handed him the first of the papers she had collected at the Temple. Lykken stared at it, screwing up his face as if to express the mental effort involved in extracting meaning from the small black marks on the page. At last he nodded reluctantly over the receipt, and without waiting to be asked, Ranira handed him the second list.

"Ah, they will ruin me!" he said after another minute's concentration. "Three rooms and food and drink for ten people. It is not possible!" Ranira grinned maliciously to herself, carefully keeping her eyes lowered so that Lykken would not guess the satisfaction she hid behind her veil. The Temple requirements would not ruin the fat innkeeper by any means, but they would put a substantial dent in one of the man's dearest possessions—his pocketbook.

"Well, don't just stand there," Lykken said, looking up. "Get to work! I didn't buy you to loaf, and you still have two years before your bond is paid. Don't start acting as though it's canceled already."

"It is the day of my half-holiday," Ranira reminded him.

Lykken paused. "Yes, and it was not well done of you to take it before returning the receipts to me," he said after a moment. "Someone might have stolen them! Still, I am generous; I will not report it this time."

"I have had no holiday, as you may guess," Ranira said, trying hard to keep her temper in check. "I am asking now only for what is my right."

The innkeeper's eyes narrowed. "All this time on one small errand?" he asked in mock disbelief. "No, you must be mistaken! Now, go on with your work! You have wasted enough time."

"My half-holiday is today," she repeated stubbornly.

"I am owner of this inn, not you! A lazy bondwoman has no right to a holiday if her work time is not properly employed. Be off; there are fires to lay before the guests return for the night!"

"I work harder than you do, you fat idiot!" Ranira shouted. "You sent me to the Temple on purpose, to cheat me of my time. Well, I won't be cheated! You have no right!''

The innkeeper's face turned purple. "I am your bond-holder, and I have the rights I choose!" he shouted. "You will learn your place, girl!''

Ranira did not quite manage to duck the heavy hand that swung with surprising speed in her direction, and she was knocked backward into one of the tables. Thrown off balance by the collision, she was unable to avoid the second blow, and she fell to the floor. Winded and dazed, she was hard put to protect her head from the continued pounding.

A cool voice broke through the haze of pain that surrounded her. "Innkeeper Lykken? If we may interrupt?''

As suddenly as it had begun, the beating stopped. After a moment, Ranira shook her head experimentally. Nothing rattled, so she looked up.

A tall, blond man dressed entirely in green leather stood near the entrance of the room. Beside him was a woman with black hair and grey eyes, wrapped in a fine wool cape of pale blue-grey. The short veil she wore identified her as one of the rare female visitors from outside the Empire of Chaldreth. Her presence was surprising; foreigners rarely patronized the Inn of Nine Doors.

Lykken was hurrying toward them, all interest in Ranira gone. "Gracious sir, gentle madam, what service may I give you?''

To Ranira's surprise, it was the woman who answered. "One of my escort has fallen ill. I wish to rent a room where he can rest for a few hours before we must leave the city.''

"So close to the Midwinter Festival there are few rooms," Lykken lied. "But perhaps we can find something that will be suitable." He turned and scowled at his bond servant. "Get up, girl! The gentlefolk will have the red room, at the rear, where it is quiet.''

Ranira climbed to her feet and began hastily straightening her veil. As she did so, she saw a strange look pass between the two foreigners. "I think something upstairs would be better," the man said. "The corner room, perhaps, where the windows can catch the breeze.''

"There are but three of you?" Lykken said, allowing a

note of doubt to creep into his voice. "The room is large for so few, and with the Festival pilgrims already crowding the city . . ."

The blond man shrugged. "Our gold is as yellow as any other, and we only plan to be here for an hour or two. Still, a little extra might be appropriate for your trouble." He named a sum nearly twice the worth of the room for a whole night.

Lykken nodded numbly, and motioned to the two to follow him. The woman stepped forward, while her companion disappeared through the open doorway, returning with a slender youth who moaned in spite of the slow, careful pace the blond man set. Ranira watched in fascination as they climbed the steps behind Lykken. Before she could decide whether to follow the fascinating foreigners or to disappear while she had the chance, Lykken's head reappeared at the top of the stairs. "Water and clean cloths for the gentlefolk. And bring a firebox as well," he hissed. "And don't be slow about it!"

Ranira turned slowly toward the kitchen. There was no chance of getting any part of her holiday now, but she found herself more interested in the strangers than in brooding. Ever since her childhood, Ranira had been fascinated by tales of the world outside the Empire of Chaldreth, but the chances offered to a bond servant to indulge such unprofitable and doctrinally suspect interests were few. She would enjoy serving the foreigners for the few hours they remained in Drinn, and if they proved generous enough to put Lykken in a good mood, she might even get back a little free time during the Festival.

Unreasonably cheered by these reflections, Ranira grabbed a water bucket from its place beside the door and stepped out into the alley behind the inn. The first of the big water jars was nearly empty, and she frowned as she replaced the heavy lid. Though there were five jars standing against the back wall of the inn, Lykken paid the water carters to fill only three regularly. If the first was empty already, the inn might well run short of water before the carters made their next rounds in the morning. With a shrug, Ranira dismissed the problem; if Lykken wanted to save coppers by shorting the water supply, he, not she, would have to deal with the angry patrons.

Picking up the bucket, she stepped toward the second jar and reached for the lid, wincing as she stretched recently beatened muscles. Just as she lifted the cover, she heard a whisper behind her.

"Psst! Renra!"

Ranira whirled and almost dropped the lid. "Shandy! Don't sneak up on me like that. If I break one of these lids, Lykken will have the cost added to my bond, and two more years is enough to be stuck here."

A small, dirty figure materialized out of an impossibly tiny space between two walls. "Ah, Renra, I just wanted to be sure he wasn't around. Get anything good on your free day?"

"I didn't have one," Ranira said with renewed bitterness as she reached for her water bucket. "Lykken sent me to the Temple with the week's offering just before noon, and with the Festival crowd and everything, I didn't get back until a little while ago."

"He musta been in a real mood," Shandy said, eyeing Ranira critically. "Another day or two, and you should have some real good bruises."

"I wouldn't call them good," Ranira snapped. "And I haven't got time to stand talking today; there are some foreigners that Lykken wants to settle in, and he'll come looking for me if I'm not back soon."

The urchin's eyes widened. "Outsiders? But Festival starts tomorrow."

"One got sick, and they wanted him to rest for a while. Lykken is going to take every copper he can wring out of them before they leave, too."

Shandy still looked worried. "But, Renra, if they don't leave and the Temple finds out, you know what will happen. You could get in real trouble!"

Ranira pressed her lips together tightly for a moment before she replied. "I know. But that's Lykken's problem, not mine. I'm only his bondwoman."

"Yeah, but your parents got burned for witchcraft," Shandy reminded her unnecessarily. "The Templemen are always meaner to people with witches around.''

"My parents weren't witches!" Ranira said angrily. "And neither am I. The Templemen had no proof, only suspicion. You don't have to remind me what they can do. Chaldon's curse on the lot of them!''

"Renra!" Shandy looked around in horror, as if he expected a Watchman or an Eye of Chaldon to materialize and arrest her at once. "You can't curse the Temple!''

Ranira laughed bitterly. "No, because it is cursed already.'' She saw that Sandy was getting more upset, and she forced a smile. "Don't worry. I don't say such things to anyone except you.''

"When you get mad you would," Shandy insisted. "You be careful, Renra.''

The boy's solemn advice was too much for Ranira; she broke out laughing, and the lingering traces of her black mood vanished. "I can take care of myself, Shandy. You just make sure that none of the Watchmen catch you sneaking food out of the farmers' stalls, or you'll be the one in trouble.''

"Ah, them!" Shandy said scornfully. "They're too fat to catch me!''

"Well, I don't think I'll be able to bring you anything from the kitchen today,'' she said, lifting the brimming bucket onto her hip. "When Lykken has special guests, he watches everything so closely that a fly couldn't sneak off with anything. You'll have to steal your own dinner today.'' Shandy nodded, and as Ranira reached for the door, the urchin vanished again into his own mysterious byways.

CHAPTER TWO

Lykken was already in the kitchen, shouting orders at the cook, when Ranira entered. The innkeeper paused for a moment in his tirade and jerked a thumb at her. "Upstairs! And don't forget the cloths! And be sure the fire is well lit before you return!"

Ranira nodded and proceeded through the kitchen as rapidly as she could without spilling water from the bucket she carried. Near the far door she stopped and lowered her burden to the floor. Reaching up, she grasped one of the large pitchers that hung beside the door. She was just about to fill it when Lykken came hurrying over.

"No, no, not that one! It's cracked; see, there! Find a good one, you lazy slattern, or you'll get the beating you deserve!"

Once more Ranira fought down anger. There were no good pitchers; Lykken refused to purchase new ones so long as those he had could hold water. Silently, she replaced the offending crockery and after a short search found one which was cracked near the handle, where it was less obvious. The innkeeper gave a cursory nod of approval when Ranira offered him the jug to inspect, and then turned back to the cook.

She filled the pitcher as quickly as she could and left the kitchen with a sigh of relief. Once out of sight, Lykken might well forget about her for a while, and as long as she had some plausible excuse when he found her again, the innkeeper was unlikely to give her another beating. She climbed the stairs and paused in the short hallway above. A narrow chest at one

9

side contained the cloths she needed. Ranira set the pitcher on the floor and knelt to open the chest.

As she started to lift the lid, she heard the muffled sound of voices coming from the far side of the wall. For a moment she hesitated; then she thought she heard the sound of her own name. Leaning forward, she strained to catch the words more clearly.

". . . help everyone, Mist," a man's voice was saying. "Besides, if you try that in Drinn you will be arrested for witchcraft, foreigner or no."

"I know, Jaren, but that poor child will have bruises for a week!" a female voice responded. "She is lucky not to have any bones broken, and by the look of things, it isn't the first time, either. Why, the innkeeper boasts of it!"

"But is it worth the risk to try to help her now? Just being here is dangerous enough as it is."

"I know, and I do not wish to add to your burden," the woman replied. "But I think there may be some talent in her that would be criminal to waste."

"You'd see genius in every mistreated puppy if you let yourself, Mist," the man said. "I don't like seeing a child in this situation either, but it is the custom here, and if we interfere now, what will we accomplish besides alienating the innkeeper?"

"There ought to be something we can do!"

"Not without giving ourselves away entirely," a third voice broke in. "And even if we managed to get her away somehow, it is much too late to find another place like this. A room close to the gates, on the second floor where we can remain unseen, is too good a piece of luck to throw away. Not to mention the risk of attracting the attention of the Temple of Chaldon."

"Arelnath's right," the man's voice said. "If the Temple of Chaldon were to get wind of a healing, or even the disappearance of a drudge, they would be scouring the city for us in no time. You haven't been in Drinn before; I have."

"Enough, my friends," the woman's voice said. "I do not like it, but I can accept the necessity for now. We will talk of this again later. As to the innkeeper . . . ." Her voice faded into a blurred murmuring as she moved farther from the wall where Ranira crouched.

Judging that she was unlikely to overhear more, Ranira lifted a pile of cloths from the chest and slowly lowered the lid. She was intrigued by the implications of the conversation. Evidently, the strangers intended to remain in Drinn throughout the Midwinter Festival. Interesting. None of them sounded ill, either. Ranira sat back on her heels. What could they possibly want at the Inn of Nine Doors?

Well, at least they seemed to mean Ranira no harm, though she knew better than to expect more than kind words from any of them. They might be shocked at the way Lykken treated her, but their concern meant no more than the horrified comments of the noblewomen of Drinn when they happened to pass through one of the poorer sections of the city.

Ranira rose to her feet and picked up the cloths and the water pitcher. A few steps brought her to the door of the corner room. She knocked firmly. The blond man opened it a moment later. "Yes?"

"Water and cloths, as the gentlefolk requested," Ranira said. The man made no move, so she added, "I am also to light the fire."

"Let her in, Jaren," said a gentle voice from the interior of the room. The blond man stepped back, somewhat reluctantly, and Ranira moved inside. She glanced around quickly. Jaren stood by the door, watching her attentively. The boy was just a head and mound of blankets on the bed. Beside him sat the grey-eyed woman with black hair. "Go quietly, please," she said softly as Ranira's eyes reached her. "He sleeps."

The woman's gaze was full of sympathy. Ranira's stomach knotted in a familiar blend of resentment and scorn. She fought down her irritation, and with an effort nodded politely as she stepped to the side of the bed.

For a moment she busied herself arranging the cloths and pitcher, deliberately avoiding the other woman's eyes by studying the supposed invalid. The youth was certainly a good actor, she thought; if she had not overheard that revealing conversation she would have assumed him to be deep in sleep. His head was turned away from her, showing only a shock of sandy brown hair and a smooth line of neck and cheek. The boy moaned and shifted, and Ranira started slightly. Looking up, she found Jaren's eyes on her, intent and wary.

Now, why is he so worried? Ranira puzzled as she dropped her gaze to the cloths. The boy's act was certainly convincing enough. She glanced at the bed again with critical appraisal. There was something else, something besides the feigned sickness. Ranira couldn't be quite sure what, but she was suddenly certain of it.

Then the boy shifted again, and Ranira froze in shock. The—person—on the bed was a woman! Unveiled and posing as a man, she risked the fire, or worse, in Drinn. No wonder the blond man was wary.

Ranira forced her gaze downward. She picked up the firebox and moved over to the hearth. For a few minutes she concentrated on rearranging the firewood to make a place for the tinder, giving the tumult of her emotions time to subside. When she was sure her voice would remain steady, she said, "Is there anything else the gentlefolk will require? Something for the sick boy, perhaps?"

"No, not now," the black-haired woman said from the bedside. "Possibly later."

Ranira nodded and bent to strike sparks from the flints. "It is well that this is a corner room," she said impulsively. "The closet will keep the conversation in the next room from disturbing your friend, and on the other side is only the stairway and the hall. During the Festival, sometimes a few of our patrons celebrate over much and you can hear them shouting all over the inn, the walls are so thin. But you will be gone by then, of course. Still, if you find the noise disturbing while you are here, you have only to mention it. I am sure Innkeeper Lykken can arrange things to suit you."

A startled silence followed. Ranira smiled behind her veil. Let them wonder whether she had overheard or not! She leaned forward and fanned the fire with her hands. Slowly the wood caught. When she was certain the fire would not go out accidentally, Ranira turned back toward the center of the room.

Jaren was still watching her, a slight smile on his face. Ranira sketched a bow toward him and repeated her question. "Is there anything else I can do?"

"Not now," Jaren said. "But we will think over your suggestions—carefully."

Ranira bowed again and slipped from the room, her head whirling. As she descended the stairs, she found herself trying to puzzle out what could have brought the strangers to Drinn, and why they intended to stay through the Midwinter Festival. It occurred to her that her oblique warning might not have been such a good idea as it had seemed at the time. Thoughtfully, she headed away from the kitchen, keeping a sharp watch for Lykken as she went.

Lykken was in an excellent mood when Ranira finally decided to return to the kitchen. The dining hall was crowded, and as the Festival did not officially begin until the next morning, the patrons were all paying customers. Nothing improved Lykken's disposition like a large profit. The innkeeper didn't even notice when Ranira slipped in, and by the time he looked in her direction she was busily scrubbing an enormous iron kettle, trying to look as if she had been occupied with that task for some time.

For several hours, Ranira was too busy to pay much attention to the innkeeper except when his voice shouted some new job for her to attend to. She was too grateful for being spared the task of serving the raucous crowd outside to object to the pace of the work in the kitchen. She hated waiting on drunken patrons, most of whom were all-too-eager to snatch at her veil or try to unfasten the ties of her tunic. So far, Lykken had prevented anything more than these small humiliations, but Ranira was under no illusion as to his motives: A virgin's bond was worth more than that of a woman who had been "used."

As the hours passed into evening, Lykken's temper began to worsen. Ranira watched in private amusement. The innkeeper's frequent glances toward the stairs made it clear what was on his mind. The gates of Drinn would soon be closed for the night, and his unexpected guests must be gone by then. The strangers did not appear, however, and time continued to slip by. Ranira knew Lykken was trying to decide whether he should risk his fat fee by disturbing them, or whether he should wait a few minutes longer.

The innkeeper had been driven nearly to distraction by the time Jaren finally sauntered into the kitchen and motioned to him. Marveling at the exactness of Jaren's timing, Ranira set down the tray she was holding and slipped behind a rack of pots near where the man stood. She was just in time; Lykken came hurrying up at once.

"Ah, sir, it grieves me that you and your friends must leave so soon!" the innkeeper said in obvious relief. "I trust the boy has recovered?"

"It says much for you that you are touched by the affairs of your guests," Jaren replied. "Few others would be so concerned about the welfare of a stranger, I think." Lykken looked at him suspiciously, but the blond man only smiled. Lykken nodded, and Jaren's expression sobered quickly. "The news is bad, I fear. The boy's constitution . . ."

Jaren's voice sank, and he stepped closer to the innkeeper. Ranira could catch only a few phrases here and there, but from Lykken's expression and the brief conversation she had overheard earlier, she could guess what Jaren was saying. The strangers were not leaving Drinn that evening, and once the Festival began it would be impossible for them to slip out of the city unnoticed, for no traffic passed out of the great wooden doors until the Festival was over.

Jaren finished, and Lykken began expostulating frantically. Jaren responded, at first firmly, then soothingly. Eventually he drew a large purse from inside his tunic. Lykken's agitation subsided almost immediately, but he did not give in at once. He seemed to feel obliged to make certain first that he was not the victim of some elaborate hoax, for a moment later the two men left the room and turned right, heading for the stairs.

Neither of the two appeared to notice Ranira crouching behind the rack of pots, though they passed within a foot of her. For a moment more, she stayed motionless; then she rose and walked briskly across the kitchen, picked up one of the tattered brooms leaning against the wall, and followed Jaren and the innkeeper out into the hallway. The men were not in sight, but she could hear the echoes of their footsteps coming from the stairs. She went to one end of the hallway and slowly began to sweep. She did not quite dare to follow them upstairs, but it hardly mattered. From where she stood, she was certain to see anyone descending.

By the time Lykken reappeared, Ranira had swept the hallway twice, even at her deliberate snail's pace. The innkeeper had a strange expression on his face—one of mingled fear and greed. His hand kept straying to a large bulge just above his sash that made a muffled clinking sound as he came down the stairs. When he saw Ranira, his expression changed to his habitual scowl.

"What are you doing?" he snapped.

"Sweeping the hall," she replied, a bit too innocently. "I am nearly done."

Lykken's frown deepened; his hand strayed to his sash once more. Abruptly, he spoke again. "Our special visitors in the corner room will be leaving very soon," he said, and paused.

"Of course," she said. "If they were to stay much longer they would not be able to reach the gates before they are locked and barred."

The innkeeper shifted uncomfortably. "Yes, of course. But there is a problem. The boy, the sick boy, must be moved in absolute quiet. So, no one will be allowed in the hall until they have gone. No one!"

"Yes, sir," she said. "But if no one is to stay in the hall, how shall we know when they have gone?"

"I will tell you!" Lykken roared. "Now, be gone; they may be coming down at any moment. Go!"

Ranira nodded and picked up her broom, thoroughly pleased with herself. She had been wondering how the innkeeper intended to arrange for the strangers' "departure." She had all the information she needed now. The only question that remained was how best to use it.

CHAPTER THREE

Ranira was up before dawn next morning. The air was cool. She shivered as she coaxed the embers of last night's fire into flames. When the wood at last began to burn, she warmed herself for a moment, then began laying out utensils for the cook. The bruises on her shoulders and arms were painfully tender, and she winced whenever she bumped them.

The cook arrived just after dawn, grumbling about the hours Lykken set. He nodded at Ranira, then grunted his approval of her work so far. He inspected the menu Lykken had left, then sent Ranira to draw water while he began preparing the first meal of the day.

The water carters had not yet made their delivery, so Ranira ignored the first two jars and went directly to the third to fill the two buckets she was carrying. When she lifted the lid, she found the jar barely a quarter full—the kitchen had used a great deal of water cleaning up after the crowd at last night's meal. She unhooked the dipper from its place inside the rim of the jar and lowered it carefully into the water.

As she finished filling the second bucket, she heard a soft scraping noise from the side of the alley. She hung the dipper back on its hook and replaced the lid of the jar, then went down the alley to look for the source of the noise.

The alley appeared deserted. She turned back toward the buckets and stopped. A thin, bare leg protruded slightly from behind the last of the empty water jars, invisible from any position closer to the mouth of the alley. Ranira smiled and moved closer.

Peering around the jar, her suspicions were confirmed. Shandy lay sprawled loosely behind the jar, fast asleep and snoring. Ranira's smile grew as she reached down and poked him. "Shandy! Wake up!"

"Huh? Renra! Where'd you come from? I thought you had to work," the boy said hazily.

"That was last night," she replied. "It's after dawn now. You'd better move. The water carts will be here soon, and you don't want them to find you."

"Wouldn't matter if they did," Shandy said as he got to his feet. "They can't catch me."

"Maybe not, but they can report you to the Temple as a stray or a runaway, and you know what would happen then. The Watchmen would be after you, and if they knew how to look for you, you would have a hard time keeping away from them. And once they caught you, they'd sell you as a bond servant—which is no fun, believe me."

"Ah, don't worry, Renra. I got lots of good hiding places!"

"Where? Halfway behind a water jar? The Watchmen won't miss you there, not during Festival. You know they're always more careful then."

"I'm not dumb!" Shandy said indignantly. "There's lots of places the Templemen don't look, and I know all of 'em. I didn't get caught last Festival, did I?"

"No, but I can't think why not," she retorted.

Shandy grinned engagingly. " 'Cause I'm smart, and I'm fast, and the Templemen are old and fat," he said.

Ranira gave up. True, the boy seemed to have an uncanny ability to avoid discovery by the Templemen. Unfortunately, Ranira thought, it was also true that the Temple would catch him eventually, especially if he continued to take chances. But try to convince Shandy of that!

"Think Lykken'll give you any time off for Firstday?" Shandy asked, breaking into her train of thought.

"Yes," she said with a malicious smile that was hidden by her veil. "Only he doesn't know it yet."

"What do you mean?" Shandy asked suspiciously.

"Oh, I think I can persuade him to give me back some of my half-holiday time," Ranira said with belated caution.

"You meant more than that," Shandy insisted. He sucked on his lower lip for a moment. "Renra, it doesn't have anything to do with those foreigners, does it?"

"Of course not," she replied automatically. She went on with forced casualness, "Except that they gave Lykken a fat purse before they left last night, which means he'll be in a good mood this morning."

"I didn't see 'em leave," Shandy said. "And I was watching 'most all night."

"The way you were watching for me to come out this morning?" she scoffed. "Just don't go telling the Temple we had foreigners at the Inn of Nine Doors," Ranira added sternly.

"Ah, Renra, I wouldn't do that!" Shandy said indignantly. Ranira laughed. "What're you going to do with your holiday?"

"I don't know," she said, relieved by the change of subject, "but I intend to enjoy every minute!"

"Too bad you can't get free tomorrow. You could watch the parade with me."

"You aren't going to stand out in the open with all the pilgrims, are you?" she asked, horrified. "Shandy, you'll get caught for sure!"

"I told you I'm not dumb. But you can see everything from under the bridge. The parade goes right over it. The Watchmen never check there; they're too lazy. I like watching, and it's always been safe before."

Interpreting this to mean that no one had looked under the bridge during last year's Festival Parade, Ranira shook her head. "You be careful, Shandy."

"Ah, Renra, you worry too much."

"Someone has to! I have to go. I won't get any free time at all if Lykken catches me out here with you. I'll see you later, Shandy."

"Tomorrow," the boy promised. With a brief backward wave, he disappeared into a small space between two buildings. Ranira smiled and went back to pick up her buckets.

● ● ●

Shandy's speculations worried Ranira more than she cared to admit. She blamed herself for letting him know about the occupants of the corner room at all, though at the time she had not suspected they would try to remain in Drinn during the Festival. She did not expect Shandy to deliberately do anything that would cause trouble for her, but if he let something slip accidentally and a rumor reached the Temple of Chaldon . . .

Ranira did not waste much time on this uncomfortable line of thought. She was too busy, for one thing. The inn was jammed. Lykken was, as usual, trying to make up for the free room and board the Temple required by cramming as many pilgrims as possible into the other rooms. Ranira was so occupied that she nearly missed seeing Lykken slip out of the kitchen with a tray of food intended, she assumed, for the occupants of the corner room.

As soon as she, too, could slip away from the kitchen, Ranira seized a broom and a firebox and went out into the main hallway. Her timing was good; she had to wait only a few minutes before she heard Lykken's heavy tread on the stairs. She immediately started for the second floor, so that she met the innkeeper halfway up the stairs. Before Lykken had a chance to say anything, Ranira burst into speech. "I'm sorry, I really am. I meant to take care of it last night, but it was so busy in the kitchen! I'm on my way now. I'll have it clean and ready right away."

"What are you babbling about, girl? Have what clean?" asked the bewildered man.

"The corner room, where the foreigners were," she said. "I meant to take care of it last night, after they went, but they slipped away so quietly."

Lykken blanched. Plainly, it had not occurred to him that he would have to keep the staff of the inn from doing the customary cleaning and laying of the fire for the next patron.

"Ah, perhaps you had best leave that for later," he said after a pause. "I can have Hindreth see to it, or Drena."

"But it's my job to clean the rooms," she insisted. She allowed a sullen note to creep into her voice. "You refused me my half-holiday yesterday because you said my time wasn't 'properly-employed.' I'm not giving you a chance to do that again!''

The innkeeper's face cleared as he saw the way out of his dilemma. "Yes, well, I may have been a little hasty. Things are rather busy the day before Festival, but now Festival is here! Why don't you take your holiday today, and enjoy Firstday to the full? Yes, an excellent idea!''

"Oh, thank you!'' Ranira said, trying to pump as much gratitude as she could into the words. "Shall I take care of the corner room first?''

"No, no,'' said Lykken expansively. "I'll have Hindreth clean it later. You go and enjoy Firstday.'' He beamed down at her, obviously pleased at being able to solve his problem and appear magnanimous at the same time.

Ranira lowered her eyes to hide the contempt she felt, and bowed briefly before she turned to go back down the stairs. "By the time I get back, he will have convinced himself that he let me go out of nothing but kindness,'' she thought cynically as she hurried toward the kitchen to replace the broom and firebox. Not that it could make any difference; the innkeeper could not reclaim her holiday once she had taken it. Feeling happier than she had in weeks, Ranira washed the dirt from her hands and went out into the street.

Firstday was always the best part of Midwinter Festival, Ranira thought as she wandered through the streets. The six-day rituals at the Temple of Chaldon, which began with the Festival Parade, did not start until the second day of Midwinter Festival. Everyone in the city was obliged to attend the rituals, but on Firstday there was nothing for the pilgrims to do but wander through Drinn and enjoy themselves. The inhabitants of Drinn were only too happy to take the coppers of their eager brethren from other parts of the Empire of Chaldreth, and the city streets were full of small booths selling everything imaginable.

Ranira spent several hours walking slowly past the vendors in the main square just outside the Temple. Though she had no money to spend, she enjoyed pretending she really was looking for a new tunic or a piece of jewelry, and it was pleasant to watch the merchants haggling with more serious buyers. Besides, the booths were the only spots of color in a city of grey stone and brown-robed pilgrims.

A small stand selling veils and the twisted silk cords that held them in place caught Ranira's eye. She edged toward it. It took her a moment to reach her goal, for the veil-maker's booth was wedged in behind a man selling fruits and jam. The shelves, loaded with berry bags and jam pots, nearly hid the little stand Ranira was aiming for.

The proprietor was a wizened little man who gave Ranira a long, appraising look and then ignored her, allowing her to rummage through the bright veils as she wished. His selection was surprisingly large—coarse linen squares mingled with the finest of embroidered wools. Ranira was wistfully fingering a veil of red silk when a hand touched her shoulder. A smooth voice behind her said, ''I believe I have seen you before, my dear.''

Even during Festival, it was not permissible to speak uninvited to a veiled woman. Ranira turned angrily, then froze in shock. Standing behind her was the priest she had noticed watching as she left the Temple the previous day.

''Revered Master,'' Ranira managed in a strangled voice, lowering her head.

''I am named Gadrath,'' the priest said. ''Since I hope we shall become better . . . acquainted, you may use it.''

Startled, Ranira glanced up; the predatory smile on the priest's face made her shiver, and it was a moment before she found her voice again. ''It would not be right for a bond servant to presume so greatly, honored sir,'' she said, lowering her eyes again.

''Such piety becomes you, my dear,'' the priest said. ''There is always a place in the House of Chaldon for a woman of humility.''

Ranira barely stopped herself from recoiling in terror and disgust. She knew, as did all Drinn, that only two types of women were welcomed into the inner sanctuaries of the Temple of Chaldon: those who were meant as sacrifices for the god, and those who were meant for the pleasure of the priests. She had seen the wretched women who had been cast out of the Temple when the priests tired of them, sometimes only weeks or months after they had entered the Temple doors. A slow anger began to rise within her. The Temple had burned her parents; did they think to degrade her as well?

"A bondwoman is seldom free to do as she wishes," she said finally. She knew it was a weak response, but she was unable to find a better one with the priest's gaze upon her.

"That need not concern you," Gadrath answered. "I am of sufficient rank to make arrangements, if it pleases me." Ranira swallowed hard and remained silent. After a moment, the priest went on, "You may be sure I shall be kinder to you than your bondholder. Shall I have him fined for mistreating you?" He reached out toward the purpling bruise at the side of Ranira's head, and the girl shrank back from his touch.

The priest frowned. "There is nothing to fear, girl," he said impatiently. "Have I not observed the courtesies? Now, I doubt that your bondholder will refuse to assign your bond to the Temple of Chaldon. In a day or two it will all be settled. But there is no reason to wait until then. Come."

Gadrath reached out and took hold of her arm. "No," Ranira whispered, and her pent-up anger burst free. "No!" she shouted. She pushed the priest violently away and wrenched free. The sudden release threw her off balance, and she staggered back into the crowded square, away from the veil-maker's stand. She had a brief glimpse of the astonishment on the priest's face before he reeled backward into the heavily laden shelves separating the veil-maker's booth from that of the fruitseller. The awkward structure teetered alarmingly, showering soft purple fruit and sticky red jam on the unfortunate priest.

Silence descended on those bystanders who were near enough to see clearly what had happened. No one dared to laugh at the spectacle of a Temple priest covered in berry-juice and sliding on the crushed pulp every time he tried to regain his feet. No one quite dared to go to his assistance, either, though the crowd edged closer until Gadrath was the center of a ring of silent, brown-robed people.

Hoping she would remain unnoticed, Ranira dropped the red veil she was holding and began edging away from the disaster. She had to force herself to go slowly. Every minute she expected to hear outraged cries from the direction of the fruit stand, ordering the crowd to seize her, bind her, return her to face the priest's vengeance. The crowded square was oppressive. There were too many people too close. She wanted to run.

An eon later, she reached the edge of the square. There were fewer people there, and she could move more freely. Trying to retain some shred of composure, she started down one of the streets with measured paces. The light hurt her eyes. Every dark-robed pilgrim looked at first glance like one of the black-clad Temple Watchmen.

Something jogged her elbow; she whirled, stifling a scream. It was only one of the pilgrims, an apologetic young man in the ubiquitous brown. A little shaken by her own reaction, Ranira exchanged polite apologies with him and continued on. Slowly, she began to recover from her panic. The priest doesn't even know my name, she reassured herself. He can't examine everyone who comes to the Temple, no matter how important he is. Unless he knows my name or Lykken's, he can't find me again except by accident.

She had almost succeeded in reassuring herself when she reached the Inn of Nine Doors. Someone was standing in front of the door, blocking her way. Ranira looked up, and her heart stood still. Three men were standing just outside the doorway of the inn. Two wore the ordinary garb of Temple Watchmen, but the third was dressed in the unmistakable robes of an Eye of Chaldon.

CHAPTER FOUR

Ranira did not have time to react. "That's another one, the bondwoman," said a voice, and her arm was seized from behind. Numb with shock, she made no protest as the guard hauled her inside the door and through the inn to the large dining hall.

The room was crowded. Lykken's servants stood huddled against the far wall, kept apart from the inn's customers by a flimsy barrier of chairs, boxes, and two Temple guards. A confused, frightened mass of people milled about the rest of the room. Most of them were customers or pilgrims unlucky enough to have chosen to dine at the Inn of Nine Doors that morning.

The guard who held Ranira stopped at one of the tables. A Temple priest sat there, amid a clutter of paper. "Another one of the staff," the guard said.

The priest made a note. "You are Ranira, bonded to Lykken who owns this inn?"

Ranira nodded. The priest looked pleased. "That is the last of them, then," he said in a satisfied tone. "Put her over there with the rest of the servants, and go help with the pilgrims. With a little luck, we can be finished with most of them before the High Master of the Eyes arrives."

The guard nodded and pushed Ranira over to the barricade that enclosed the employees of the Inn of Nine Doors. Ranira stumbled into the midst of the crowd. Her hands came up instinctively as she collided with someone, and she barely managed to keep from falling. As she regained her balance,

24

she looked up to apologize. She found herself staring into the red, angry face of Lykken.

"You!" he hissed, seizing her arm in a painfully tight grasp. "You pit snake! After I've kept you fed and clothed and given you a place for six years. It was you! I should have known better than to take the bond of a witch-child!"

Ranira's teeth rattled as Lykken shook her. She could not have replied even if she had wished to. Suddenly Lykken pushed her away, and she stumbled again. "You hate me!" the innkeeper shouted. "That's why you did this—to ruin me!"

"I . . . I have not done anything," Ranira said jerkily. "What do you mean?"

Lykken's face became even redder, and he raised a hand. Ranira cringed, but the innkeeper was only pointing. "There! Can you deny you told the Templemen they were here?"

As Ranira's eyes followed the pointing finger, she suddenly understood. The three strangers were sitting calmly at the rear of the room, just on the other side of the chairs and a little apart from the rest of the customers. Two more Temple guards and an Eye of Chaldon stood close beside them, watching. The veiled woman did not appear to notice. She was speaking in a low voice to Jaren, who did not seem quite so much at ease. From time to time the man's hand moved unconsciously to his empty scabbard. The "sick boy" drooped over the table, still keeping up the pretense of illness.

Ranira looked back at Lykken. "I didn't tell anyone!" she said angrily. "You have no one but yourself to blame. If you weren't so greedy, this would not have happened."

"How dare you!" The innkeeper reached out, but Ranira dodged away in time. "You slimy little thief! Witch-child! You should have burned with your parents!"

Most of the room was watching now, but Ranira knew better than to expect any of them to help her. She continued to duck Lykken's wild swings, backing away as best she could. It was impossible to run. Suddenly Lykken bellowed and lunged forward. Ranira jumped back and bumped against the low barricade that separated the staff of the inn from the rest

of the room. For a long moment, she fought for balance.
Then something shifted, and she crashed to the floor in a pile
of rope and broken chairs. Lykken moved forward in
triumph. Ranira pulled against the ruins of the barricade,
frantically trying to avoid him. The innkeeper's first kick
landed hard against her side. Through the explosion of pain,
she felt ribs grind together. Another blow fell, and she
twisted away and rolled to her knees. Lykken grinned and
shifted to aim another kick before she could rise.

A shadow fell across Ranira's face. She had a glimpse of
green leather just before Lykken went reeling backward into
the wall. Suddenly, Jaren stood in front of her, turned slightly
so that she could see the almost imperceptible smile on his
face.

Lykken climbed slowly to his feet as the Temple guards
came hurrying over. The innkeeper pointed a thick finger at
Ranira. "I knew it! She has been in league with them all
along. It is all her fault!"

"Whatever this girl has done or not done, you will think
twice before abusing her again, innkeeper. Even if she is your
bondwoman," Jaren said, spitting out the last word as if it
left a bad taste in his mouth.

Before Lykken could do more than turn red, one of the
Temple guards had shoved himself between the two men.
"Back where you belong," he said brusquely to Jaren. "We
will not permit brawling among prisoners."

Jaren looked at him coldly. "You did not seem so anxious
to avoid a disturbance when it was a large man beating a small
girl."

The Templeman drew his sword and stepped forward.
"The High Master will deal with all of you when he arrives.
Now, go." Jaren did not move. The guard smiled and moved
closer until the point of his sword was touching the leather
Jaren wore. But Jaren still did not move.

"Jaren." The soft voice broke the tension between the two
men. Ranira let out the breath she did not know she had been
holding in and turned her head. The woman called Mist had
risen and was standing by the table. She made no movement,
spoke no other word, but those closest to her backed away.
Ranira looked back toward Jaren. He had not moved, but

some indefinable tension had drained out of him. He no longer looked like a cat preparing to spring.

Jaren looked past the Temple guard to Lykken. "Don't trouble her again, innkeeper. Next time I will not stop with one blow." He turned and started back toward the table where Mist was standing.

Lykken's face twisted into a grotesque mask of anger and hate. He lunged forward, ripping the sword from the surprised Templeman's hand, and thrust for Jaren's back. Ranira cried a warning, and without thinking, she grabbed one of the pieces of broken chair from the floor and threw it at the innkeeper. She saw Jaren whirl and duck, saw the sword in Lykken's hand grow red, saw the broken chair leg hit the innkeeper just before the Temple guard knocked him unconscious. As Lykken slumped to the floor, the Temple guard stepped forward to recover his sword.

In the stunned silence that followed, Jaren turned toward Ranira. Blood welled from between the fingers he pressed tight to his side, and the half-bow he gave her made him wince. "Little sister, I owe you a life," he said.

The Templeman standing beside Jaren laughed. "Much good may it do her! Chaldon will have you both before long."

Jaren turned his head. The Templeman fell back a pace, and his sword came up. Jaren smiled. "I am Cilhar," he said softly. "What will come is never sure. Remember that, Templeman."

"When you have finished discussing the nature of the future, Hirnlan, perhaps you can find time to explain to me just what has been going on," said a new voice.

The Templeman lowered his sword and straightened abruptly. "High Master," he croaked.

Cold chills ran down Ranira's back as she scrambled to her feet. The High Master of the Eyes of Chaldon was the most feared of the Temple priests, for he controlled the Eyes, and the Eyes of Chaldon hunted down disbelievers and witches and punished those who dared to disobey the dictates of the god. It was a measure of the gravity of Lykken's offense that the High Master himself had come to the Inn of Nine Doors. In all her life, Ranira could not remember hearing of a foreigner attempting to stay in Drinn during the Festival.

The crowd parted as the new arrival moved toward the Templeman. In the first instant that she saw him clearly, Ranira swayed in shock. The High Master of the Eyes of Chaldon was the priest Gadrath! She bit back a gasp of fear and dismay, and tried to melt into the press of people.

He did not notice her at once; his attention was on the unfortunate Templeman. "I asked for an explanation," he said in a tone of exaggerated patience.

The guard paled and swallowed. "Lord, there was a disturbance. He," pointing at Jaren, "struck this man before we could intervene. I ordered him back to await your pleasure and judgment. The other attacked him as he turned to go, but I knocked him out before he could do any real harm."

"Indeed?" Gadrath's eyes narrowed. "You must think me a fool, Hirnlan. I am not blind, to overlook a wounded man and a bloody sword. Make your tale complete, or share the fate I choose for this one!" Gadrath nudged Lykken's recumbent form. The innkeeper stirred and moaned.

"High Master, Revered Lord, he wrenched my sword from my hand without warning and struck the foreigner before I could stop him," the guard stammered.

"Without warning?" Gadrath's smile was half sneer. "Then you shall tend the snakepits in the Temple until you know the meaning of the words. If you survive, that is; the snakes of Chaldon are swift as well as silent."

The Temple guard stumbled back, and people recoiled from him in horror, as if the mere touch of his clothing might force them to share his punishment. Gadrath smiled again and turned to another of the Temple guardsmen. "To lay hands upon a Templeman is death. The innkeeper is of no use to us. See to it."

The guard hauled Lykken to his feet and prodded him toward the door of the dining hall. Ranira was too numb to feel horror as she watched them leave. A muffled scream came a moment later, cut off abruptly. Ranira shuddered, and tears came unbidden to her eyes. Lykken had been cruel, greedy, and stupid, but at least he had been familiar; now she was alone.

Her reverie was broken by the sound of her name. "Ranira? Oh, a bondwoman. You say he accused her of bewitching him? Well, where is the girl, then?'' A priest gestured in answer to Gadrath's question. The High Master turned toward her.

Gadrath's eyes met hers, and the priest was suddenly, dangerously, still. Then he drew a long breath, and smiled coldly. ''So? I must think on your fate, my dear. It will take a moment or two to find something appropriate.'' Ranira shivered at the menace in his voice.

With a brief nod of satisfaction, Gadrath turned away from Ranira to the three foreigners. ''These you will take to the Temple. Hold them in the House of Correction until tomorrow. We will begin the rites of purification after the procession.'' The priest paused thoughtfully. ''Yes. We will make a public spectacle of the unbelievers. Mid-Festival will be suitable, I think. The inn is confiscated; call an ironsmith to see to the binding of the staff.''

Someone on Ranira's right moaned. Gadrath ignored the sound and looked speculatively toward the frightened crowd of customers. ''These others—a fine. You have their names recorded? Then, release them once they have paid; it will give the tale a chance to spread.''

Turning back to Ranira, Gadrath smiled with cruel satisfaction. ''This one comes with us as well. Truly, this will be a great Midwinter Festival! We will revive an old ritual to accompany the new ones. It has been far too long since anyone was chosen to be the Bride of Chaldon.'' He looked sharply at Ranira as he spoke, but she was too numb to react. Gadrath's smile faded, and he turned abruptly away. ''See to it!''

The Temple guards bowed as the High Master of the Eyes of Chaldon left the room in a swirl of black robes. A murmur of relief swept through the crowd. The remaining Temple priests pulled a table into position beside the door, and brown-robed pilgrims began filing slowly past. Coins clinked as they paused briefly at the table. None of them dared to glance toward Ranira or the foreigners; few paid any attention to the small group of servants, soon to be bound and then sold to enrich the Temple.

A guard materialized beside Ranira. ''It is time to go,

Chosen One,'' he said. His tone was respectful, but his hand rested on the hilt of his sword and his eyes were hard. Ranira shuddered once, then gave a jerk of her head. She saw five other guards close in around the three strangers before the Templeman put a hand on her arm and turned her toward the door. Like a sleepwalker, she moved forward into the hall and then out of the inn. She hardly noticed the sound of the door closing behind her, and she did not look back.

CHAPTER FIVE

The streets of Drinn were even more crowded than they had been when Ranira reached the inn, but the people moved back with a murmuring that died into silence as the Templemen went by. Ranira followed mindlessly, still dazed by the rapid sequence of events. She saw the fear she could not feel herself in the faces that drew away from the circle of black robes surrounding her. Twice she thought she saw Shandy among them, but the glimpses were too brief for her to be certain.

It did not take long to reach the Temple. Ranira was not surprised when the guards headed around the wall of the Temple, away from the great iron gates that opened into the Temple courtyard. At a small wooden door in the black stone wall, the guards stopped and knocked. A moment later a wizened man in black robes pulled the door open a crack. One of the guards stepped forward, and after a whispered consultation, the door swung wide.

The hallway they entered was dark and windowless. Only the Templeman's hand on her arm kept Ranira from stumbling during the time it took her eyes to adjust to the gloom. The doorkeeper-priest moved silently in front of the guards, carrying a torch that gave off almost as much smoke as it did light. Three times the party halted while the doorkeeper opened heavy doors of wood and iron to allow them to pass.

The last door, at the end of the hallway, opened into a small open area not really large enough to be called a room. In the opposite wall were two more doors. The doorkeeper

31

went straight to the one on the left and began fumbling with his keys.

"There," he said as the door opened. He held out a key to the first guard. "Use the empty cell right at the bottom of the stairs. It will do nicely for now."

The Templemen exchanged looks, and the first one stepped forward. "Master Lanarsh," he said, bowing deeply as he took the key, "I would not presume to question you. But the High Master Gadrath has chosen this one as the Bride of Chaldon. Is there nowhere more suitable?"

"Not if he wants her guarded well," the little priest snapped. "And I assume she didn't volunteer for the honor." His eyes narrowed as he looked at Ranira. Suddenly he darted forward and ripped the veil away from her face.

Ranira's hands came up in a belated reflex to hide her face. The doorkeeper-priest chuckled. He crumpled the little square of linen and tossed it aside. "She's pretty enough, but if she's to be a Bride, something will have to be done about those bruises."

"The High Master Gadrath has declared her the Bride of Chaldon," the guard repeated stiffly.

"Gadrath is not yet High Priest of the Temple, though he acts like it," Lanarsh said. "And in this House I am High Master. As soon as Benillath sends the official declaration, I will set up another room and move her, but not before."

The guard bowed again. "As you will it, my lord."

The doorkeeper chuckled again and turned away. He handed the single torch to the first guard in an almost absentminded gesture. The guard bowed a third time, then waved the rest forward with his free hand.

The stairs were narrow and slippery, and the dim light cast by the torch did not make it any easier for Ranira to keep her footing. Behind her she heard grunts and muffled curses as the guards slid on the polished stone. At the foot of the stairs, the guard with the torch stopped and waited while the others finished their descent.

"Hold this." The first guard thrust the torch at one of his fellows and began fumbling with the lock on the heavy wooden door at the foot of the stairs. It swung back unexpectedly, and the Templeman stumbled into the cell. One of the other guards snickered, then coughed as the stench reached him.

"Phew! Smells like Lanarsh hasn't cleaned these cells since the last Festival," someone muttered.

"*High Master* Lanarsh to you," another guard said. "And if you want to stay out of the House of Correction, you'll remember it, too."

"But we can't put them in there!" the first speaker objected. The voice sounded young, but Ranira could not tell which of the guards was speaking.

"Correction isn't supposed to be pleasant. Come on, let's get them in and get out of here," another guard said. There was a mutter of agreement, and Ranira found herself pushed forward into the small, dark opening. She heard a curse as the strangers were shoved in after her—probably Jaren's voice, from the sound of it. The door clanged shut, plunging the small cell into darkness, and Ranira heard a key turn in the lock.

No one spoke as the muffled sounds of the guards retreated up the stairs. Ranira reached out gingerly in the darkness, trying to touch a wall, a person, anything to give herself a sense of direction. She found nothing. Behind her, she heard a rustling sigh, then a sudden, startled exclamation. "Mist!" Simultaneously, there was a flash of light inside the cell. Ranira whirled, blinking against the sudden brightness.

"It is all right, Jaren. No one is watching us, and I would see this place," said the dark-haired woman. Ranira's eyes cleared, and she saw Mist standing near the door of the cell. Her left hand was clenched around something at her breast. The right was outstretched, and on her open palm was a globe of silver-blue light.

Ranira watched in horrified fascination. "Lykken was right. You *are* witches!"

Jaren turned his head to look at her. "Not all of us, and certainly not as you mean the word. Have patience; we have no choice now but to explain." He looked back at Mist.

"She will not betray us," the woman said with serene confidence. Ranira felt a sudden, irrational dislike of her.

"How can you be sure?" the third member of the group, the "sick boy," demanded. "She is frightened enough already to call in one of those Temple people, if they could hear her.''

''Arelnath, you are too suspicious. But if you wish, and she permits, I will use truth-trance after we have explained,'' Mist said. ''Will that content you?''

''You won't!'' Ranira burst out before the other could reply. In her mind, remembered screams sounded in an old dream of terror. ''Anything's better than burning! You can't make me!''

There was a shocked silence. The silver-blue light in Mist's hand wavered. ''They burn witches in Drinn? No, I cannot believe it,'' Mist said at last. ''Surely you are mistaken, child.''

''They burned my parents.'' Ranira flung the words at that soft, reasonable voice. ''They burned my *parents*!''

She turned away, shaking with sobs. From far away, she heard Jaren's low murmur, ''It is no wonder she is frightened.''

''And it is no wonder the Empire of Chaldreth does not wish to be open about itself,'' Mist responded with anger. ''I knew the Temple of Chaldon did not approve of magic—but this!''

''There is worse, I fear,'' Jaren said grimly. ''I tried to warn you, but you insisted.''

''On staying? But it was the only way to find out what we need to know,'' Mist said.

''What good will knowing do us, or your Temple, if we don't survive?'' Arelnath asked.

Ranira jerked around. ''Survive? You're dreaming.'' Suddenly she was shaking uncontrollably, and her voice began to climb. ''We are all going to die. Die!''

''She's hysterical,'' a voice said beside her.

''No, Arelnath, I will see to her,'' Mist said just as Ranira was seized in a strong grip. For a moment, she fought back; then the silver light flared once, blindingly bright. Ranira fell back as if she had been slapped, and the hands loosened their hold. Ranira found herself staring into the face of Arelnath.

''I'm all right now,'' Ranira said. ''Just leave me alone.''

Ignoring Arelnath's raised eyebrows and Mist's look of hurt, Ranira turned away. She had to clench her hands to keep them from trembling. None of these foreign fools seemed to realize what was going to happen to them, she thought. Were they so ignorant that they expected to be released at the end of the Festival?

Jaren's voice cut across her reflections, shaking her back into present reality. "What is it you fear?" Ranira did not respond, but the voice came again, insistently. "As the Bride of Chaldon, you surely will not share our fate, whatever that may be. What is it you fear?"

Ranira turned slowly to face him. A cold calmness descended on her. The only way to stop these stupid questions and unrealistic attempts at reassurance was to tell these people exactly what was happening, so that they would no longer pretend there was some way out of this. Well, she would do so, and she hoped they would appreciate what they heard. Her voice surprised her by being low and steady as she began to speak.

"You still do not understand, do you? The Midwinter Festival of Chaldon will run for six more days. When the Highest Born agrees that I am to be the Bride of Chaldon, I will be moved to another room. They will give me fine robes, and before the rites begin I will be paraded through the streets in them, and the pilgrims will give me gifts. Of course, the Temple guards will only be there to protect me. Why would anyone chosen for such an honor want to run away?

"For three days more I will be seated in the place of honor in the Temple, next to the High Priest, while he teaches the people the new rites and leads them in the old ones. Then the High Priest himself will perform the wedding ceremony. And consummate it. Publicly," she added as an afterthought. She stared resolutely at the door of the cell. She was determined to finish, to make them understand, so that they would leave her to whatever little peace and sanity she could find and cling to. "When he is finished, the god will take me. For two days, Chaldon will walk in my body and speak with my voice, and there will be nothing left of me at all. On the last day of the Festival, when both moons are full and Chaldon has accepted the other sacrifices, the nine High Masters will kill me as well.''

''Other sacrifices?'' whispered Mist. Her face was white above the short veil she still wore.

''There are always other sacrifices,'' Ranira said with a shrug. ''You will not be among them, for witches are burned at mid-Festival. Of course, since you are foreigners who have disobeyed the Law of the Festival, the priests may choose some other death for you, but it will certainly happen at that time.''

''Then we have at least two days,'' Jaren said calmly. He exchanged a long look with Arelnath, then turned to Mist. ''Have you learned enough to satisfy you?''

Mist shook her head. ''No, but as we are this close to the Temple of Chaldon, I should have no difficulty. Make your plans. I will be ready.''

''What do you mean?'' Ranira burst out almost against her will. ''You can't escape; the Eyes of Chaldon can find out anything! They are probably listening right now.''

''According to you, we will all die anyway,'' Arelnath pointed out. ''What does it matter if we try to escape?''

''Don't you understand? The Eyes of Chaldon can hear everything you say!'' Ranira repeated.

''We are not being watched now,'' Mist said. ''I will know if they try.'' She gestured with the globe of light.

''More witchcraft,'' Ranira said. She was not reassured; she had seen too many witches and rebels die at the command of the Temple to have any real hope of escape by witchcraft. Still, in spite of herself, she was interested in the magic that seemed to give Jaren, Mist, and Arelnath such confidence.

''If you are certain no one watches, Mist, perhaps you would be willing to make a few repairs?'' Jaren said. He gestured toward his left side, and suddenly Ranira realized that it was not the blue-white light that made him look so strange.

''Jaren! You should have said something sooner.'' Mist's voice was full of concern as she walked over to him. She examined his side briefly, then motioned to Arelnath. ''I have not the concentration to maintain the light, keep watch, and heal as well. You have some training, do you not?''

"A little, but I am a Cilhar mercenary, not one of your sorcerer folk. I spent four months on your island. I can hold the light and the watch-spell for you, but I do not have enough sensitivity to give much warning if someone comes. It would be better if you could watch as well as heal.''

Mist frowned. "We will have to take the chance," she decided. "He has lost too much blood for this to be an easy task." She gestured at a darkening of Jaren's green leather tunic that seemed to cover much of his left side.

Arelnath nodded and reached out. The ball of light shivered as she touched it. For a moment, shadows flickered eerily in the room. Then the light steadied and brightened. The shining globe, yellow now instead of silver-blue, rested lightly in Arelnath's palm.

With a nod of approval, Mist turned toward Jaren. Her fingers moved gently, peeling back the leather to expose the place where Lykken's swordstroke had landed. Ranira watched in silence, feeling both fascinated and embarrassed. She was no stranger to blood and injury, but a sword thrust was a more serious matter than the bones broken in a drunken brawl. Still, the injury looked more painful than serious, except for the unusual amount of blood lost because Jaren had been forced to walk to the Temple with the wound untreated.

Both of Mist's hands were stretched out before her, hovering barely a hairbreadth above Jaren's side while Arelnath held the light steady above them. The only sound was the low, continuous murmuring of Mist's voice chanting the spell. Ranira found herself holding her breath and willing this attempt, whatever it was, to succeed. Suddenly, the tension drained from Mist's body and her hands fell away. Beneath them was unbroken skin; not even a scar remained.

"Thank you," Jaren said as he pulled his leather garb back into place. "Whatever we have to face will be easier now that I am in one piece."

"I have never done so difficult a healing," Mist said absently. Her brows were contracted. She stared thoughtfully into the air. "Something was opposing it; the injury itself was not unusual. Almost until the end, I feared I would not succeed; then the resistance collapsed.''

Before Jaren could reply, the yellow glow illuminating the cell winked out. Into the startled silence came the sound of a key scraping in the lock. ''Someone comes,'' Arelnath said unnecessarily.

CHAPTER SIX

The door of the cell swung inward. Through the rectangular opening spilled a smoky yellow light, silhouetting five of the dark figures in the corridor beyond. The sixth, standing at the rear with a torch, was the only one whose face was visible, but the voice that came from the small shape in front instantly identified it as the High Master Lanarsh.

"Come here, girl. The High Priest Benillath has sent the proclamation, and you are to be moved at once."

"That's no way to speak to the Chosen One," muttered one of the guards.

Lanarsh chuckled. "I doubt you can do anything about it. Not even Benillath dares to trifle too much with this House. Well, come along, girl. Don't just stand there! I would imagine you'd be glad to be out of here."

Ranira felt fear rising in her once more as she moved slowly forward. Somehow this seemed to be the final separation, the death of hope. She swallowed hard, determined not to show her fear before the Templemen, yet knowing they saw through her pretended bravery. She looked at the three foreigners, their faces dim and shadowy in the torchlight, and blinked to clear away the tears. As she passed Jaren, she heard him whisper, too softly for the guards to hear, "I owe you a life. Remember."

Though she did not see what good the implied promise could do her, Ranira found Jaren's words oddly comforting. She paused a moment before the torchlight could make her

39

fully visible, and her hand jerked upward toward her uncovered face. She saw Lanarsh's face twist into a smile, and
suddenly her fear was drowned in a wave of anger. With an
abruptly determined motion, she threw back her hair and
stepped forward.

"Benillath may not dare to trifle with you, old man, but I
have no such reservations," she said in the most arrogant
tone she could muster. "You will treat me with proper
respect or know the wrath of Chaldon when he comes for
me."

Behind her she heard a crow of delight from Arelnath and a
smothered chuckle that she was certain came from Jaren. For
a moment, she was astonished at herself; then she gave a
mental shrug. What did she have to lose? The priests would
never allow her to interfere with anything really important,
but in little things, at least, she could force them to bend to
her wishes. The thought gave her confidence to meet
Lanarsh's startled stare with a cold look of her own. The
priest bent his head a fraction of an inch.

"If you will join us, Chosen One?"

Ranira allowed herself an infinitesimal, cold smile, copied
from a seamstress who had occasionally deigned to patronize
the Inn of Nine Doors, and stepped forward. She would have
liked to take one last look at Mist and Jaren and Arelnath, but
it would have spoiled the part she was playing, so she let the
cell door clang shut behind her without turning.

"This way, Chosen One," said Lanarsh, beckoning toward the stairs. The High Master of the House of Correction
looked as if he had bitten into a sour string-fruit. She nodded
as gravely as she could and began the long climb up the stairs.

When they reached the top, the guards paused while
Lanarsh locked the door and opened one of the others. In
silence, they escorted Ranira down a long hall that twisted
and turned and branched until she ceased trying to remember
which turns they had taken. At last the guards stopped, and
Lanarsh flung open a door. Ranira gasped in spite of her
determination to maintain a cold demeanor.

The room was almost as large as the dining hall of the Inn
of Nine Doors. Intricately embroidered hangings covered
the walls and draped the chairs, golden candelabra stood on

marble tables, and the floor was buried under a thick wool carpet. An inner door stood open, revealing the barest glimpse of a bedchamber furnished in equal luxury. In the doorway stood a veiled figure, which bowed deeply as soon as Ranira entered the room.

"Mornah, the Chosen One is to be bathed and suitably attired," said Lanarsh. "The High Master Gadrath will wish to see for himself that the ceremonial robes for tomorrow are perfect. You may expect him later."

Despite herself, Ranira shivered; Lanarsh chuckled as he bowed and left the room. She stood staring at the door without moving until she heard the key turn in the lock. Only then did she become conscious of Mornah's patient silence. Forcing a smile, Ranira turned.

Immediately, the other woman bowed again. "I am yours to command, Chosen One. What will you prefer? There is a bath with many perfumes, or you may choose more suitable raiment. There are healing ointments." Her eyes flickered briefly over the bruises on Ranira's face and then dropped again. "And there are rare dishes and wine. You have only to request, Chosen One."

The woman bowed a third time. It made Ranira uncomfortable. "My name is Ranira," she said. "Call me that; I am not used to titles."

"I could not dare to be so greatly familiar, Chosen One," said Mornah with yet another bow. "I am but a humble serving woman."

Ranira looked at the woman with growing irritation. "Until a few hours ago, so was I. And stop bobbing like that. It makes me dizzy."

"The Chosen One must have the respect that is due her exalted station," Mornah recited. "I am here only to wait upon your wishes. I may not presume upon my great good fortune in being permitted to serve you, Chosen One, for when the Festival is over, I will return to my regular duties in the Temple."

I can guess what those are, thought Ranira. Then comprehension dawned. "You're afraid of the Eyes!" she said. "You think you'll be punished later if you do something they don't like."

Fear flashed in Mornah's eyes before she bent forward again. "I am here to serve the Chosen One," she murmured.

"Oh, I give up," Ranira said in exasperation. "Go get me a veil; I don't want to walk around like this any longer than I have to."

The serving woman trembled, but did not move. "Alas, Chosen One, I am not permitted to bring a veil, for the High Priest has decreed that nothing shall hide the radiance of the Chosen One. I sorrow that I cannot obey, for I am here only to serve the Chosen One."

Ranira sighed. "Yes, I know; you must have said so at least a dozen times. Well, if you can't bring me a veil, at least you can show me what other clothes you have here. And you did say something about a bath, didn't you?"

"Oh yes, Chosen One," Mornah said in obvious relief. She beckoned Ranira into the bedchamber and drew aside a curtain that covered one wall, revealing a long row of elaborate garments. Ranira made a show of examining them, but her mind was on other things. The wave of anger which had supported her spirits was receding, leaving a deep depression in its wake. She found Mornah's pathetic eagerness to please oppressive, and she could not forget Lanarsh's parting words.

Why did Gadrath want to see her again? Ranira could not believe it was her appearance that drew him; she was attractive enough, she supposed, but not out of the ordinary. Gadrath's interest was no more than the casual arrogance common to all Temple priests, who assumed that no one would dare to refuse their slightest whim. At least, she was sure that was all Gadrath had felt until her overly enthusiastic refusal had humiliated him and prompted this revenge. But surely the High Master would not be spared from his Festival duties simply to gloat over her!

The problem preoccupied Ranira throughout the long afternoon. She submitted to Mornah's ministrations; the long bath and the healing ointments were welcome indeed. Even more welcome was the smith, who made a brief visit late in the afternoon to remove the iron bracelets that she had worn for six years. The luxuries could do little to set her mind at rest, however, and by the time she was ready to dress, she could not muster even a token enthusiasm for any of the rich garments.

Finally, Ranira allowed Mornah to choose one of the gowns herself and coax her into it, but to the serving woman's dismay, Ranira refused even to sample the carefully prepared dishes laid out in the main room. As the woman became more insistent, Ranira grew more and more exasperated. Finally she ordered the serving woman from the room. When a knock sounded at the door, Ranira was seated at the marble table, staring moodily at an empty silver goblet.

The sound made her jump. She forced herself to remain seated, and called as steadily as she could, "Enter."

The door was already swinging open; the knock had been a warning, rather than a request for permission to enter. Gadrath's eyes met hers as he stepped into the room. "You may go," he said over his shoulder. Two Temple guards behind him bowed and stepped back into the hallway. Gadrath's eyes never left Ranira. "Quite an improvement, my dear," he said as the door swung shut behind him. "You do credit to your position."

"Should you not address me with more respect? Or are you exempt from the rules of the Festival, since it is to you that I owe my . . . position?"

Gadrath's lips curled. "Lanarsh told me of this amusing conceit of yours. He was a fool to encourage you. Your 'position' in this Temple, my dear, is exactly the same as it was this morning, except that you are permitted to enjoy a few of the lesser comforts that are available here. What the pilgrims outside think, is of little concern to any of us."

Ranira's hands tightened on the silver goblet. Gadrath's smile broadened. "But you have not tasted any of these excellent dishes!" he said. "You should certainly do so while you still have the opportunity. After all, your time here will be brief." When Ranira did not respond, the priest went on. "Perhaps you do not care for the food, but the wine at least you should enjoy. Allow me to pour you some."

Without waiting for her to answer, Gadrath reached for the crystal decanter in the center of the table, along with the mate to the goblet in Ranira's hand. He poured wine for himself, then stretched his arm toward Ranira's goblet. She held it while he poured, not trusting herself to speak. Silently, she raised the goblet to her lips.

The High Master returned the decanter to the table and seated himself across from her. "I drink to your very good health, my dear."

Ranira angrily set the goblet down and demanded, "What is it you want of me, High Master Gadrath?"

"What I want of you, my dear, you seem curiously unwilling to give," he said, leaning back in the chair. "Or did I only imagine being pushed so rudely into a fruit stand?"

Shaken, Ranira gulped at the wine. She could not prevent her eyes from turning toward the door to the bedchamber. Gadrath smiled. "There is no need for you to be afraid yet, my dear. It will be three days before you are given to the god; no one will touch you until then."

"You are disgusting!" Ranira cried, jumping up. "Leave me alone. Haven't you done enough?"

"Why, I have done nothing at all," Gadrath replied. "I would think you would welcome my company. After all, this is a great improvement over a small, unlit cell filled with foreign witches, is it not?" He waved a hand negligently at the luxurious room.

Something in Gadrath's tone seemed false to Ranira, but she was too angry to pinpoint what. "At least the foreigners were courteous," she said, turning away.

"I am not concerned with their manners," Gadrath said. "After all, they are witches, are they not?"

That was it. Ranira was glad she was not facing the priest—he would surely have seen her reaction and guessed the cause. Gadrath wanted evidence against Jaren and his companions; that was what he was here for. Another thought struck her—Mist had been right! If the cell had been watched, there would certainly be no need for Gadrath to seek proof by questioning Ranira.

"How should I know whether they are witches?" she said. "I was only with them for a little while, and in a dark cell, as you say." She turned back toward the table, careful to keep her eyes from meeting Gadrath's.

The priest shrugged casually, but Ranira could feel tension in him. "It is easy enough for people to forget they are not alone in the dark. I thought perhaps you might have heard something we could use as proof. Of course, it does not really matter; they will die at mid-Festival in any case.''

Ranira thought of the flames and wondered why Gadrath was so anxious to burn Mist and the others. ''They sounded like ordinary, frightened people to me.'' She sipped her wine.

''You are certain?'' Gadrath's eyes were sharp and oddly bright. Ranira took another swallow of wine to avoid his gaze. ''It might be that another could become the Bride of Chaldon if you can help me. Such things have happened.''

''You lie!'' Ranira hissed. The violence of her reaction surprised her. ''Do not toy with me. The High Priest has already sent out word that I will be the Bride of Chaldon. You cannot change that.''

''Why should I deceive you, my dear?'' Gadrath said. ''It is very simple, really; a false name for you and a pretty slave to take your place during Festival are all that are needed. Surely the foreigners said something while you were with them.''

Unexpected hope turned Ranira's bones to water. For a moment she could not speak. It was possible; someone else could take her place. Words jostled against each other in her mind, framed in a glow of silver light: ''We are not being watched.'' ''I can hold the watch-spell.'' Softly, a voice whispered among them, ''I owe you a life.'' Her head ached; she fought to think clearly. Why would Gadrath give up his revenge so easily?

The silence was growing uncomfortable. Ranira raised her head and looked at Gadrath. Instead of speaking, she deliberately took another sip of wine. She set the goblet down carefully and looked up again.

''Why should you keep your promises once you have what you want? Even if I thought you would do as you say, I do not like the idea of owing my life to you, nor of giving you so great a hold over me,'' she said. ''In any case, it does not matter; the foreigners said nothing unusual. Or would you have me make up tales so that you may prove them false? What good would that do me?''

Gadrath laughed. ''You are cleverer than I thought, my

dear. I will have to resort to other methods.'' He smiled and shook his head regretfully. ''Unfortunately, none of them will involve you. The Bride of Chaldon must not have a marred body. Still, are you certain there is nothing you can tell me? There are ways to make your fate easier.''

''Nothing,'' Ranira repeated. Her tongue felt thick. She blinked, trying to clear away a sudden fuzziness in her vision. Gadrath was standing over her now. How strange; he was supposed to be sitting on the other side of the table.

''Perhaps I was wrong,'' Gadrath said, half to himself. ''Perhaps there is nothing for you to tell. You have lasted far longer than I expected. I doubt that you could lie to me now. No, they were careful, and I will have to find some other way to accuse them. Now, finish your wine, my dear. You must be in good spirits tomorrow, you know. The pilgrims will expect the Bride of Chaldon to smile.''

The priest lifted the goblet to her lips and forced the remaining contents down her throat. Ranira's last lucid thought was that she should have guessed he would drug the wine.

CHAPTER SEVEN

For a long time, Ranira floated in a world of light and color. She did not notice at what point she again began to be aware of what was going on around her; the change was much too gradual. It began with voices, fading in and out. Gadrath, peremptory and brusk: "See that she is ready in time, or you will be beaten again. If the drug seems to be wearing off, give her this. But be careful. We cannot have her unconscious during the procession." Mornah, soft and appealing: "Your robes, Chosen One. Your slippers, Chosen One. Allow me to braid your hair, Chosen One. . . . ." Lanarsh, sharp-edged and perpetually cross: "She's still that far away? No, don't give her that; can't you see she's drugged enough already? Gadrath overestimated again. Well, we haven't time to do anything. At least she'll do as she's told, and this time it will not matter if there are permanent effects. The god demands an unmarred body, not a sound mind."

Footsteps echoed in a long, twisted corridor. "This way, Chosen One." Unfamiliar skirts rustled around her feet, gold and silver embroidered on black. How pretty! Black crystal jewels glinted from lacy waves around her throat. She twisted, trying to see them more clearly. A sudden wash of light made her blink. "Wait here, Chosen One." Why should she move? People milled in the Temple courtyard. Such fascinating patterns they made!

A face appeared in front of her—Gadrath. She blinked at him; her vision was blurred. "You are fuzzy around the edges," she told him.

"Listen to me, my dear," he said. "You are the Chosen

47

One. You want to please the people. You will sit and smile at
them while we move through the city. Sit and smile. Do you
understand?''

Ranira was confused. She did want to make the people
happy, but how could she move and sit at the same time? It
would be so much easier to stay here and smile. She didn't
like Gadrath; she couldn't remember why. She wished he
would go away, but he was coming closer. "Sit and smile,
my dear. Do you understand? Or I will hurt you, like this.''

A knifing pain in her arm penetrated the haze surrounding
her. She cried out. The pain stopped. She whimpered and
rubbed her arm. Gadrath's face thrust itself close to hers.
"Do as I say, my dear. Sit and smile. It is really very easy.''
Still confused, but too frightened to antagonize him further,
Ranira nodded.

"Good," said the priest. "This way, my dear.''

Just then she caught sight of the three foreigners. Mist,
Jaren, and . . . Arelnath. She was very pleased with herself
for remembering their names. They were standing in a group
at one side of the courtyard, surrounded by guards. She
wanted to wave, but Gadrath was holding her arm. Then she
remembered—she was supposed to sit and smile, not wave.
But there was nowhere to sit. She frowned. There was something she wanted to remember.

Gadrath stopped, ending Ranira's speculations. "You will
sit here, my dear. Sit and smile. Remember.''

Ranira was barely listening. Her eyes were on the huge
open carriage drawing up in front of her. It was gold, with
three black horses and three white ones harnessed in front. A
tall throne of carved gold rose from the seat at the back. It was
even larger than the High Priest's conveyance standing just in
front of the courtyard gates. Why, she would be sitting far
above everyone. She would be able to see everything!

There was a rattling noise, and a group of Templemen
came up to the rear of the carriage. A moment later, more
guards arrived with Mist and her companions. The foreign
witches were being chained to the rear of the carriage. How
nice! she thought. They will be close by. But she could not
remember why it would be nice.

Temple guards lifted her into the carriage. A priest arrived, muttering, and spread her heavy skirts over the cushions of the throne. She sat and smiled. Her head was beginning to ache, and the courtyard swam before her eyes, but she smiled; Gadrath was watching. The iron gates ahead swung open, and Templemen began marching out of the courtyard. It seemed to take a very long time.

A small man in black climbed onto the driver's platform at the front of the carriage. He raised his whip and made a chuckling noise. The carriage moved forward. She smiled. They were through the iron gates and into the streets of Drinn. A blurred sea of faces surrounded the carriage, shouting and cheering. Ranira still could not think. She was beginning to be annoyed by the way her mind was wandering. She could not remember why she was here, and somehow she was sure it was important.

The procession approached the river. In spite of the Temple guards striving to clear a way for the carriages, the bridge was crowded. Progress slowed to a crawl, then stopped altogether. Ranira heard angry shouts and curses from the Templemen. The horses pranced nervously, and her driver whistled softly through his teeth as his fingers worked the reins.

The carriage inched onto the bridge, its sides so close to the edge that Ranira could easily have stepped from her seat onto the guard wall. She looked curiously down at the river, already swollen with the early winter rains.

Suddenly, one of the horses reared and plunged forward. Its companion shied, and in another instant all six of the horses were bucking and rearing in a tangle of harness. Guards ran forward from the rear of the carriage, pushing past the screaming pilgrims. The throne lurched sickeningly; Ranira grabbed at the side to keep from falling. The carved metal cut into her hands. Fear and pain cleared away the drug haze for a moment, and all at once she saw a way out of the trap Gadrath had sprung on her.

She stood up in the carriage, bracing herself with one hand. Seeing her, the crowd quieted briefly, and she shouted as loudly as she could, "Chaldon's curse on you, Gadrath, and my deathwish as well!" Before the reaching hands could grab her, she turned. Calmly, as if she were alighting from the carriage, she took one step out onto the thick stone rail. And then another.

The water was cold, dark, and dirty. Ranira's wide skirts trapped enough air to keep her afloat, but she knew it would not last long. The current had already swept her under the bridge. She caught at one of the supporting pillars, trying to keep herself out of sight until the water could soak her gown and drag her safely down, away from Gadrath and the Temple of Chaldon and the god. Her nails scrabbled on the rough stone surface, then found a hold.

She could feel the weight beginning to pull at her, but the fear-induced clarity of thought was fading as well; the drug was reasserting its hold. Her fingers began to relax, and she felt them slide on the wet stone. Dreamily, she saw the pillar sliding sideways across her line of vision. Suddenly there were hands on her shoulders, pulling. She struggled weakly, but the effort only made it easier for her to be dragged to the shore. Stones scraped beneath her feet; she felt only a dim regret that she had failed to escape. She stumbled onto the narrow bank below the end of the bridge.

"Come *on*, Renra!" whispered a voice. "We got to get out of here!"

"Shandy!" She ought to be surprised, she thought. No, she was under the bridge, and Shandy always watched the parade from under the bridge. What was she doing under the bridge? She could not remember.

Ranira could hear shouts above her, but they seemed distant and meaningless. She looked at Shandy and smiled. "You didn't get caught," she said.

"Renra!" The boy was tugging at her. "The Temple guards will be here in a minute. Hurry up! Do you want them to catch us?"

The urgency in Shandy's voice penetrated at last. Ranira rose. The wet gown dragged like an iron weight at her legs. She plucked at it ineffectively. "I can't . . ."

"This way." Shandy slipped away. Ranira followed. The heavy skirts seemed to catch at the stone supports of the bridge, clinging and holding her back. Dark water lapped inches from her feet, and her slippers did not grip the narrow, wet stone ledge. She was panting when she caught up with Shandy, though they were barely three body-lengths from the place where she had reached the bank.

"In here, Renra. You go first," he whispered. He pointed to a rounded opening just above the water. Something oozed sluggishly out of it, staining the stone below. Ranira shook her head, but the drug left her no will to resist. "Go on!" Shandy urged, and she obediently dropped to her knees and crawled into the hole.

Darkness wrapped around her like a cloak. Her skirts caught on something. She pulled and felt the fabric tear. The tunnel floor was wet and slippery; her hand landed on something soft and slimy that wriggled. With a cry, she jerked back, and her head slammed against the top of the tunnel. Dizzy and frightened, she stayed motionless, waiting for the sick feeling to go away. Something touched her foot and she whimpered; it was the only remaining effort she was capable of.

"Go on, Renra. It isn't far," came a whisper from behind her. Fuzzily, she recognized Shandy's voice. With a sigh, she started forward again. Maybe he wouldn't make her do anything else when she got to the end. Perhaps she should have stayed in the carriage. It wasn't wet or cold or dark, and Gadrath only wanted her to sit and smile. No, she didn't like Gadrath, and there was a reason why she hadn't stayed. She couldn't remember it just now, but she would. Now she had to keep crawling.

Ranira crawled. The tunnel narrowed, the floor rose, and she was forced to creep along almost on her stomach. The embroidered gown was long since in rags. She would have stopped if it had not been for the insistent shoves from behind. Suddenly there was a little light in front of her—a stone in the roof of the tunnel had cracked. A few feet further she came to another, then three stones in a row with pieces broken out of them. Then the tunnel was a shallow trench half-filled with broken rocks. She sat up, blinking in the sunlight.

Beside her, Shandy wriggled out of a dark space between two stones and grinned at her. "I *told* you I didn't have to worry about Templemen, Renra. I bet they don't even know the tunnel's here. But we got to find someplace they won't look for you, or they'll catch you again soon as they start hunting.''

Dizziness overwhelmed Ranira as she tried to stand, and she put out a shaking hand to steady herself. From miles away she heard Shandy's exclamation. ''Renra! What's the *matter* with you?''

Ranira fought to think clearly. ''They gave me some kind of drug,'' she said hazily. ''I don't know how long it will last. I think someone said it could be permanent.'' Memory swam up out of the shifting cloud that threatened to engulf her: silver light turning yellow, and a voice murmuring. ''Mist. Did she get away?''

''What?'' Shandy looked confused, then began tugging at her hand determinedly. ''Come on, Renra. We got to get out of here. You can tell me about the mist later.''

''No!'' She jerked back. ''Mist is the foreign woman, the one in the short veil. She can heal; I saw her. Did she get away too? You have to find her, Shandy. She can heal.''

''I told you those foreigners would be trouble. Why do you want to find a bunch of witches? This way. Duck your head; you're too tall.''

''They can heal! Will you find them?'' Ranira asked, clinging desperately to her fading lucidity. ''Mist and Jaren and Arelnath. Will you?''

''All right,'' Shandy said. ''But not now. Come on, Renra!''

Mental tension flowed out of her like a sigh. As she relaxed back into the drugged fog, she tried to murmur her thanks, but she could not even be certain she had spoken. Part of her was still aware of the awkward scrambling over broken pavement and the twisting route that Shandy followed, but most of her mind was in a pleasant stupor.

''Renra! Renra?''

Slowly, Ranira realized Shandy was talking to her. He seemed to want a response. ''Shandy?'' she said tentatively.

''Ah, Renra,'' he said disgustedly, ''You didn't even hear. You have to climb over that wall. I'll help. You understand?''

She looked doubtfully at the high wall of crumbling bricks

that stretched from one side of the alley to the other, but she nodded. Shandy pushed at her. "Go on!" Dutifully, Ranira stepped forward.

Climbing the wall was almost as difficult as crawling through the tunnel had been. Though her skirts were now in rags, they still hampered her movement, and her thin slippers slid treacherously on the ancient brick. Twice she slipped back when one of her handholds broke free of the wall. At last she reached the top. She was too tired to climb down, and it looked like an uncomfortably long drop. She was still sitting there when Shandy popped up beside her.

"You crazy? Anybody looks down this way, they'll see you for sure. Get down, Renra!" The boy followed his own advice immediately, swinging down to the ground with the ease of long practice. She blinked at him for a moment, then slide her feet over the side of the wall.

The drug was still distorting her perceptions; and she was not prepared for the wrenching drop from sitting atop the wall to hanging from her hands. She grabbed in panic as she realized her mistake. Her hands slid along the brick, scraping the skin painfully. She missed the hold she was reaching for and slipped from the top of the wall to land in a crumpled heap on the other side.

Shandy was beside her immediately, wanting to know if she was all right. Ranira shifted and started to respond, but a stabbing pain in her right leg made her bite back a scream and shake her head instead. Shandy stood over her, frowning.

"Can't you walk, Renra? If you rest for a while? The Templemen don't know about this place, but if they really start hunting . . ." The boy's voice trailed off.

Even drugged, Ranira knew what a full Temple search would mean. Again, she tried to move, and almost fainted. "No," she whispered, biting her lip. "I can't. You have to find Mist, Shandy. She can heal. She could do something."

"That witch you were talking about?" Shandy shook his head. "But the Temple will catch us right away if we use magic! And it'll take all day just to find her. Those foreigners may not even have gotten away. And there are too many places to look. Are you sure you can't walk?"

"I can hardly move my leg at all," Ranira said hazily.

"Try, Shandy. You know where to look; you can find them. They got away. They're hiding over by the old market. You *have* to find them." She did not even wonder at the certainty of her knowledge.

"All *right*, Renra. I'll go look," Shandy said. "But I don't like it."

Ranira sank back, relieved. She wanted to say more, to explain, but she had no energy left to do so. As she watched Shandy climb the wall once more, a wave of dizziness pulled her, unresisting, into darkness.

CHAPTER EIGHT

She woke alone and miserably uncomfortable. Her head ached, and her injured leg throbbed painfully. The ragged black gown was still damp with river water and clung with unpleasant coldness to her back and legs. The effects of the drug still lingered; she felt slow and stupid. She found herself staring intently at a broken piece of brick and could not remember why. Irritated, she forced herself to look around.

She still lay where she had fallen, at one side of a small, rectangular courtyard, barely a few feet wide. There were no exits; the two short ends of her shelter were blocked by the blank stone walls of buildings, and the two brick walls ran unbroken from side to side.

For a moment Ranira was puzzled. Then she laughed weakly. Years ago the Temple of Chaldon had decreed that all of the alleys in the city must be blocked at regular intervals so that fleeing thieves, witches, and other undesirables could not lose their pursuers in the narrow maze behind the buildings. Evidently someone at the Temple had made a mistake when the walls were positioned, and no one ever dared to question it. Erecting two walls in the same alley would be a small price to pay to escape the notice of the Eyes of Chaldon. Ranira wondered how many other such places there were in Drinn. Shandy would know, she was sure.

The shadows of the walls crept closer. She began to wonder where Shandy was, but with the drug in her system she could not stay worried long. There were other effects as well—she felt cold, and her mind began to alternate between a fuzzy semiconsciousness and nightmarish hallucinations. Only when she shifted, trying to escape her dream-pursuers, did the pain in her leg bring her back to herself for a moment or two.

Time ceased to have meaning. Ranira woke for perhaps the third or fourth time to find herself in darkness with her leg twisted painfully. A shadow moved beside her, and she stifled a scream. "It's me, Renra," came Shandy's whisper. "And I found those foreigners."

The note of disapproval in his voice was unmistakable, but Ranira ignored it. "Mist?" she said, straining to see into the darkness.

"No, little sister. Jaren," another voice whispered. "I will take you to her. Can you stand?"

"No," she said. "I think my leg is broken."

"Then I will carry you." Ranira felt arms around her, lifting. Then agony flared up her leg, and she fainted.

She awoke with cool water streaming down her face. She was outside the walls; Jaren was bending over her. Silver-green moonlight poured into the alley—Elewyth had risen. Though it was five days from being full, its light was bright. In the greenish glow she could see Shandy standing next to Jaren, holding a dipper. She leaned against a brick wall. On her other side stood a pair of stone water jars.

"I am sorry," she said hazily. "Did I faint?"

"You did," Jaren replied. "I will be gentler this time, but I am afraid it won't be easy. We must move quickly. There are Watchmen about, and this place is too open to linger."

As if to emphasize Jaren's words, a robed figure appeared at the end of the alley, silhouetted in moonlight. Almost by reflex, Shandy melted into the shadows. Ranira shrank back, seeing her recent nightmares become reality. The Temple guard strode forward, peering into doorways and shadowed places. A hand caught her, forcing her to remain motionless. It was Jaren, crouched tense and unmoving beside her.

The Templeman moved slowly in their direction, sword in hand. He had not yet seen them crouching behind the water jars, but he was sure to do so if he came much closer. She held her breath, willing him to turn away. The guard hesitated, and she felt a sudden surge of hope; then the Templeman shook his head and started forward again.

When the guard reached the water jars, Jaren sprang. His leap carried him in one graceful motion from his frozen crouch beside Ranira to a stance directly in front of the Templeman. The startled Temple guard opened his mouth to cry out, but it was already too late. Jaren's right hand locked around the guard's neck; his left grabbed the Templeman's sword arm and held it motionless.

The guard's left hand was still free. It clawed at Jaren's face, but the foreigner twisted away without losing his hold. The Templeman tried again, but Jaren seemed to anticipate his every move. Finally, the guard abandoned his attempt to break the grip that was slowly strangling him. He reached instead for his dagger. Jaren's knee came up as the weapon left its sheath, and the dagger went skittering across the stones. The battle continued in silence.

The guard's dagger lay just beyond Ranira's reach. She bit her lip and began inching carefully forward with the vague idea of helping Jaren if she could reach the dagger in time. Pain brought tears to her eyes with each movement of her leg, but as long as the movements were small, the pain was not unbearable. It seemed to take hours to cross the small stretch of alley. Finally her hands closed around the dagger's hilt. She looked up.

The guard was still clawing at Jaren, but more weakly—he was evidently beginning to feel the lack of air. Ranira relaxed; Jaren needed no help from her. A scraping noise behind her made her jerk her head toward the mouth of the alley just as a new voice said, "What's this?"

A second Templeman stood silhouetted briefly at the mouth of the alley, his attention focused on the combatants. Ranira's hands closed around the dagger as he stepped swiftly forward. Jaren and his opponent were too intent on their own struggle to show any sign that they had noticed the new arrival, though they must have heard his voice. The newcomer drew his sword. Ranira caught her breath. He was too far away for her to reach him, and there was no way she could move that far in time.

Suddenly the shadows behind the Temple guard shifted. Something long and round flashed in the moonlight as it came down on the back of the second guard's head. He stumbled and fell to his knees immediately in front of Ranira. His eyes widened as he took in the unmistakable garments she wore, and he opened his mouth to shout. Without thinking, Ranira leaned forward and, with all her strength, drove the dagger into his chest.

The guard choked. Ranira had a fleeting glimpse of utter astonishment on his face before he fell sideways, carrying the dagger with him. Shandy appeared behind the body, still holding the water dipper. He swung it at the remaining guard, but the blow was unnecessary. The man was already collapsing.

As the second guard fell, Jaren twisted the sword from his grasp and neatly cut the man's throat, stepping a little to one side as he did so. Blood spurted briefly, then the Templeman pitched forward on his face. Beneath his head, a dark pool began to grow, glistening wetly in the moonlight.

Jaren turned and bent to inspect the other corpse. He retrieved the dagger and wiped it on the Templeman's robes, then turned and offered it to Ranira. She accepted it silently. Suddenly she found herself shaking, and she forced herself to look away from the bodies.

When she recovered her composure enough to look again, Jaren was removing the swordbelts from the two corpses. He donned one, settling it around his waist with a relieved sigh. He picked up the other, then hesitated. He drew the unused dagger and gestured at Shandy, but the boy shook his head. With a shrug, Jaren replaced the weapon and slung the entire belt over one shoulder. He looked at the bodies again and shook his head regretfully, then began dragging them to less conspicuous positions in the shadows.

By the time Jaren turned back to her, Ranira was under control again. This time she was ready for the surge of pain as he lifted her. She did not faint, but the alley swam before her eyes as Jaren glided silently forward.

Shandy led then cautiously through the streets and alleys of Drinn. Several times they had to stop, crouching behind water jars or flattened against doorways while groups of

Templemen strode past. Jaren moved so smoothly that the swordbelt dangling from his shoulder never scraped a wall or banged against the sword he wore.

Well as she knew the city, Ranira was soon lost. She quickly stopped trying to remember the turnings and concentrated instead on remaining awake. Between exhaustion and pain, this was no easy task, and she was surprised and relieved when Jaren slid into an alley and knocked a curious rhythm on one of the doors.

The door swung inward and closed hastily behind them as they entered. It was dark inside. No hint of moonlight crept through any window slits. Ranira realized they must be in one of the abandoned buildings not yet claimed by the Temple of Chaldon. She could not see even a dim outline of the room, but she could feel Jaren moving surely forward, and she wondered how he could find his way through the blackness. She heard the click of a door latch opening; then they were descending a flight of stairs.

A light shone below, dim and wavering. Ranira found herself looking down into a deserted wine cellar. Empty racks stood along the walls, dusty and broken. Pieces of glass and pottery littered the floor. Seated on a pile of warped and rotting boards on the far side of the room was Mist, carefully shielding a flaming candle stub from any draft. The foreign witch had discarded her short veil, and Ranira was shocked by the weariness that showed in every line of her face. Embarrassed, she hastily averted her eyes. Though she knew few women went veiled outside the Empire of Chaldreth, the sight made her uncomfortable.

Jaren set Ranira gently down on the floor. She glimpsed Shandy and Arelnath descending the stairs. Shandy's eyes shifted nervously from side to side; Ranira suspected that the boy disliked hiding in a wine cellar with only one exit almost as much as he disapproved of the three non-Chalders. Arelnath moved to stand beside Ranira, looking down at her.

"I see the boy spoke truly," she said. "How did you get out of the river? I did not really expect to see you again." Her voice was cool.

"Shandy pulled me out." Ranira started to explain the details of her rescue. Halfway through, Jaren interrupted.

"Tunnel?" he asked, looking at Shandy.

Shandy was smug. "Sure. The Watchmen don't care about it 'cause they're too fat and lazy for it to do them any good. I got lots of good hiding spots like that."

"Shandy knows more about getting around Drinn than anyone," Ranira confirmed.

Jaren nodded. "I can well believe it. I've seen what he can do." He turned to the boy. "Would you be willing to assist us in getting out of Drinn? I don't think we could find a better guide."

Shandy's thin chest swelled with pride at Jaren's words, but almost immediately his eyes narrowed. Ranira could see his suspicion of the foreigners warring with his desire to be rid of them. "Maybe."

Arelnath looked disapprovingly from Jaren to Shandy, but said nothing. Shandy glared back. There was a brief silence. "I brought something for you, Arelnath," Jaren said then. He rose and unslung the extra swordbelt from his shoulder. "Here, catch."

Arelnath's face lit up as she saw the weapons, and she jumped forward and caught them easily. She buckled the belt in place, then drew the sword. She examined it closely, testing its edge against her thumb. She hefted it to test its weight, then stepped back and swung the weapon several times as if feinting at some imaginary opponent. She repeated the process with the dagger.

"Not the best weapons I've seen," she said at last, "and not sharp enough, but better than none."

"I hadn't checked." Jaren drew his own sword. He flicked a fingernail against the side, producing a faint ringing. He shrugged. "It'll do."

"Jaren, you're too casual about things," Arelnath said, shaking her head. Her frown returned, and she looked at Jaren suspiciously. "Where did you come by them?"

Jaren shrugged again. "A couple of Templemen who won't need them anymore. Nowhere near here, though we may have spoiled one of Shandy's better hiding places for a while."

"If they come from Templemen, I must examine them, Jaren. Give them to me, please," Mist's voice interrupted.

The black-haired woman had risen and come slowly forward. Even her voice sounded tired. Jaren looked at her and raised both eyebrows almost to his hairline, but he unbuckled his swordbelt and handed it to her without comment. The woman's face went blank for a moment as she fingered the sword and sheath. Then she relaxed with a sigh.

"Nothing," she said in response to Jaren's look of inquiry. She returned the belt and looked toward Arelnath. "Yours next."

The other woman had already unbuckled the belt, but she made no move to hand it to Mist. "You are tired already, and there is more work here that only you can do," she said, glancing at Ranira. "Is this necessary? Is it wise to spend your strength so freely?"

"I am afraid I must," Mist replied. "I must be sure we cannot be traced through the weapons Jaren has brought. Our protections are thin enough now. They could not withstand any added strain, and I am not familiar with much of the magic the Temple uses."

"The Temple doesn't use magic," Shandy objected. "Magic is forbidden." He frowned at Arelnath, who ignored him and handed Mist her swordbelt. The examination took longer this time, for there were two weapons for Mist to handle. Finally she relaxed and shook her head. "Nothing."

"I *told* you the Temple doesn't use magic!" Shandy said triumphantly.

Mist turned toward him. "Your Temple *does* use magic," she said flatly. "I have felt it. I feel it now, and I must find its source or the priests will track us down once more. Please do not distract me again."

Arelnath seemed startled by Mist's reaction, and Shandy squirmed uncomfortably. Jaren only smiled slightly and pointed to Ranira. "There is one more dagger," he said.

Mist nodded and walked to Ranira's side. She stooped and reached for the dagger that Ranira held out. As her fingers touched the hilt, she gasped and lost her hold. The weapon fell to the floor between the two women. Jaren bent to retrieve it.

"What have you found?" Arelnath demanded as Mist stepped back.

"I do not know," Mist replied. "There was not enough time. I will have to try again." Reluctantly, she reached once more for the dagger. Her face was tight as her fingers brushed Jaren's on the hilt. Then her expression relaxed into astonishment. She blinked; her face became remote. It was a long time before she shook her head and handed the dagger back to Jaren.

"There is nothing here, either. How could I have been so mistaken?"

"Then it wasn't the dagger you felt," Arelnath said. Her eyes were on Ranira as she spoke.

"What do you mean? Why are you staring at me?" Ranira asked peevishly. Her head was aching again, and her mind felt suddenly fuzzy. She heard an exclamation from Jaren, but she couldn't seem to focus her attention on what was happening. There was a flash of pain from her leg; then another. But her leg didn't hurt like that unless she moved, and she wasn't moving—was she?

"It is the jewels!" someone said above her. "Smash them!" A moment later Ranira felt hands at her shoulders. She cried out in pain as the jeweled lace was ripped away from her throat. She felt as if hooks were tearing her flesh as the jewels pulled away. She choked, unable to breathe. As she fought for air, Ranira heard Jaren's voice cry faintly, "Mist! We must smash these. Look to her!"

Ranira's vision cleared for a moment. She saw Mist kneeling beside her while behind her Jaren and Arelnath stamped the black crystal jewels into powder. Then Mist took her hands, and white fire ran through Ranira's bones like lightning. She would have cried out again, but she had no breath left.

As the fire grew stronger, Ranira felt something within her stir in answer to the storm of power and magic that poured through her body. Even as it did so, she saw orange flames leap before her eyes and smelled the black smoke of old nightmares. Then she did scream. Dimly, she heard Mist's cry, an echo of her own, but she was too stunned to respond to anything other than the flames that crept nearer and nearer.

Abruptly, Mist's hands let go their hold. The sensation of power flooding through her vanished, and with it the flickers of fire. Ranira looked around wildly for a moment, searching for the flames she knew she had seen—but there were none. A wave of dizziness swept over her. She closed her eyes against the sudden distortion of the room, grateful that the fire had been an illusion but too tired to wonder how or why it had occurred.

CHAPTER NINE

The disorientation lasted only a few moments, then subsided, leaving Ranira relaxed and once more aware of her surroundings. She opened her eyes at once and glanced quickly around as she sat up. Mist lay nearby, with Arelnath bending over her in concern. Shandy hovered near the foot of the stairs, watching suspiciously as Jaren scattered the fine black dust that was all that remained of Ranira's jewels. As Ranira watched, the blond man finished his task, dusted his hands, and turned to look at her.

"What happened?" she asked before he could say anything. She shifted to a more comfortable position, and suddenly realized that there was no pain in her leg. Her mind was clear as well. She looked toward Mist with a feeling of mingled curiosity and respect—tinged with suspicion. Jaren began to speak, and she jerked her wandering attention back to him.

"You were acting strangely," Jaren said. "Then the jewels on your gown started smoking. I ripped them off, and Arelnath and I smashed them while Mist did . . . whatever she did. You'll have to ask her, if you wish to know more."

"The jewels?" Ranira said, staring. "I thought it was the drug that made my mind feel so strange."

Jaren shrugged. "I am not trained in magic. Ask Mist or Arelnath," he repeated. He glanced toward the two women and frowned, then called something in a language unfamiliar to Ranira. Arelnath answered in the same tongue, and Jaren nodded. "Mist is waking now, if you wish to ask any questions."

64

His voice carried the length of the cellar easily, and Mist struggled to a sitting position. "There is no time for questions," she said. "We must leave at once. The Temple will not take long to find us now."

"What? But your protective spells!" Jaren said. He was not objecting; even as he spoke, he stretched out a hand to help Ranira to her feet.

"I could not hope to hide such a burst of power, even if the Temple could not trace the jewels," Mist said. "We must go."

"At once," Arelnath said, nodding. She rose and offered an arm to Mist, then bent to retrieve the candle stub. Mist started toward the stairs. Jaren and Ranira followed close behind.

As they passed Shandy, the boy nodded in some satisfaction. "I told you magic was forbidden," he said as he started up the stairs behind Ranira.

Ranira started to reply, but Jaren motioned her to silence. He leaned forward to listen at the door, then nodded. "Ranira, Shandy, let us guide you until we are outside and you can see again. Arelnath!"

Ranira heard the soft puff of breath below her on the stairs as Arelnath blew out the flame of the candle stub she carried. The flickering light vanished, plunging the room into darkness. Ranira heard the click of the door latch and felt a hand on her shoulder. She stumbled forward in the darkness and heard a second door open. Moonlight flooded in. She did not stop to look around, but hurried forward into the alley.

Without waiting to be asked, Shandy slid by her and gestured for them all to follow him. Halfway up the alley he stopped and pointed at a narrow space between two buildings, then vanished inside it. A moment later he reappeared and beckoned. Mist nodded, and Arelnath stepped forward and also disappeared. Mist followed; then it was Ranira's turn.

She looked dubiously at the dark, narrow opening. Jaren stood in the shadows beside her, silent and still, but plainly waiting for Ranira to go ahead. Reluctantly, she started to slide between the walls. As she did so, she heard a quick intake of breath from Jaren, and instinctively her head turned. She had just time enough to see and grasp the significance of the eight robed figures at the end of the alley before Jaren shoved her forward. She felt him squeeze into the opening behind her, and she forced herself to move faster. She could not run; there was too little space.

Abruptly, the walls ended and Ranira stumbled into another alley. "Renra! This way," Shandy hissed beside her.

"There are Templemen back there," Ranira whispered back as she followed. "Hurry!"

The boy's eyes widened, and he nodded. He paused a moment for Jaren to join them, then set off. Two shapes moved to join them as they passed along the edge of the alley: Mist and Arelnath. They did not need Jaren's whispered "Templemen!" to warn them to move quietly; both were as silent as shadows.

Under Shandy's direction they moved up the alley. Ranira was tense, expecting any moment to hear Templemen behind them or see guards blocking their way in front. None appeared. Undisturbed, the little group worked its way across a narrow street and another alley, until a wordless shout from the direction of the old building announced that their former hiding place had been found.

Now their way became more difficult. Groups of Watchmen sped by, heading toward the source of the cry. Kaldarin had joined Elewyth in the sky, a thin red crescent split by the beginnings of a black stripe. The additional light, dim as it was, made dodging the Templemen harder, and Ranira was soon exhausted by tension from the constant wariness that was required.

For hours they wove through the streets and alleys of Drinn, barely able to keep ahead of the Temple searchers. There were no pilgrims on the streets. They themselves were the only moving things besides the Temple guards and the rats. Wearily, Ranira wondered where all the people were. The inns never had enough space for all those visiting Drinn during Festival, but there was no sign of anyone too poor or too unlucky to find a room. The only place in Drinn big enough to hold them all was the Temple. She shivered at the implications of that thought and tried to thrust it out of her mind, but it would not go away.

They reached a small sheltered area, out of sight of the street. Ranira touched Jaren's shoulder to attract his attention. If she could tell him her suspicions, perhaps they would cease to preoccupy her. The blond man turned and shook his head, then pointed. Ahead, Shandy was standing in front of a pile of rubble. The front wall of the building still stood, but the rest of it appeared to be simply a heap of boards and broken bricks. There was no sign of Mist or Arelnath.

Shandy grinned and pointed as they came closer. Ranira bent down. Near the base of the pile was an opening, hardly more than an irregular gap in the tumbled brick. She looked up and Shandy pointed again, insistently. Ranira bent once more and began squirming into the hole.

It was not as difficult as she had feared. The opening was larger than it looked, and though the passage beyond was lumpy and far more uncomfortable than she expected, it was passable. It twisted right, then sloped sharply downward, toward the interior of the pile. At the top of the incline, Ranira found it impossible to move forward. Her hands scratched ahead of her. Then her feet found a securely embedded rock, and she twisted and shoved. Suddenly she was sliding down the slope. A moment later, in a shower of brick dust, she rolled into an open area and collided with someone.

"Who are you?" a voice whispered. Ranira was coughing too hard to answer at once. She felt a knife point prick her throat.

"Ranira," she whispered hastily between spasms, and the pressure vanished. "Shandy and Jaren are behind me," she added when the coughing finally subsided.

"It took you long enough," Arelnath grumbled in the darkness. "I thought a Templeman might have found you."

She was spared a reply by Jaren's arrival. She could not see him, but curses mixed with coughing were more than enough to identify him. Beside her, Arelnath snorted. "Quiet, Jaren. We don't know how far sound carries here," she whispered.

"You can't hear anything outside," Shandy's voice informed them in a normal tone. " 'Long as nobody shouts, they won't notice, even if a Templeman is standing on top of the rocks. And nobody can see lights, either. I blocked the entrance.''

"That's good to know," Arelnath said. "You are thorough.'' A moment later the candle stub flared to life in her hand.

They were in a rough cave formed by part of a collapsing floor and a few strong beams that held the rest of the rubble at bay. In the middle of the floor, next to a dusty green bottle, lay a little bag which Ranira recognized as the one Shandy sometimes carried to collect kitchen scraps. Somewhere was an opening for air to enter; Ranira could feel a slow draft on her face.

The quarters were crowded for five people, but no one complained. Jaren coiled down against the beam nearest the exit and looked expectantly at Mist. "What now?" he asked.

"We must find a way out of Drinn. Today, or tonight,'' Mist said. Her eyes were closed; she seemed far more exhausted than the effort of dodging Templemen should have warranted.

"How do you think you can do that?" Shandy asked. ''The Templemen will be watching the gates in double shifts, and nobody could sneak out even when there was only two of them.''

"We must find a way,'' Mist repeated in a low voice. Her eyes opened in a long, slow motion. Ranira saw something like desperation in them. ''I cannot hold out longer than that.''

"What do you mean?" Arelnath demanded. "Protective spells are not that draining. With food and water, this place will be safe for days. By then it should be easier to slip past the guards. Venran will not be at our meeting place for another four days, at least, and it's certainly possible that his caravan may be delayed.''

"If we wait beyond tonight, there is no place in the city that will be safe for us,'' Mist said. "The Temple watches constantly, and that pressure is draining, especially since I do not dare to use any but the most subtle spells. Even those I cannot keep secret for long. Yet, without them we would be detected at once. I do not know how they channel such power! You have some training; can you not feel it?"

Arelnath frowned in concentration. "No, I do not, but I have very little skill. I will have to trust to your abilities."

"The watchers must rest sometime," Jaren said thoughtfully. "Magic is so hated that there cannot be many priests in Drinn with the knowledge to trace us. Can you not rest when they do?"

Mist shook her head. "It is easier then, but not enough. I must be prepared for them to begin again. I fear, too, that they prepare some other magic against us; I have felt the edges of it brushing by. We must be out of Drinn before they are ready."

"Then we will leave today," Jaren said calmly. He turned to Arelnath. "Will you have any difficulty leading us to the spot Venran picked?"

"No, but he won't be anywhere near there for several days yet," Arelnath said. "We had not planned on leaving until just before the end of Festival, remember. Venran is a Trader. He won't waste time waiting for us in a forest when he could be making money elsewhere."

"How are you planning to get out of Drinn?" Ranira asked pointedly. "You can't meet your friend at all if you are still in the city."

"When the streets fill with people, it will be easier to avoid the guards," Jaren said, "and it should not be hard to find some of those brown robes and a couple of veils. You . . ."

"Jaren, I will not wear one of those things!" Arelnath interrupted. "I am a Cilhar warrior. I will not pretend to be a brainless slave. I thought we settled this when I agreed to this harebrained scheme of yours."

"I, too, am Cilhar, and I do not ask lightly," Jaren said, ignoring Arelnath's last comment. "But the Templemen are looking for a man, a youth, and two women. They are not looking for a family of pilgrims with three women and a young boy. It will be far easier to avoid them if you go veiled, at least until we are out of the city."

Arelnath's mouth set in a stubborn line, but before she could respond, Shandy broke in. "Women don't have short hair," he said scornfully. "A veil won't hide that. Anyway, no one leaves during Festival. Don't you know anything?"

"If we knew more of Drinn, we would have no need to be here," Jaren said.

Arelnath snorted. "I thought you had been in Drinn before! Why don't you know all this?"

"I have been in Drinn before," Jaren said. "Exactly once. But I wasn't interested enough in local custom to spend much time asking questions."

"Now he tells us!" Arelnath said.

"We had to come," Jaren said. "It doesn't really matter now. Shandy, I cannot believe the gates are completely closed. How could the priests feed all these people?"

Ranira said, "The gates are only opened for a few hours to let the farmers in with food. No one goes out at all. And there are always two Temple guards there; probably more than that since we got away." She looked at Mist. "Unless your magic can kill the Templemen, we can't get out that way."

"I am a healer," Mist said. "There are rules which govern such magic. It would be my death to strike them. A healer cannot kill."

Arelnath gave Mist an odd look, but said nothing. Jaren looked briefly from Mist to Ranira and then back to Arelnath. "I see. We shall have to find another way, then."

The two foreigners began discussing alternative ways of getting out of the city, with Shandy putting in an occasional word of advice while Mist leaned against the wall, resting. Ranira retreated as well as she could into the shadowed edges of the cave and curled into an unhappy ball. In the frantic race for safety, she had all but forgotten her own disheveled condition. Her skirts were in filthy rags, the bodice of her gown was hardly better, and she had no veil at all. It might not bother foreign women, but Ranira felt naked without one.

She glanced toward Mist, then her eyes slid away from the woman's uncovered face. Curiously enough, she was more disturbed by Mist's unveiled condition than by Arelnath's. Once she got over the shock of seeing a woman dressed in male attire, it was easy for Ranira to accept Arelnath as someone foreign, unusual, not bound by the Temple codes. Mist, on the other hand, might easily have passed for one of the noblewomen of Drinn. Yet, watching her, Ranira saw that she felt no reluctance to walk unveiled, and that disturbed Ranira more than she had at first realized.

A tiny thread of doubt wove through Ranira's thoughts. She knew very little about the three foreigners. Why did they want to spend Midwinter Festival in Drinn? A more troubling thought then occurred to her. Why had she automatically sent Shandy to find them when she was drugged and injured? And how had she known where Shandy would find them? Had they put some spell on her?

The sound of her own name jerked her thoughts back to the present. ". . . Ranira, at least," Jaren was arguing. "She can't walk around in that costume much longer; it is much too obvious. Anyone who sees it will recognize her."

"True," Arelnath agreed, glancing at Ranira. "We will try to get a robe for her, then."

"And a veil," Ranira put in, then bit her lip. She did not know how hard it would be to steal clothing, but adding another item could hardly make it safer.

"A veil," Arelnath said in a flat voice. "Do you know what you ask? It is unlikely that we will find robes and a veil in the same place, and the guards will certainly be watching more carefully than usual. Is it necessary?"

"I'm sorry," Ranira said. "I didn't think."

"I can get a veil," Shandy put in. "It'll be easy, Renra."

"There is no need," Mist's voice said quietly. "I would have offered sooner, had I thought you were uncomfortable. Here. I have no further need to wear this, and it will put you more at ease." From a pocket in her skirt she drew the short veil she had herself worn and handed it to Ranira.

Ranira reached for the veil and tied it in place. In spite of Jaren's amused glance and Arelnath's unconcealed contempt, she felt better immediately, and the thanks she offered Mist were sincere. When she had finished, Arelnath turned to Mist. "If you are rested enough, lady, we can discuss ways of leaving the city," she said.

Mist nodded, and Arelnath went on. "There are only two ways to leave Drinn: through the city gates or on the river. The gates will be carefully watched. We might be able to contrive a way of slipping past the guards, but from what

Shandy and Ranira say, it is not likely. That leaves the river. The city walls are too close to the water for us to get out that way, even if we could steal a boat. However, the river does go under the walls, and the Temple of Chaldon will probably not expect us to swim in midwinter.

"I think we should try."

Visions of dark water rose in front of Ranira's eyes as she stared at Arelnath, appalled. "Swim the river? You cannot be serious!" she gasped.

"Why not? The current is steady, but not too swift, and the banks are high enough to hide us until we are well past the farms outside the walls. The water will be cold, but as long as we do not stay in it too long, we should not have to worry about freezing."

"If the Temple snakes let you live," Ranira said. "Why do you think the river is left unguarded?"

"Snakes?" Arelnath asked. "In midwinter? Drinn is not far enough south for that."

"The Temple snakes do not sleep in winter," Ranira said. She shivered. "They do not have to. They live in a pit below the lowest chambers in the House of Correction, and every night they are loosed into the river. They return in the morning, because they know the Templemen will feed them. They are fast and silent and deadly. No one can swim the river and live."

"But you jumped into the river to escape," Jaren objected.

Ranira looked away. "I jumped into the river to die," she corrected him. There was a moment's silence, then she added, "I saw a man die of the bite of a river-snake once. It is a painful and lingering way to reach the Gates of Mist. I was lucky."

"If the Temple releases the snakes each night, it will take time for them to swim the entire length of Drinn," Arelnath mused. "When are they set free?"

"When the evening trumpet blows to close the gates," Ranira said. "But they do not all return to the Temple each day, even in winter. There are always some in the river."

"Of course, but there will certainly be far fewer of them if we start from close by the city walls at the time when the gates are closing," Arelnath said impatiently. She turned to Mist. "Have you strength enough to control snakes as well as horses?"

Mist hesitated. "Control is not necessary; only warning. I do not know if I can keep the spell undetected, but the charm itself is simple."

"What do horses have to do with snakes?" Shandy demanded abruptly.

"Nothing," Jaren told him. The blond man smiled. "Only that Mist was responsible for the confusion that Ranira's carriage horses caused this morning. If she can do as well with snakes, we will have little to fear from them."

"*You* made the horses rear?" Ranira said. "You were chained at the back of the carriage! How could you have frightened them?"

"It was not difficult," Mist replied quietly. "The spell is a minor one, and the horses were already nervous in that crowd. Frightening blameless animals was not pleasant. I do not wish to do so again unless I must."

"But how did you get out of the chains?" Ranira persisted. "The Temple forges use a metal that is proof against witchcraft. Or so they claim."

Jaren's laugh rang out in the enclosed space. "So they may, little sister. But the locks are as easy to open as any other smith's. Easier. Your Temple trusts too much to its reputation, and I have some little skill at lock-picking." His hand brushed his boot top; a moment later he displayed a piece of stiff wire about twice as long as Ranira's forefinger. "It was not so mysterious as you think."

"Particularly since everyone was staring at Ranira just then," Arelnath commented. "I'll wager the Temple guards did not even miss us. They were too busy trying to find a way down to the river."

"Which we intend to swim," Jaren said. "If you can keep the snakes away, Mist, it will not matter whether the Temple notices the spell. By the time they can reach us, we will be out of the city."

Mist seemed troubled by Jaren's confidence, but she did not speak. Beside her, Shandy shifted uncomfortably. "I guess Ranira and I can show you how to get to the river, if you really want to," he said after a moment. "But I'm not going near those snakes."

The frown on Mist's face vanished in a wave of surprise. "Won't you come with us? I do not think you will be able to dodge the Temple guards for long if you stay. The snakes will not harm you; I will see to that."

Shandy ducked his head and mumbled something. "What is it, Shandy?" Mist asked gently.

"I don't like witches, and I don't like snakes," Shandy said sullenly. He hesitated. "And I can't swim."

"Neither can I," Ranira said as Arelnath frowned. She glared at the two foreigners. "It is hardly a common skill in Drinn, though it may be so in your home."

"Jaren and I can carry you, if that is your only worry," Arelnath said abruptly. As she turned away, Ranira heard her mutter, "I wouldn't leave anyone in this Mother-lost city."

"Carry us?" Ranira said incredulously. "In the river?"

"Well, not exactly," Jaren said. "It is more like towing, but you won't drown. So, tell us—will you come?"

Ranira hesitated. She still did not completely trust the foreigners' magic, in spite of the dramatic demonstrations she had seen and experienced, and the idea of leaving Drinn with them disturbed her. The only one of the three non-Chalders that she really liked was Jaren. Arelnath was too touchy, and Mist's witchcraft troubled Ranira despite the healer's kindness. Yet she had no real choice. To remain in the city was a guarantee that she would be recaptured by the Temple. Outside Drinn, she at least had a chance.

She looked over at Shandy. The boy's eyes were on hers, but Ranira could not read any expression in them in the dim candlelight. Shandy would be caught by the Templemen soon, she was sure; his luck had already stretched far beyond that of most other street children. At best, he would be bonded. If the Temple discovered his role in her escape, he would certainly be tortured, or perhaps even sacrificed. She knew Shandy would join her, however reluctantly, if she left Drinn, and that knowledge decided her. "I will come," she said, firmly setting her doubts aside.

"Renra!" Shandy exclaimed, aghast. "You're going to

leave Drinn? In the river? With witches and snakes and everything?''

"Yes, and so are you," Ranira said. "How long do you think we can manage to stay alive with the Temple after us if we don't go?"

"Ah, Renra, I can do it," Shandy protested. "I haven't got caught yet, have I?"

"No, but you haven't had the Eyes of Chaldon after you before, either," she said tartly. "And they will be, as soon as the Temple finds out you helped me get away."

Shandy's mouth opened, but no words came out.

"Well, that seems to be settled," Jaren said after a moment. He stretched his legs carefully, to avoid kicking one of the others in the cramped quarters. "There are still a few things puzzling me, though. Perhaps you could explain how you came to be involved in all this, Ranira."

Ranira looked at Jaren in surprise, but his interest seemed sincere. With a shrug, she began her story. The three foreigners listened intently. When she finished, Arelnath looked at her. "What is an Eye of Chaldon?" she asked. "And why are you so afraid of them?"

"The Eyes?" Ranira repeated. "They are special servants of Chaldon. They do not take part in the Temple rites, though some of them are always at the sacrifices. No one knows how many there are. They go all over the Empire, looking for witches and people who disobey Temple edicts." She shivered. "No one can keep a secret from them. They find out everything, and when they return to the Temple, they tell the god all they have learned."

"The Eyes of Chaldon, indeed," Jaren murmured. "I begin to see."

Ranira nodded. "And their commands are the voice of Chaldon. Whatever they say must be done. They can order a whole village burned for sheltering a witch—or even on the suspicion of it."

"They do not sound like pleasant people," Jaren said. "No wonder you are afraid of them." He himself did not sound very worried. Ranira looked at him sharply.

"I have answered your question; now I have one of my own," she said. "Will you tell me why you are in Drinn?"

Jaren shot a thoughtful glance at Mist. The woman shook her head regretfully. "I am sorry, Ranira, but we cannot tell you until we are out of Drinn," Mist said. "It would be too dangerous, for you as well as for us. The Temple suspects already, but is not sure."

"How can I be in any more danger than I already am?" Ranira demanded. "I have publicly cursed the High Master of the Eyes of Chaldon—which is punishable by beheading; I have consorted with witches—which is burning; I have killed a Templeman—which is death by torture; and I have run away from being the Bride of Chaldon. I don't think they have a punishment awful enough for that. They'll probably throw me to the snakes, at least. How many times can they kill me?" She glared at Mist.

Arelnath laughed dryly. "She's right, Mist. The Temple isn't going to look for her any harder because she knows your secrets. She deserves to know."

Ranira turned, surprised by this unexpected support. Mist sighed. "Do you agree, Jaren? Very well. Ranira, what do you know of the Melyranne Sea and the lands around it? Have you ever heard of the Temple of the Third Moon?"

"Third Moon?" Shandy said scornfully before Ranira could answer. "There's only two moons, Kaldarin and Elewyth. Everybody knows that!"

"There are only two moons now," Mist said. "But once there were three. One was destroyed, so long ago that we know nothing of the cause. There are pieces of it all over the world, but they are hard to find." Unconsciously, the woman's hand moved upward to close around a small white stone dangling from a chain around her neck. Ranira recognized the gesture; it was the same one Mist had used when she was healing Jaren, only then her veil had hidden the stone from Ranira's eyes.

"Three moons?" Shandy said, wavering between disbelief and awe.

Mist nodded, and the boy blinked and lapsed into a thoughtful silence. She looked at Ranira. "You have not answered my question. Do you know of the Temple?"

"No." Ranira shook her head. "The Melyranne Sea is east, beyond the boundaries of the Empire of Chaldreth, but I have never heard of those other places.'' Shandy started to speak, but Ranira frowned him into silence. She was not going to let him antagonize these people again, just when they might be ready to tell her something.

Mist sighed again. ''I thought as much. Well, to make matters simple, there are more than thirty countries and independent cities on this side of the Melyranne Sea alone. The Temple of the Third Moon is on an island south of the Sea, and it is older than all of them. Because we are small and have no interest in conquest, we have come to play the role of arbitrators and advisers among the countries that ring the Sea. We . . .''

''You said 'we'! You're a heretic!'' Shandy interrupted. ''Renra, did you hear?''

''What do you expect from a foreign witch?'' Arelnath asked irritably. ''She isn't a priest of Chaldon!''

''But the Temple catches heretics,'' Shandy said. ''Just like they do if you think about magic too much. That's how they caught Cilla, and Parlin.''

Jaren looked at Mist, a startled expression on his face. ''Could the Temple of Chaldon actually detect people who merely think about magic?'' he asked.

''It is possible,'' Mist said thoughtfully. ''I am still not sure how they found us so quickly. If they can locate people who merely do not think as the Temple wishes, they certainly would have noticed us. But there is no need to fear now, Shandy. The Temple cannot find you while I am hiding us.''

''Huh,'' Shandy replied skeptically, but he did not object again.

''I already know how Shandy feels about the Temple,'' Ranira said crossly. ''I want to know what you are doing in Drinn. If it is safe for Shandy to talk heresy about the Temple of Chaldon, it is safe for you to explain why you are here.''

''You are probably right,'' Mist said. She was silent for a moment, then looked up. ''I am a . . . servant of the Temple of the Third Moon. We are trained in magic and healing, and as I have said, some of us are advisers to the countries that ring the Melyranne Sea. A little over two years ago, the Temple of the Third Moon was asked to judge a dispute between the Empire of Chaldreth and Basirth. We agreed, though we had never dealt with the Empire before. The delegation went to Basirth and returned safely, but shortly after that there were disturbances, sendings against the Island of the Moon.

"At first the spells were minor, irritations only, but lately they have grown more serious. It is no longer safe for ships to visit us because of the storms, and there are a hundred lesser things. We have been able to counter some of these magics, but for each spell we overcome, another two begin.

"When we realized what was happening, we tried to trace the spells, but they are subtle. It took us days to follow them even as far as the Empire of Chaldreth, and no one could learn more. The Assembly of the Temple chose to send me into the Empire to find out why the Empire is doing this and to stop it, if I can. Arelnath and Jaren are Cilhar mercenaries, hired by the Temple Speaker to help me. Do you understand now?"

Ranira started to nod, then frowned. "Why did you have to be in Drinn during the Festival in order to do this? If you had come just before or just after it, there would have been no reason for the Temple of Chaldon to arrest you. Foreigners are only banned during Festival."

A fleeting grin crossed Jaren's face, but Mist looked uncomfortable. "We have traveled through the Empire of Chaldreth for weeks," she said. "I have learned little, but enough to know that the Temple of Chaldon is the real authority here. Drinn is the center of the Empire and the home of the main Temple, and Midwinter Festival is the greatest of your feasts. I could sense the power flowing from the Temple of Chaldon toward the Island, and I hoped to learn the answers to my questions here."

"Did you?" Ranira asked. Mist shook her head.

"There is a darkness about the Temple of Chaldon that I cannot penetrate. Even in the House of Correction I could not discover the source of the Temple's power, nor the reason it attacks us."

Once more Mist's hand closed around the white stone she wore. Suddenly she looked very tired. "I will try again to read them, but not until we are at the river. I am sure the priests will notice at once, so we must be able to leave quickly when I have finished."

"Is that necessary?" Arelnath said, scowling. "We have already learned a great deal. If the priests of Chaldon notice your spells quickly enough to guess what we're doing, they may be able to catch us, and the Island will learn nothing."

Mist hesitated; then her mouth set in a determined line. "The Temple of Chaldon is the key to the Empire. Yes, we have learned much, but we still do not know why they would destroy us. I must find out why, and how, and this is the only way left."

"I think they fear your magic and your influence among their neighbors," Arelnath said. "A Temple that freely teaches the use of magic is not likely to be popular with those who burn witches."

"Perhaps that is part of their reason, but I am sure there is more," Mist said. "I must try to find out what other motives they have. Only once more. That is all I ask."

"If you insist," Jaren said. "I am not magician enough to stop you. But will you have enough strength to deal with the snakes if you make this attempt?"

"I will do what I must," Mist replied. "Do not worry. The charm against snakes is an easy one. Unless I am dead or unconscious, I will be able to warn them away. It takes very little strength."

The blond man did not look completely reassured, but all he said was, "Since we are leaving tomorrow, I suggest we try to sleep now. We may not get so good a chance again for a while."

"Sleep?" Ranira said incredulously.

"Of course," Arelnath said. "You'll feel much better after you have rested, and so will Mist. Match straws for first watch, Jaren?"

The blond man nodded, and a few moments later Arelnath sighed. "You always were luckier than I. Dream of home." She crawled over him to the exit hole and vanished.

Mist leaned forward and pinched out the candle stub. "The Moon watch you," her disembodied voice said in the darkness. Ranira heard a low chuckle from Jaren, but her eyes were already closing of their own weight. A moment later, she was asleep.

CHAPTER TEN

"Ranira, wake up." Someone was shaking her shoulder. With a groan, Ranira lifted her head and opened her eyes. Her muscles were stiff and sore. The uneven, rocky surface on which she lay seemed to have bruised her everywhere. Jaren was crouching over her, holding a small bundle. She blinked at him for a moment before she realized that someone had lit the candle stub once more.

"Here," Jaren said, tossing the bundle at her. "Put this on. It's probably more comfortable than what you're wearing, and it's certainly less noticeable."

Ranira automatically caught the soft, awkward mass—a brown pilgrim's robe. She held it for a moment, then pulled it over her head without removing any of her other garments. She tried to belt it in place, but gave up after a brief struggle; there simply was not enough space. The belt would have to wait until she was outside in the alley again. An icy finger traced a line down the middle of her back as she thought of going out to dodge the Templemen once more. She shook her head, checked her borrowed veil, and looked up.

Jaren was watching her, an amused expression on his face, but all he said was, "Here. Breakfast. Don't look too closely, just eat it. You'll need the energy by the end of the night." He handed her a crumbling lump of bread and a hard, squarish object which proved to be cheese—the standard fare of the poor Drinn. In the flickering candlelight she could not see the food clearly, but she had certainly eaten far more dubious-looking meals. She realized suddenly that the last food she remembered eating was nearly two days in the past. If the Temple had fed her after Gadrath had made her drink his drugged wine, she had no memory of it. She bit eagerly into the bread.

There was not enough to satisfy her, but she was no longer painfully hungry when she finished. She licked the crumbs from her fingers and looked up. Except for Shandy, the others were still eating; evidently, the unappetizing appearance of the food affected the foreigners more than it did the two Chalders. Ranira noticed several more lumpish bundles lying beside Jaren. "Where did you get all this?" she asked, waving at both the robes and the food.

"Shandy and I stole them while you were asleep," he replied with a grin. "We got a firebox, too, and some cord. Nobody watches pilgrims closely; after the first robe it was easy. We can walk right to the river without being noticed in these."

"We might be able to," Arelnath put in, "but we aren't going to try. Walking openly through Drinn would be like going up to a Temple guard and saying 'Excuse me, I'm one of the people you're looking for. Would you mind arresting me?' You're crazy to even suggest it. We don't know enough of the customs of Drinn to fake being pilgrims. I'll wager it's more complicated than it looks. Haven't your harebrained ideas gotten us into enough trouble?"

"As you wish," Jaren said with an unrepentant shrug. He rose and made his way to the entrance hole. "In any case, we had best be on our way."

"Don't forget your own disguise," Arelnath said. She picked up one of the bundles and pitched it at Jaren. "It will be easy enough to spot you even with the robe; you're too tall for a Chalder."

Jaren caught the robe, then dropped on all fours and vanished into the small opening that led to the alley outside. Shandy followed immediately. The ease with which he negotiated the tunnel showed how often he had used it. Arelnath looked at Mist and sighed. "I'm next, I suppose. Mother of Mountains, but I'll be glad to be out of this city! Crawling through holes isn't much to my liking." She scooped up the two remaining bundles and pushed them into the tunnel. In a moment more she was gone.

Ranira slid over to the tunnel mouth and started inching her way uphill to the bend. It was more awkward this time because of the robe, but she managed the trip without any major difficulty. When she reached the alley, Arelnath was waiting to help her to her feet and brush the dust from the robe.

The sun had already set, but enough light remained for Ranira to see Arelnath and Jaren clearly. The two had donned the brown pilgrim's robes. Ranira surveyed them critically. Their swords made odd bulges beneath the coarse brown cloth, but with luck no one would come near enough to notice. Far more serious was their manner. Even in the fading light, it was plain that neither had the bearing of a pilgrim.

"Can't you look a bit more frightened?" Ranira asked. "No one will believe you're pilgrims if you walk like that!"

"Ranira is right," Mist said as she emerged from the tunnel and slid her own robe over her head. "Try to seem less sure of yourselves. We have no wish to attract attention."

"Come then," Jaren said softly. He turned and, to Ranira's amazement, scuttled down the alley in perfect imitation of a frightened old man. The others followed more slowly. When they reached the mouth of the alley, Shandy took the lead, and again they began a twisting progress through the streets of Drinn.

There were few people about. Once again Ranira wondered what had become of all the pilgrims. The few they saw were hurrying toward the center of the city, where the Temple of Chaldon loomed. Not even Templemen were in evidence. The city seemed more deserted as the darkness deepened, and she grew more and more uneasy as they drew nearer to the walls of Drinn.

At the end of a short, dirty sidestreet, Shandy turned and wriggled through a crack where two buildings did not quite meet. The others followed with more difficulty and soon found themselves standing on a small stone ledge, about two paces wide. On one side rose the featureless wall of the building; on the other, the stone dropped toward the river, forming a low wall along the bank. Ahead, the walls of Drinn arched low over the dark waters, barely visible against the now completely darkened sky.

"Well, who is first?" Jaren asked, breaking the silence. He looked at Mist.

"Not yet," Mist said. "I wish to try my strength against the Temple one last time, now that I will not be hampered by the need for secrecy. But be ready; we will have to leave quickly."

"That is easy enough," Jaren murmured, looking down at the river. "All that is necessary is to jump." Mist seated herself on the wall above the river. She reached up and cupped the stone she wore in both her hands. The stone began to glow softly, and Mist's face went still and remote. Ranira watched in fascination until she was distracted by a touch on her arm.

"The robe will hamper you dangerously in the water," Arelnath was saying. "Leave it here, but be sure to take the knife." She and Jaren had already discarded their pilgrim's garb, and Jaren was making a bundle of the swords, the remains of the food, the firebox, and Shandy's water bottle.

Ranira hesitated. She could not dispute the advice, but she was reluctant to part with the only decent clothes she had. Arelnath smiled slightly and said, "Add it to Jaren's pack. It will not absorb much water, if it is tightly rolled and tied." Ranira complied, and after a moment's thought, added the veil and her knife to the pile as well.

"Good," Jaren said as he dropped his leather boots on top of the stack. He strapped the bundle together with the cords that had belted the pilgrims' robes. It made a surprisingly compact parcel. Jaren looked up. "I think . . ."

He was cut off in midsentence by a bright silver light flashing from the riverbank where Mist was seated. Ranira heard the woman's voice cry strange words, and she felt a tingle run down her spine. She heard Jaren say, "That's done it. The river now, and quickly!" Ranira paused, blinking. Before she could gather her wits, a hand grabbed her arm and propelled her over the edge of the wall.

As she fell, she heard splashes and a brief wail that sounded like Shandy. Then she hit the water. The river was deep and far colder than she remembered. The current pulled her along. In panic, she tried to fight her way to the surface. Her head broke water at last, and she gasped in relief, then gasped again as she started to sink once more. Her second breath sucked in a mouthful of water, and she choked. Most of her breath was gone, but she could not keep her head in the air long enough to draw another.

A wave of water smothered her, but a moment later an arm encircled her waist. Almost at once she found her head above water. She coughed and gasped. "Stop thrashing around like that," a voice said in her ear. "It won't do any good, and it will certainly attract the Templemen if you keep it up. Relax."

Ranira recognized Jaren's voice and tried to do as he said. Under his guidance she found herself floating on her back while the man supported her head. When at last she became convinced that she was not going to drown, she tried to look around. She was rewarded with a glimpse of several dark shapes above the water nearby before she started sinking again.

"Relax, I said," Jaren whispered. "Everyone's all right; you don't need to see them."

"But Shandy," Ranira spluttered. "He can't swim either."

"Arelnath has him. It's all right, I tell you. Be quiet."

As if to confirm Jaren's words, a second voice whispered in the darkness. The echoes from the water distorted the sound slightly, but Ranira could still identify the speaker as Mist. "The Temple will send men soon, and probably the snakes as well," she said. "We must . . . ." Ranira lost the rest of the sentence in a little wave that covered her ears briefly. She knew that Jaren must have heard, though, for almost immediately he shifted his grip on her and she felt a surge of water as his legs kicked.

Between Jaren's efforts and the increasing current, they began to move more quickly. The river narrowed as it approached the city walls, where it flowed faster and deeper. Ranira grew more nervous, but quickly discovered that whenever she began to grow tense she also began to sink. Jaren was concentrating on swimming; he had no attention to spare for advising her. Somehow he seemed able to consistently choose the fastest part of the river. They were approaching the arching walls of the city with frightening speed.

Just as they swept under the wall, Ranira saw lights along the bank they had just vacated. She stiffened and cried out, pointing, but the movement pushed her mouth under water and the cry came out in bubbles. Then they were under the city wall. Jaren stopped swimming and clamped a hand over Ranira's mouth. She heard the water slapping softly at the sides of the tunnel, and nodded understanding. The walls multiplied even that slight noise into an eerie murmur; any additional sound, at least until they reached the end of the tunnel, was almost certain to carry back to the Templemen. Jaren's hand loosened its hold, but remained ready in case he had not interpreted her nod correctly.

The tunnel was pitch-black. Ranira had no idea how wide it was, or how long. It seemed to her that they had been in darkness far longer than it would take to pass under the thickness of the city walls. Just as that thought occurred to her, her head scraped the top of the tunnel, then scraped it again. Jaren pulled her backward, so that only her nose and mouth were above water. The top of the tunnel continued to drop. Jaren tapped her head with his finger. Guessing what was coming, Ranira took a deep breath just before the roof of the tunnel met the water and they had to dive. Jaren held her under one arm like a sack of flour and began to kick again, assisting the current now that no splash could betray them to the Templemen.

Without warning, the current swirled into a confusing mass of eddies, then slowed. Jaren kicked again, and they bobbed to the surface. Ranira gasped air and felt Jaren's warning touch on her shoulder. They had surfaced just outside the city wall, where the river widened into a broad pool. Elewyth was just rising over the horizon, and silver-green sparkles of moonlight lit the ripples on the water. It made the swimmers very conspicuous, Ranira realized as she watched first a single dark head and then two more break water nearby. Behind them was the wall of the city, dead-black against the stars. She blinked as a shadow passed along the top of the wall, then realized that a guard was patroling there.

She swallowed hard. If he looked in their direction, he would surely see them.

Her attention was then distracted by an S-shaped rippled in the water. She blinked, then saw another, and realized what they were. Snakes! She froze. As a result, she started to sink at once, but her fear of the snakes outweighed her fear of drowning. Jaren's grip on her shoulders was all that kept her from going completely under before she saw one of the snakes turn aside. Unbelieving, her eyes flickered to the second ripple. It, too, changed direction before it came within an arm's length of the swimmers. "It's working," she whispered, too softly even for Jaren to hear. "It really is working."

The current slowly carried the little group past the wide section of the river, to where it turned and narrowed once more. Ranira grew impatient. Even with Jaren's cautious kicks and one-handed strokes to aid the current, they were moving far more slowly than a walking man. Then she remembered the guards. A group of people clambering up the banks of the river would be easy to see at this distance, and it would be hard to avoid making noise that might attract a Watchman's attention.

The river narrowed again at last and the current quickened. The banks grew higher, hiding the swimmers from the city walls. Jaren began to swim more strongly, angling toward the south bank of the river where a little grove of trees near the water's edge could give the fugitives some shelter. The water grew shallower. Ranira's feet touched bottom. Thankfully, she stood on it and, with Jaren steadying her, began moving slowly toward the shore.

The trees were still nearly twenty paces downstream, and the bank was nearly as far. The river was shallower only because some quirk of flow had deposited layer upon layer of pebbles and sand along a wide band from the riverbank to the place where Ranira and Jaren stood, creating a low shoal. She could hear small watery noises behind her—Mist and Arelnath were still swimming. She turned her head, but the distance was too great for her to find them in the darkness.

Suddenly something like a heavy club hit Ranira between the eyes. She stumbled, pulling on Jaren's supporting arm.

Her head rang. It was a moment before she realized that there had been no physical blow; Jaren had noticed nothing until she pulled at him. A second blow fell, but this time Ranira was almost ready for it, and she did not fall. Blood pounded painfully in her ears. Simultaneously, she heard a gasp and a low moan from the direction of the deeper water. Between the darkness and her own discomfort, she could not identify the speakers. Then, as unexpectedly as it had come, the pressure vanished.

Ranira shook her head to clear it. Beside her, Jaren stood chest-deep in water, still holding her arm, his head twisted to look backward. Ranira turned with him, eyes and ears straining over the dark water, until Arelnath's whisper came floating back from just beyond the shallows. "Jaren! Mist is unconscious. Help me with her!"

Jaren dropped Ranira's arm and lunged back out into the river. Water surged up in waves on either side of him. Ranira stood frozen for a moment, listening to the indeterminate sounds coming from the middle of the river. The high banks that hid them from the city walls also blocked out the moonlight, so she could not see any of her companions.

Suddenly a group of dark, dripping figures materialized in front of her. Jaren was carrying Mist while Arelnath stumbled along beside him, one hand braced on his shoulders, the other supporting a whimpering Shandy. "Ranira, take Shandy and get out of the river," Jaren said shortly.

Ranira reached for Shandy. The boy was too big for her to carry, but too small to stand alone in the water. She settled for an awkward grip and half-carried, half-dragged him away from Arelnath. The water was deeper for her than it was for Jaren, and she felt uneasy with the floating sensation it imparted to the simple act of walking.

"Hurry," Jaren said. Obediently, Ranira tried to increase her speed, but almost at once she slipped. She started to panic as her head went under. One foot hit bottom and held long enough for her to lift her head out of the water, then it slid and she went down again. Twice more she regained her balance just long enough to take a brief gulp of air, only to lose it again. Finally she floundered into water shallow enough for her to find sure footing once more.

Water sheeted off her head as she pulled herself upright at last, coughing and choking. Shandy was in no better shape, though at least here he could stand unaided. She had dragged him along in her stumbling progress, and the boy had spent at least as much time under water as she had. He spluttered and splashed forward. Ranira kept one hand firmly locked on his shoulder, as much for her own sake as for Shandy's.

Jaren and Arelnath went past on her right without stopping. Arelnath no longer leaned on Jaren's shoulders, though she looked far from steady on her feet. Jaren, too, seemed unbalanced. He was holding Mist high above the water, so that not even the hem of her robe dipped into the river. Suddenly Ranira realized why he wanted her to hurry and why he was carrying Mist in such an awkward position: With Mist unconscious, there was nothing to keep the Temple snakes away from them!

In a panicky rush, Ranira splashed toward the riverbank, coughing and dragging Shandy with her. Her flight was halted by a dark figure that blocked her path. "Quiet!" Arelnath said sternly. "Do you want to attract every snake in the river?"

Ranira swallowed hard and began wading more slowly. Arelnath turned and accompanied her. In a matter of moments they reached the bank of the river. A weedy, tangled growth of plants bent toward the water from an almost vertical slope that rose from the ankle-deep river to just above Ranira's head. There were no trees above them. In their hurry to leave the river, she and her companions had moved straight to the riverbank instead of at the angle that would have brought them to cover.

Without stopping to think, she reached up, trying to find a good grip among the weeds. She quickly discovered that they were too shallow-rooted to support her weight. Almost frantic from her fear of the snakes, she dug her hands into the mud behind the plants. Roots and water made it too slippery to find a firm hold. Arelnath was having a similar problem. Jaren stood unmoving behind her, holding Mist carefully. Shandy was the only one who had found a spot to climb; he was already halfway up the slope.

Frustrated and afraid, Ranira moved toward where Shandy

had been standing. She immediately found the reason for his success: A small bush was growing halfway up the bank, twisted but still anchored strongly enough to give a good starting point to a climber. Ranira grasped the base of the bush in one hand while her other clawed at the damp weeds and finally found purchase. Slowly, she dragged herself upward.

upward.

CHAPTER ELEVEN

Moonlight washed over Ranira as she reached the top of
the bank and slid over a slight rise into the grassy weeds.
Shandy was squatting just in front of her. Below, she heard
Arelnath hiss something at Jaren, but she was unable to make
out the words. Soon there were rustling noises as Arelnath
struggled upward. Ranira rolled out of the way, then turned
to help Arelnath over the top of the bank.

As soon as she reached the top of the riverbank, Arelnath
turned and squatted at the edge of the slope she had just
ascended. "Brace me!" she hissed over her shoulder. Confused, Ranira hesitated. Arelnath leaned forward precari-
ously, stretching into the darkness below. Ranira slid up next
to her just in time to see Jaren lifting Mist upward.

Without thinking, Ranira too leaned forward to support the
unconscious woman. She heard a pained grunt from below,
then Arelnath whispered, "Ready? Pull!" Ranira pulled.
The two women went sprawling backwards with Mist's body
on top of them. Jaren had given the unconscious woman an
additional shove at the same time as they had started to pull,
and the unexpected force was enough to overbalance the two
women at the top of the riverbank.

Ranira heard a smothered yelp from the river as she and
Arelnath struggled to untangle themselves. The sound was
followed by rustling noises as Jaren began to climb. By the
time the two women regained their feet, he had reached the

top of the bank and was untying the bundle he still wore strapped to his waist.

"Never mind that," Arelnath said as soon as she realized what Jaren was doing. "Come help me wake Mist. We must get as far from here as we can before daylight. It will be easier traveling if she can walk instead of being carried."

"I doubt that Mist will be in any condition to heal, even if you are able to wake her," Jaren replied, kneeling and starting to unwrap the bundle. "Therefore I would rather continue with this."

Arelnath's right hand dropped to her waist, as if she were unconsciously feeling for a weapon. Even in the shadowy moonlight, Ranira could see the set expression on the woman's face, and the tension in her voice was obvious. "Jaren, not the snakes?"

"I am afraid so, mihaya," Jaren replied. "The leather stopped the first couple of bites, but the last one got my ankle." He looked ruefully at the misshapen pile in front of him, then picked up one of the soft leather boots he had included at the last minute. "If I'd been wearing these, it wouldn't have happened."

"You couldn't swim in boots," Arelnath said. Her voice was shaking slightly, but her hand was steady as she reached down for one of the knives Jaren had taken from the Templemen. "Let me do it. You never have been good at things like this."

"All right." Jaren sounded almost relieved as he leaned back and stretched out his left leg toward her.

"What are you doing?" Ranira asked. She was still stunned by the news that Jaren had been bitten. She also had the distinct feeling that she had only heard half of the conversation; she could sense undercurrents she did not understand.

Arelnath ignored her. Pulling one of the swordbelts from the soggy pile, she started toward Jaren's leg, only to be stopped by Ranira's sudden cry, "Wait!"

"Why?" Arelnath snapped, but Ranira saw that her hands had stopped moving.

"If a snake bit Jaren's leather, it must be full of poison," Ranira explained. "If you touch it with bare skin, it will poison you also. When it soaks all the way through, it will kill

Jaren. I mean, it would if . . .'' Her voice choked on the
large lump in her throat, and she stopped in midsentence.

"Enough about dying!" Arelnath said sharply. She looked
toward Jaren, but he was lying back with his eyes closed and
gave no sign of having heard. "Those snakes can't be so
dangerous that even touching their poison kills.'' Despite her
words, Arelnath's hands were already busy with the knife,
slicing through the upper part of Jaren's close-fitting leather
pants, well above where any snake could have bitten.

"Get any of it in a scratch, and it'll kill you," Shandy said
suddenly, coming to Ranira's support. "But I bet you didn't
scrape your hands at all climbing up here, so you don't need
to worry," he added sarcastically.

Arelnath did not reply, but Ranira saw that she was moving
more carefully. The leather was slow to yield, but at last it fell
away from Jaren's leg. Arelnath speared the leather piece
with the point of her blade and, with a snap of her wrist, sent
it flying back into the river. Ranira jumped at the splash.
Then Arelnath knotted the belt from one of the pilgrims'
robes around Jaren's leg.

Ranira watched with a feeling of helplessness. She had no
confidence in Arelnath's ability to save Jaren, yet she had
seen these people do one impossible thing after another. She
wanted to help, but she had neither knowledge nor skill to
offer, and Arelnath's grimly purposeful movements seemed
to forbid speech.

Ranira and Shandy watched in silence while Arelnath
finished tightening the belt around Jaren's leg. Then she
picked up the knife again, hesitated for a moment, and bent to
wipe it carefully on the grass. When it was clean enough to
suit her, she leaned forward and inspected the leg closely,
searching for the puncture marks made by the snake's bite.
The knife came up in a swift, decisive movement, and Ranira
gasped in shock as blood trickled from the slash. Jaren made
no sound.

Ignoring her audience, Arelnath laid her mouth against the
wound. Ranira's shock deepened; she had heard the tales of
foreigners who drank blood, but she had never believed
them. Arelnath straightened up and spat, then bent once
more, and Ranira realized that she was trying to suck the

poison out of the bite. This sudden understanding made her relax somewhat, but the sight of Arelnath's efforts still made her feel queasy.

A thought struck Ranira, and then she turned away, glad to have an excuse to avoid watching. She had to rummage for a moment among the pile of odds and ends that Jaren had been carrying, but she soon found the small bottle she was seeking. She shook it, and there was a sloshing noise as the water shifted inside. Only half-full. Well, that was better than she had expected. She risked a look in Arelnath's direction. The woman seemed to have finished. Ranira walked over to her.

"Here, rinse your mouth," she said, handing the bottle to Arelnath. "If you swallow any of the poison . . ." She did not have to finish the sentence.

"Thanks," Arelnath said, taking the bottle. She uncapped it and poured water into her open mouth, swished it around, and spat. She repeated the action, then poured water over Jaren's leg for good measure. The effort all but emptied the bottle. Arelnath grimaced as she replaced the cap. "Too bad, but it can't be helped. We can fill it later. How is Mist?"

With a guilty start, Ranira turned to look. She had completely forgotten the unconscious woman. The healer-witch still lay unmoving where Arelnath and Ranira had left her. Pale green moonlight gave a cold, corpselike appearance to her face, and Ranira had to touch one of the motionless hands in order to convince herself that the woman still lived.

Arelnath moved to Mist's side. She placed a hand at the woman's temple and went rigid. Ranira hardly dared to breathe. A moment later, Arelnath relaxed with a sigh. "I cannot reach her," she said. Her eyes flicked from Mist to Jaren and back; her mouth was set in a grim line.

As if aware of Arelnath's gaze, Jaren shifted and sat up. "How long until she wakes?" he asked.

"I do not know. I think tomorrow, at the least. And we cannot stay here until then." Her eyes met Jaren's, and the man nodded.

"I can manage, for a while," he said. He untied the belt Arelnath had knotted about his leg, then reached for his boots. Arelnath's hand came up in a gesture of protest that stopped almost before it was begun, but Jaren saw the movement and looked up. "I can't walk far or fast without boots, especially on this ground. And I can't wear boots with that thing tied to my leg," he said.

"I know," Arelnath answered.

Ranira looked from one to the other, appalled. "You aren't going to try to walk with a Temple-snake bite, are you?" she demanded. "You'll just kill yourself faster. The poison . . ."

"According to you, I am a dead man anyway," Jaren said shortly. Disregarding Arelnath's protest, he went on, "If we stay here, we are all dead. In the daylight, anyone on the city walls could spot us at once. We have to get as far from here as we can before dawn, and you cannot carry me. How long will it be before the poison starts to affect me?"

Ranira blinked at the abrupt question. "I don't know. I've only seen one person who was bitten before—people in Drinn are careful around the river. I heard someone say that it took four days for him to die, but he was only at the inn for the last two." She shivered, remembering.

"With luck, you'll make it through the night," Arelnath said, sounding relieved. "Mist is sure to be awake by tomorrow evening. She can heal you then."

"Heal a Temple-snake bite?" Shandy said incredulously. "She can't do that."

"How do you know?" Arelnath demanded irritably as she sorted through the little pile of belongings. "Poison is difficult to heal, but not impossible. I am sure Mist will have no difficulty. She has been using her power freely these last three days, but she will have strength enough. It is not as if warding spells were a major enchantment, and outside Drinn we may not even need them."

Looking at Mist's face, Ranira wondered. She did not voice her doubts, though. Her knowledge of magic was not great, and the Cilhar woman might well be right. Arelnath was still picking through the remains of Jaren's bundle. "Here, you carry this. Ranira, if you don't want this robe, throw it in the river. We can't haul it around forever. But take the knife, or give it to Jaren; we may need it."

A shapeless blob landed at Ranira's feet with a squishing

sound. Gingerly, she picked it up. It was the tightly rolled pilgrim's robe and the dagger Jaren had taken from the Templeman. The remnant of the Temple gown Ranira wore was so tattered it hardly managed to meet the most minimal standards of decency. Her face grew hot in the darkness as she struggled with the knots that held the package together. The water had tightened them into hard, slippery balls. She made several unsuccessful attempts before she finally worked them loose. The outer layers of the compact bundle were wet, but the interior was barely damp. As the robe unrolled between her hands, something small and crumpled fell out of it—Mist's veil. Ranira stooped to pick it up. She put it on and started to pull the robe over her head, then paused and looked up.

Arelnath sat on the ground beside Mist with the two swordbelts, the extra robe, and the brown cords from the pilgrims' robes, knotting them together. Shandy looked on in fascination. Jaren was easing a boot onto his injured leg. No one was watching Ranira. Still, she hesitated.

Finally, she backed into the grass until she was hidden from her companions. In a few quick movements, she rid herself of the last of the black-and-silver gown of the Bride of Chaldon. Shivering with cold and from fear of discovery, she hastily pulled the heavy robe over her head and readjusted the borrowed veil. She fingered the knife for a moment, then carefully made a small slit in her robes and thrust the dagger inside, where it would be hidden.

Ranira's brief disappearance caused no comment among her companions. Arelnath insisted on throwing the scraps of Ranira's gown into the river after weighting them carefully with a rock. But for that, Ranira could have believed that her absence had gone completely unnoticed.

They started off almost at once, following the river. Jaren and Arelnath carried Mist between them on an awkward and uncomfortable-looking contraption made of swordbelts and cord. At first, Ranira tried to take Jaren's place at one end of the litter, but though she was strong enough to lift it, she was not tall enough to carry the makeshift litter comfortably with the taller Arelnath holding up the other end. Their progress slowed to a crawl, and Arelnath ordered Ranira to give up her place to Jaren once more.

Both moons had risen. The night was clear and cool. Ranira soon found herself shivering in her damp robes, and her own clothing was far dryer than Shandy's or Arelnath's. None of the others complained, so Ranira kept on in silence as well, trying to generate warmth through the sheer exertion of walking.

They had to detour frequently to avoid the ramshackle farmhouses that dotted the land near the river. This close to the city the farms were small and poor, and the cottages were close together, so that the path Ranira and her companions traced was a twisting one. In spite of their winding trail, Arelnath seemed sure of the direction they should take. As they moved into the area owned by the Temple of Chaldon and worked by the poor of Drinn for the benefit of the priests, the land became emptier.

As the night wore on, Ranira became more and more wrapped up in her own thoughts. The country darkness was unnerving for a girl who had spent all of her life within the narrow confines of Drinn. There was too much open space, and while the lack of cover allowed no cover for Temple spies, Ranira was too aware of the dark mass of the city behind her to enjoy the freedom. The Temple must already know they had tried to swim the river; she was sure that soon the priests would learn of their survival as well.

Ranira's thoughts shied away from the inevitable pursuit. Instead, she found herself remembering her years at the Inn of Nine Doors. Lykken didn't seem so horrible, now that she did not have to deal with him any more. Even the Temple of Chaldon began to take on an aura of grim but familiar authority. She almost began to wonder if she had been wise to leave.

A touch on her arm recalled her to the present. Shandy was standing beside her, and his voice was worried. "Renra? You all right? I spoke to you twice and you didn't hear me."

"Yes, I'm sorry," Ranira said, shaking off the reminiscent mood. "What is it?"

"Arelnath says we're going to hide over there in the trees," he said, pointing to a wooded area that showed dark and shadowy against the moonlit sky. "Come on."

Shandy started off at once, and after a moment's hesitation Ranira followed. Arelnath and Jaren were well ahead of them, but Ranira saw with a sinking feeling that they were moving far more slowly than they had been before. Jaren was swaying and stumbling on practically every step. No wonder Arelnath decided to stop, Ranira thought as she hurried to catch up to the others. The wooded area was a perfect hiding place, and there was no guarantee they would be able to reach another before dawn made further travel too dangerous.

In fact, they were barely able to reach the edge of the woods. Arelnath forced her way easily through the bushes that screened the trees, but Jaren seemed to have difficulty following. Finally, he reached the outer ring of trees and stopped. With a slow, deliberate motion, he dropped to his knees, placed the end of the carrying hammock gently on the ground, and collapsed.

Ranira was the first to reach him. His hands were icy, but his forehead was burning hot. Ranira looked up as Arelnath joined her. "Why did you make him walk so far?" she asked angrily. "You knew this would happen!"

"I had no choice!" Arelnath blazed, and Ranira winced at the anger and pain in her voice. "At least this way we have a chance. What good would it do him for all of us to be caught by Temple guards? Be glad that you did not have such a decision to make, and do not reproach me for what it is too late to change."

With an abrupt, jerky motion, Arelnath turned away. Ranira was too astonished to speak again. She had not expected such a violent outburst of emotion from the cool, practical foreigner. Tentatively, she stretched out a hand to assist Arelnath with Jaren, but the other woman brushed it away. Torn between anger and sympathy, Ranira judged it better to leave Arelnath alone with her thoughts, at least for the moment.

As she rose to her feet, she nearly tripped over Mist. With a pang of guilt, she realized that once again she had forgotten the gentle healer. She immediately set about moving the woman to a more comfortable position. Mist was still unconscious, and Ranira was worried as well as puzzled. The only similar instance of prolonged unconsciousness her limited experience provided was that of a man clubbed heavily on the head in a brawl at the inn, and he had eventually died without awakening. Ranira frowned and looked up.

"Arelnath? Do you know what is wrong with Mist?"

"She was hurt badly when the Temple spell hit us," Arelnath answered without looking away from Jaren. "It drove her mind into itself, for protection. She will wake tomorrow, but she may be drained. She was tired already when the spell struck."

If Mist should awaken in a weakened condition, it did not seem to Ranira that she would be likely to heal Jaren at once. She had wit enough not to say that aloud, however, and instead she asked, "Was it a spell that I felt out in the river? It felt more like a club."

"You noticed the spell?" Arelnath turned in surprise.

"Notice? I thought someone had dropped a rock on my head. Jaren didn't seem to feel anything, though."

"I thought Mist was protecting the rest of us, and so was hit hardest," Arelnath said thoughtfully. "Shandy did not feel anything either. I felt the blow more than you, but I was not hurt very badly. But if the Temple was striking only at those who can work magic, Mist would have been hurt the worst, because she is the most powerful. Have you ever been tested? No, of course not."

"I do not cast spells," Ranira said in shock.

"You may be capable of doing so, nonetheless," Arelnath said. "You have no training, but that does not mean that magic is impossible for you."

"No!" Ranira cried. She found herself standing without remembering how she had gained her feet. She glared into the darkness at the dim form that was Arelnath. "I am not a witch!"

"Magic doesn't mean witchcraft, and witchcraft doesn't mean what you seem to think it does," Arelnath said. Her voice was tinged with exasperation. "You have seen enough in the past few days to realize that, haven't you?"

"I can't work magic," Ranira insisted. "I'm not like you. Leave me alone!"

"As you wish. I suggest you follow Shandy's example and get some sleep while you can."

Arelnath turned away abruptly. After a moment, Ranira followed her advice and lay down at the base of one of the trees. She was glad that Shandy had not heard Arelnath's accusations. Shaken and confused, it was a long time before she finally slept.

CHAPTER TWELVE

Ranira awoke screaming from a nightmare of shadows and Temple priests. The black-clad figure in her dream had chased her with drawn dagger through the streets of Drinn and out into the fields while Gadrath had looked on and smiled and a dark, cold presence had brooded menacingly over everything. She looked wildly about her, only to find the nightmare becoming reality—the trees seemed twisted and menacing. She struck out in terror at a figure bending over her.

Hands caught and held her. Ranira thrashed violently, but she could not break free. She heard voices above, but they made no sense. Pain shot through her like a knife wound, and in Ranira's mind something writhed blackly before it burned away. Ranira found herself staring up at the worried faces of Shandy and Mist.

"I'm all right now. You can let me go," she said, and Mist leaned back with a sigh of relief. Ranira sat up. The forest spun around her, and she had to brace herself to keep from toppling over once more. After a moment, she looked up cautiously. "What happened?"

"You were shouting and yelling in your sleep," Shandy informed her. "I tried to wake you up and you wouldn't, and then Mist woke up and tried and you started hitting her. I sat on you, and Mist did something, and you stopped. Why were you yelling?"

Ranira laughed shakily. "You'd yell, too, if you had dreams like that. I'm glad it's over."

"It was more than a dream, Ranira," Mist said. Her face was lined with weariness, but Ranira was glad to see her also awake. "And I am afraid it may not be over, my dear. I am sorry; if I had done a thorough job when Jaren first brought you to me, I do not think you would have had to suffer this."

"What do you mean?" Ranira asked warily.

"Before I explain, will you tell me your dream?" Mist asked. "And do you know anything about the drug the Temple gave you before you escaped?"

The questions surprised Ranira. She frowned for a moment, trying to recall the nightmare from the rapidly fading wisps and shreds of memory that remained. Then she plunged into a description of the dream and the disorientation that followed. Mist listened in silence. When Ranira finished, she nodded and said, "And the drug?"

"I do not know what it was. The High Master Gadrath put something in my wine. I don't really remember anything after that until I was riding in the carriage." She frowned again as a fragment of memory brushed the surface of her mind, then hovered tantalizingly just out of reach. She shook her head in frustration.

"You told me someone said it was permanent," Shandy volunteered. "Remember, Renra?"

"No, but I'm sure I ought to," she said in exasperation. Instinctively, she looked around for something to jog her memory, and for the first time realized consciously that it was day. As she automatically reached up to adjust her veil, she noticed that not everyone was present. "Where is Arelnath?"

"Getting wood," Shandy said. "She left right before you started shouting."

"Yes, what was all that noise about?" a voice said from beyond the screening brush. Ranira jumped as Arelnath slid out of the bushes. The woman snorted. "It is a good thing there was no one else within hearing," she said. "I was afraid you'd been attacked by Templemen."

"Renra had a nightmare," Shandy explained. "But Mist fixed it."

"All that noise over a nightmare?" Arelnath said disapprovingly. "You could have given us all away!"

"It was more than a nightmare," Mist said. "Ranira was given a drug at the Temple to make her more tractable during the parade. There seems at least the possibility that some of the effects were more long-lasting than I had thought. And remember the jewels you and Jaren smashed? They were all part of a spell to bind Ranira's mind and will to the Temple of Chaldon."

"Didn't you stop that when you healed her leg, back in the cellar?" Arelnath asked.

"I removed most of the bindings," Mist replied. "But I did not expect there to be more than one spell. Obviously, there were others I did not recognize. Someone at the Temple was trying to use them to control Ranira while she was sleeping, and without protective spells around us it was easy for them to reach her. I have broken that spell, but there may still be more such; they are very difficult to find unless they are active."

"Would it be easier or more difficult for the Temple of Chaldon to control Ranira if she had the power to work magic?" Arelnath asked thoughtfully.

"I told you, I am no witch!" Ranira cried vehemently before Mist could reply.

"You have had no training, so you obviously cannot cast spells," Mist said calmly. "If that is your definition of 'witch,' then you cannot be one now. What Arelnath refers to, I think, is the ability to learn, which is very different. Have you reason to believe she is capable?" she asked, turning to the other woman.

"She felt something last night when the Temple attacked us," Arelnath said. "I am not sure it means anything."

"It would certainly be much harder for the priests to bind Ranira if she were trained," Mist said slowly. "I am not sure whether it would make any difference if she had only potential, although it may have made the priests more anxious to be sure of their control."

"I don't want anything to do with witchcraft!" Ranira said. "Work your magic without me. Consorting with witches is bad enough without being one."

"She's right," Shandy agreed. "You leave Renra alone!"

Arelnath started to speak, but Mist motioned her to silence. "There is no reason why you should learn if you do not wish to," she said to Ranira. "But I fear you will have to allow me to study you more carefully. I must find out if there are any more of these bindings and remove them; they are a danger to us as well as to you. It will be the last time, I think. I know now what to look for."

Ranira hesitated. Although she hated the Temple and was horrified by the thought of the priests controlling her, she was not entirely comfortable with the idea of submitting willingly to an enchantment. It occurred to her that she had already accepted magical aid several times, but it did not seem to make any difference. She was both afraid of magic and fascinated by it; the conflicting feelings were very unpleasant. Still, she could not object to Mist's proposal. If the Temple still had a way of controlling her, she was dangerous to all her companions. "I suppose you're right," she said reluctantly.

"Then try to sit quietly and relax," Mist said. "It will not take long." She leaned forward as she spoke, and began to murmur softly. Her hands hovered just above Ranira's head, but the healer did not fade into the trancelike state Ranira had come to associate with magic, nor was there any of the silvery light. In fact, Ranira did not notice anything in particular happening, and she began to fidget. The drone of Mist's voice was hypnotic, but instead of relaxing, Ranira became even more restless. Mist began to speak more softly, until her voice was barely audible. Now Ranira found it easier to sit still. Finally the chanting stopped, and Mist's hands dropped away.

"That is all?" Ranira asked uneasily. From her previous experiences, she had expected something more spectacular. "Wasn't there anything for you to find?"

"There were at least two more spells, but I have neutralized them," Mist said wearily. "Fortunately, the Temple had already used its most powerful bindings; those that remained were not difficult to break." The woman's appearance belied her words—she looked bone-tired.

There was a brief silence. "Thank you," Ranira said

finally. She could not think of anything else to say, and she felt unreasonably guilty because she had noticed neither the spells nor their breaking.

"Do not thank me yet," Mist said. "The magic of the Temple of Chaldon has a subtle and powerful source, and I may yet have missed something. I do not think so, but your own innate ability should make you able to fight anything that remains. Arelnath is right. You do have power—at least as much as she does, and probably more. I felt it when I removed the bindings."

"No!" Ranira said fiercely. Yet, the idea again both repelled and attracted her. But overlaying the clashing emotions were memories of fear and flames. "I am not a witch!"

"You are not a witch," Arelnath agreed cordially, "but you still have power." She turned away from the dumbfounded Ranira to face Mist. "I know you are tired, Mist, but can you tend to Jaren now? He was bitten by one of the river-snakes, and he has been feverish since dawn."

Color drained from Mist's face. Her head dropped. "I cannot," she whispered. "Forgive me, but I must refuse."

Arelnath stared at Mist blankly. "But *why*?" she said at last. Her voice broke. Ranira could almost see the woman's nerves fraying. "I have enough training to assist you, and I will help you all I can. You cannot be too drained to heal if you have aid."

"Even with your help, I have not the strength for two major enchantments," Mist said. "And I must contact the Temple of the Third Moon at once. I should have done it immediately, but I could not chance it while there was a possibility that Ranira could be controlled."

"You can contact the Temple later!" Arelnath snapped. "It is Jaren's life you are playing with, healer!"

Mist winced. Though her face was white, her manner was determined. "I know what he is to you, and I am sorry. But the lives of everyone on the island will be endangered if I do not reach them, and I may have no second chance. Where now do you say my duty lies?"

"If what you say is true, you . . . must try to reach the island," Arelnath agreed. Anxiety and hopelessness colored her voice. "But I still do not understand why."

Mist bowed her head. "I owe you that, at least," she admitted quietly. "I will explain my choice, but I cannot change it."

"You mean you are going to let Jaren *die*?" Ranira interrupted. "But you could heal him if you tried! I thought he was your friend. What kind of people are you?"

"I have spent my strength too freely these past three days, turning away the Temple seeking-spells and warding us all," Mist replied with the same frozen calm. "I cannot heal Jaren and still reach my Temple; the distance is too great."

"I should have known," Ranira said bitterly. "Temple priests are all the same. You can heal and cast spells, but you don't really care what happens to other people any more than Gadrath does. And *you* support her!" Ranira added, turning to Arelnath in disgust. "You are going to let Jaren die without even trying to make Mist heal him. You don't care about him at all!"

Arelnath's eyes narrowed. Her hand dropped to the hilt of her sword. "If you truly knew what you said, I would kill you," she said in a flat voice. "Jaren and I accepted the risk when Mist's Temple hired us in the Mountains of Morravik. He would not thank you for suggesting that I betray our trust; Jaren is my sword-mate, and you have no right to question my choice. No healer can be *forced* to heal. And furthermore—you have heard us say that you have power. If you will not offer it to help Jaren, you cannot criticize Mist, or me."

"I have no power!" Ranira shouted.

"Mist has said it, and you must know it is true or you would not deny it so fiercely," Arelnath said relentlessly. "Mist could tap the power that you hold and use it when her own is exhausted. With the added strength, she might be able to help Jaren as well as warn her Temple. Will you let her try?"

Vertigo struck Ranira dumb for a moment. The trees wheeled around her, and she closed her eyes. She felt the heat of a huge fire on her face and back, and though she could not see them, she knew that the flames were coming nearer. "No!" she shrieked with all the strength of her terror, and her eyes opened.

The word hung in the air before Ranira like a tangible thing, a barrier separating her from Arelnath and Mist. "I can't," she whispered, but she knew it was too late for explanation. Arelnath turned away. Mist's eyes were full of sorrow and hurt. Even Shandy looked surprised.

"You were going to explain, Mist," Arelnath said abruptly after a moment's silence.

"Do not judge Ranira too harshly," Mist said, ignoring Arelnath's comment. Ranira opened her mouth, then stopped. There was nothing she could say. Arelnath shrugged, not meeting Mist's eyes. "The explanation?" she said stubbornly.

The healer sighed and raised her head. "Very well. When I probed the Temple of Chaldon at the riverside, I learned far more than I could have hoped, though little of it is a joy to me.

"The 'god' Chaldon is really a Shadow-born, held captive beneath the Temple. Those who were meant to guard the Shadow-born have become its servants, though they are not foolhardy enough to release it from the ancient binding spell that holds it. The Temple priests draw on its power through their rituals. On the Night of Two Moons, at the climax of the Midwinter Festival, they will use it to attack the Island of the Moon."

"Why would the Temple of Chaldon want to attack the island so openly?" Arelnath asked. "I know you judged against them in that border problem with Basirth, but they certainly cannot intend such a strike simply out of spite! Are you certain it is not another of their sendings?"

"Not with such power behind it," Mist said. "Until now, they have been testing us, and perhaps trying to weaken us. Now they are ready to destroy us completely. Strange things are possible on the Night of Two Moons."

"But why?" Arelnath asked again.

"Did I not say that the priests of Chaldon are servants of Shadow?" Mist said. "In some way, the Temple of the Third Moon is a danger to the Shadow-born, a danger it seeks to remove before it is damaged." As she spoke, Mist's hand rose to touch the white stone she wore.

"What's a Shadow-born?" Shandy asked.

"The Shadow-born are ancient beings, spirits of a sort," Mist replied. "They remember old ways of magic, things we have forgotten. They have no physical form of their own; instead, they take over the bodies of others for a time."

"For a time?" Ranira said.

"A body possessed by a Shadow-born gradually fades into shadow itself. They caused great suffering when they went freely among men, but three thousand years ago the last of them were bound during the great wars."

Ranira shuddered. "You mean there are other gods like Chaldon? One is bad enough."

"They are not gods," Mist said firmly. "Once they may even have been men; no one knows their origins now. Yes, there are others. Most of them were bound in the north, near Alkyra, during the Wars of Binding. But your Chaldon is more dangerous than most."

"Why?" asked Arelnath. "I have never heard that the powers of Shadow-born vary greatly from one to another. What makes Chaldon more dangerous than those others?"

"Chaldon has willing servants," Mist said. "For centuries the Temple priests have kept him strong with their sacrifices. The Shadow-born of the north are not so fortunate; they were weakened greatly during their long captivity. In addition, it is rumored that the new Queen of Alkyra has found the four Gifts that were used during the Wars to bind the Shadow-born. If they escape the bonds that have held them this long, the Queen can restrain them with such weapons in her possession."

Arelnath nodded, but Ranira was by no means convinced. She found it difficult to believe that anything resembling Chaldon could be defeated as effortlessly as Mist made it sound. Not that it mattered; Chaldon and his priests were what they would have to deal with. Shandy's incredulous voice broke in on Ranira's thoughts.

"They let a woman rule a whole country?" the boy said. Mist nodded, amused. "We aren't going anywhere near there, are we?" he went on suspiciously.

"No," Mist replied. "The Island of the Moon is east and south; Alkyra is north of the Melyranne Sea."

"Good," Shandy said in relief. "I'm not going to any woman's country. And those other things don't sound very nice either."

The corners of Mist's mouth twitched. Before she could reply, Arelnath frowned and asked, "How can the Temple of the Third Moon be a threat to a Shadow-born? The Island of the Moon is a place of magic and learning, but I do not think that you could defeat Chaldon with knowledge alone."

"Perhaps it fears we will bring the Gifts from Alkyra to use against it," Mist said with a shrug. "Or perhaps there is some way to use the Third Moon itself to harm it. I am no scholar on the subject of Shadow-born; there are others at the Temple who will know, if I can only reach them."

Arelnath frowned again. "How can the Temple of Chaldon reach the island to attack? Magic is far more difficult over distances. Are you sure they are a real threat?"

"For an individual, it would be impossible to harm the island from this distance," Mist agreed. "But you have seen the sendings they have used against us. Can you doubt their power? It will take all my strength and skill to send a simple speaking-spell to the island to warn them; the Temple of Chaldon, however, will not rely on a single sorcerer. You yourself suggested that Ranira loan me her power; you know how a group of people can be joined to provide more power than any one person could produce alone. That is how the Temple of Chaldon will work its spell."

"I have seen nine or ten people linked like that," Arelnath admitted. "But it would take more than that to channel such power!"

"The Temple of Chaldon is not limited to ten," Mist said reluctantly. "Somehow the priests of Chaldon have found a way to simultaneously tap the power of everyone in the city, whether they are trained or not. I do not know how they are able to coordinate so large a group, but they do. That is how they reached us in the river outside Drinn. If they had known exactly where to aim their blast, we would all be dead."

"The new Temple rites!" Ranira exclaimed suddenly. Mist turned to her. Arelnath's head came around more reluctantly.

"What do you mean?" Mist asked.

"That must be why there were no people on the streets except Temple guards and Watchmen. Everyone was at the Temple! That is how the priests can use all the people of Drinn at once—they have made it part of the ritual this year. Everyone has to participate during Midwinter Festival if they are in Drinn, and there are always changes in the rites. Even if someone suspected, no one would dare to question the Temple."

"I think you are right," Mist said thoughtfully. "I do not know any other way it could be done."

"But that much power would burn out whoever was the focus," Arelnath objected. "Surely the Temple of Chaldon cannot waste trained sorcerers so freely."

"The power would certainly destroy a human being," Mist replied gravely. "A Shadow-born, however, would have no such difficulty. The priests will focus their power through Chaldon. Unwarned, the Temple of the Third Moon has no chance of resisting."

Silence followed Mist's words. At last Arelnath looked up. "I will help you if I can," she said. She hesitated. "How soon do you wish to try? I would like to build a fire. Now that it is day, we are not so likely to be seen and it will make all of us more comfortable." She looked in Jaren's direction as she spoke.

"I will be glad of your help," Mist said. Her eyes followed Arelnath's. "But make the fire first. It will take me a little time to prepare, and it will certainly be easier to concentrate if I am warmer."

Shandy sneezed, and in spite of herself, Ranira laughed. Between the nightmare and the conversation she had not noticed how cold she was, but now she realized that she was shivering and that her fingers were almost too stiff to move. "Can I help?" she asked timidly.

Mist looked at her in surprise. "I would appreciate whatever assistance you can give," she said. "But are you certain?"

"I—I didn't mean *that!*" Ranira stammered, reddening. "I mean with the fire. It's not that I don't want to help with your spells," she went on in a rush, trying to keep the hurt from Mist's face. "But whenever I even think about magic, the flames . . ." She stopped short, appalled by the extent of her self-revelation. Why, she had as good as told Mist that she was willing to become a witch!

"I have heard of such barriers before," Mist said, looking thoughtfully at Ranira. "Sometimes they can be removed. I cannot do anything until I have contacted my home, but after that I may be able to help you, if you are still willing."

Ranira looked blankly at the other woman. "I can't."

"I will not press you," Mist said, looking disappointed. "But tell me if you should change your mind." The healer turned away to talk to Arelnath, leaving Ranira feeling very much like a traitor. 'I can't,' she thought defensively. 'How can she ask it of me?' But even in her own mind the words rang false. After all, she had never actually been hurt by her imaginary flames. She began to feel childish as well as guilty.

Ranira looked toward Mist, and her hand rose in a habitual gesture to finger the hem of her veil. When she realized what she was doing, she jerked her hand away as if it had been burned. Neither Mist nor Arelnath wore veils, and she was beginning to feel self-conscious about continuing to wear one herself. Yet she did not feel comfortable without it. She pushed the problem to the back of her mind and walked toward the warmth of the tiny blaze that Arelnath was just beginning to coax out of the firewood.

CHAPTER THIRTEEN

Mist and Arelnath sat on the ground near the fire. Arelnath had made a bed of leaves to insulate Jaren from the cold ground of the little wood, and as soon as the fire caught, she turned to adjust the pile so that Jaren could have the full benefit of the warmth without danger of the leaves catching fire. She had also, Ranira noted, wrapped Jaren's injured leg in one of the heavy brown pilgrim's robes. Beside Ranira, Mist carefully fed small branches into the slowly growing blaze.

"Now, if we only had something to eat," Ranira said as she stretched her hands toward the warmth.

"There are other things to think of first," Arelnath said shortly, turning back toward the fire. She moved to one side, so that her body did not keep the heat from reaching Jaren, and looked up. "I am ready, Mist."

"Then we had best begin at once," Mist said. She dropped the last of the branches onto the fire and glanced at Ranira, but did not speak again. Arelnath nodded and extended a hand toward the healer.

Almost reluctantly, Mist grasped the proffered hand in one of her own. Her free hand rose and folded itself about the white stone on her breast, then clenched until the knuckles whitened. Mist bowed her head and began the low, murmuring chant that had accompanied all of her spell-casting. This time, Ranira tried to listen more closely. Though the language was unfamiliar, she thought she could sense a searching note in the rise and fall of Mist's voice.

The enchantress's head bent lower, as if she strained to carry some heavy burden. Arelnath sat straight, but her eyes were unfocused and the lines of strain in her face seemed to deepen even as Ranira watched. The murmuring went on and on, but now the sound seemed to intensify, as if it could cover the distance to the island by sheer force. Ranira was tempted to cover her ears, but some streak of pride kept her hands at her sides.

Abruptly, the chanting stopped. Mist's hands released Arelnath and the stone, only to bury themselves in her own thick black hair. Arelnath sighed and massaged her temples as she looked at Mist. "So, we have exhausted our strength for nothing," the Cilhar woman said.

"You did not succeed?" Ranira asked.

"No," Arelnath said.

"Why?" Ranira asked when no more explanation was forthcoming. "Can't you try again?"

Mist sighed and raised her head. "The priests of Chaldon have raised a barrier about the Empire of Chaldreth that I could not break, even with Arelnath's help. I cannot try again until we have rested and our strength is restored. I doubt I will have the time for that."

"Why?" Ranira asked again. "There are still three days before the Night of Two Moons. Isn't that enough time?"

"The Temple of Chaldon is preparing to deal with us," Mist replied. "They must suspect that I, at least, am from the Island of the Moon, or they would not have raised the barrier. If they had been better prepared, we would have died in the river last night. They will certainly strike again, and this time they will not miss."

Silence followed Mist's words. "Won't your people notice the barrier?" Ranira offered at last. "Maybe they could break it from outside."

Mist raised her head, and an expression of hope flashed across her face. Then she shook her head. "They will notice, and they will worry, but they will not try to force a way through it until it is too late. They know little of the Empire of Chaldreth, remember; they will not wish to act openly against it without provocation."

"At least the Temple of Chaldon is not likely to find us

soon," Arelnath said. "Even a Shadow-born cannot barricade the entire Empire and still hunt for us."

"It will not have to," Mist said. "Each night the Temple priests will be more practiced in linking the people of Drinn so that Chaldon can use their power. Soon the Shadow-born will have strength, and to spare."

"Even with the extra power, it will still take them time to find us," Arelnath said a little less confidently. "They cannot strike without knowing where we are."

"They did last night," Mist pointed out. "Chaldon spread his power over a wide stretch of land to be sure of reaching us, and even though the blast was stretched thin, it was painful for you. You know the effect it had on me. Tonight he will be stronger. You may survive another such random blow, but I do not think I can."

Arelnath looked at the other woman in dismay. "Distance would weaken the spell, would it not? Can we get far enough in a day to make a difference?"

"Without food, and with Jaren ill?" Mist said. "I doubt it. If Chaldon could not refresh his power every night, then perhaps—or if I had a source of power to equal his. But we are tired, and I am too drained to fight. Indeed, I am too drained even to heal—and for nothing," she finished with a touch of bitterness.

"If you cannot fight, can you hide?" Ranira asked.

Arelnath snorted. "Bushes and holes are no good as protection against magic."

Ranira turned to Mist and forced herself to speak through lips that had gone suddenly stiff. "You said I had as much power as Arelnath, but when that spell or blast or whatever it was hit us last night, it hurt Arelnath more than it did me. Why?"

"The spell was aimed at people who work magic," Arelnath said impatiently, before Mist could reply.

"If it was just power, it wouldn't have hurt you any worse than it did me," Ranira insisted. "It has to have something to do with the training you have." Mist nodded, and, encouraged, Ranira went on. "Couldn't you try to, well, forget some of the training? So the spell would not be able to hurt you as much?"

"Forget in a few hours what it takes years to learn? Deliberately?" Arelnath said scornfully. "You do not know what you are asking. I might be able to do it, but Mist has been trained until it is almost a reflex. It would take months to do what you suggest."

"Not necessarily," said Mist in a thoughtful tone. "I cannot wipe my knowledge from my mind, but perhaps I can disguise it." She looked at Ranira. "I will need your help, and it may be dangerous for you. There will be magic involved as well; I cannot deceive you about that. Are you willing to try?"

Ranira frowned and moved further away from the fire. "I won't have to do any spells myself, will I?"

"No, I will do what is necessary," Mist assured her. "It will be like the spell I used in order to find and remove the Temple buildings, only this time I will be trying to make myself as much like you as I can."

"Like me?" Ranira said incredulously. "Why?"

"It is the quickest and easiest way to hide my experience," Mist said, smiling. "I only hope it will work."

"Even if you are going to try this 'hiding,' we should still get as far away from Drinn as possible," said Arelnath. "I don't like the idea of being hit by a spell stronger than the last one, and I cannot use your method of avoiding it."

"Why not?" Ranira asked. "You helped Mist try to contact her people. Why can't you join her in this as well?"

"Linking too many people would make us more noticeable, not less," Mist said. "The Temple spell would hit us harder, and we might all be killed. Arelnath is right; we must go on as far as we can."

"But Jaren cannot walk far!" Ranira said, appalled. "He almost didn't make it to the woods last night. How can we keep going?"

"I can walk as far as I have to," a somewhat slurred voice said behind them. Ranira and the others turned to see Jaren trying to haul himself upright. Arelnath hurried over to him and shoved him back into a prone position.

"You are not going to try walking anywhere yet," she said. "And you aren't going to walk at all if I can stop you. Ranira was right—it only makes the poison work more quickly, and it isn't necessary."

Jaren did not object to this summary statement; his brief effort appeared to have tired him. Mist frowned. "If Jaren cannot walk, how are we to carry him?"

Arelnath smiled. She rose and walked to the place where the awkward hammock was lying. "This is what we used to bring you here," she said, picking up one end and displaying it to Mist. She ignored Jaren's groan and went on, "If I stretch it a little, it will do for Jaren as well."

"No wonder I feel so sore," Mist said, studying the odd-looking contraption. "I think we can make a better litter if you or Shandy can find a couple of long sticks to use as poles. It will be far more comfortable, and easier to carry as well."

"Where *is* Shandy?" Ranira asked, looking around. There was no sign of the boy, and no one could remember seeing him since Arelnath started building the fire. Accustomed though she was to the urchin's abrupt appearances and disappearances, Ranira began to feel worried. Like herself, Shandy had lived in Drinn all his life; his city-tested wiles might not serve him as well in a field or forest.

"We can't look for him now," Arelnath said. "There isn't time."

"But what if the Templemen have followed us?" Ranira said anxiously.

"If Shandy has been caught by Temple guards, we have even less time to stand around worrying," Arelnath snapped. She was already threading her way through the bushes in search of suitable branches for the litter.

Ranira glared after her. She knew Arelnath was right, but she resented it. Mist's quiet voice interrupted her angry thoughts. "Making a litter will take time. If Shandy has not returned by the time we finish, we can look for him then. But I do not think we will need to; he is a resourceful boy."

Ranira nodded without turning. Mist was right; she was probably worrying needlessly. Still, she was offended by Arelnath's attitude toward her friend. Resentment, however, was a poor reason to avoid her share of the work. With a sigh, she started after Arelnath.

She found the Cilhar woman at the edge of the woods, near two slender saplings. The trees were barely three fingers wide—just right for the poles of a litter. Arelnath and Ranira each set to work on one of the trees. With only the Temple daggers to use, it took some time to cut them down, but Arelnath persisted. "Green wood is better than dry for a litter," she explained as she stripped the two trees of their branches. "It is more flexible, and not so likely to break."

When they finished trimming the saplings, Arelnath and Ranira carried them back to the campsite, where Mist waited. The three women used the cords and belts of the hammock to make a loose web between the two poles. They were just finishing when they heard a commotion coming from the other side of the bushes. Arelnath frowned and drew her sword. Before either of the others could say a word, the Cilhar woman had faded into the shadows among the trees.

For a long moment, the noise grew closer without interruption. Then Ranira heard Arelnath's laugh ringing through the bushes, and simultaneously the noise resolved into an unsuccessfully smothered squawking accompanied by a frustrated, "Shhhh! Stop it! Ow! Shhh!"

The bushes parted, revealing Shandy holding tightly onto the feet of two large and very angry chickens, who did not seem at all interested in being carried upside down. Ranira burst into laughter, as much from relief as from amusement. "What are you doing with those?"

"I was hungry," Shandy said defensively. Mist had relieved him of the birds, but the boy was a sorry sight. His clothes were, if possible, more tattered than they had been when he left Drinn, and he was covered with scratches and angry red marks where the birds had pecked at him.

"So are we all hungry," Arelnath said, coming up behind him and sheathing her sword as she spoke. "But we are not carrying chickens. Where did you steal them?"

"I went back up to one of the houses we passed last night," Shandy said. "It wasn't very far. There wasn't anyone around, and then I saw those birds." He looked disgustedly at the chickens Mist was holding.

"So you took a couple of them and came back," Arelnath finished. "Very simple. But why didn't you hold them so their heads couldn't reach you? It shouldn't be hard to guess they would be unhappy about being snatched up. Didn't you know they peck?"

Shandy looked a little sheepish. "I was in a hurry," he said. "And the farmers at the booths in Drinn never have any trouble. How was I supposed to know? And then, once I had them, I couldn't let go."

Arelnath laughed again. "We are certainly indebted to you," she said. "I have not had such a feast in days!"

"I thought we had to leave quickly," Ranira said. She was hungry, too, but she was still annoyed with Arelnath.

"We will all be able to travel faster if we have eaten," Arelnath said firmly. "And the birds will not take long to cook." She looked toward Mist, then started forward, drawing her knife as she went.

Cooking over an open fire without benefit of pots or utensils was a new experience for Ranira. At first she thought the hardest task was holding the fowl far enough over the flames to cook them without burning either her hands or the wooden stake that Arelnath had used to spit the birds. As the chickens began to cook, Ranira changed her mind. The most difficult part of cooking over an open fire was clearly going to be leaving the birds in the flame long enough for them to be thoroughly roasted. Though they were barely half-done, the aroma rising from the two fowl was already making Ranira's mouth water in anticipation.

At last Arelnath pronounced the first of the chickens completely cooked. It was quickly removed from the fire and divided; everyone began eating at once, in spite of burned fingers and tongues. Arelnath kept a watchful eye on the second bird, turning it from time to time as she ate. When it was finally finished, she removed it from the fire and tied it to a short branch, which she gave to Shandy to carry.

Mist had been able to coax Jaren to swallow a little of the meat and some water, but by the time the others had finished eating, he had lapsed into a delirium. Mist's face was tight with concern as, in silence, she helped Arelnath and Ranira lift the semiconscious bodyguard onto the litter. Mist insisted on taking one of the ends. "I am not drained physically," she said when Arelnath objected. "It is only my spell-casting ability that is weak, not my arms."

Without further argument, they started walking. Travel by

day was far more agreeable than stumbling along at night, Ranira decided. The wind had died, and though the air was cool, it was not acutely uncomfortable as long as she kept moving. Furthermore, it was much easier to see the various rocks, roots, and branches that littered the ground.

The woods were larger than they had appeared the previous night. They walked for several hours before they finally reached the other side. Ranira took turns with Mist and Arelnath as a litter carrier. The wooden poles were much easier for her to handle than the unsupported netting had been, and she was able to carry either end of the litter without stumbling or slowing down the party. Even Shandy was able to take a turn, though he preferred carrying the extra chicken.

A little before midday they broke through another screen of bushes into tilled fields. A little to the north, a green ribbon snaked through the neat squares, marking the course of the river Annylith. Here and there a square patch of green or gold marked the place where winter crops were growing, but most of the land was a furrowed, barren brown.

At first, Arelnath insisted that they continue to walk across the plowed land, but their feet sank deep into the loosened soil, slowing progress to a crawl and leaving a clear trail across the fields behind them. Furthermore, it was difficult to hoist the litter over the occasional fence that blocked their way. At last Arelnath was persuaded to turn south along one of the narrow paths that ran by the edges of the fields. Eventually they reached one of the small, deeply rutted roads that led through the farms to Drinn, and they turned east once more.

Homes and storage bins stood by the road in periodic clumps, and Arelnath worried aloud about their being observed. A little irritably, Ranira pointed out that they were much more likely to attract comment tramping across the open fields than walking down a well-traveled road, though she had to admit that anyone taking a close look at the group would find it more than a little unusual.

In fact, the road did not seem particularly busy. Once, they did see a man pulling a small cart turn onto the road ahead of them, but he did not look back. Soon he had completely outdistanced them, and no other travelers appeared all day.

At noon they stopped to eat. Ranira found a ditch with a little muddy water in the bottom, and they all drank from it. Arelnath carefully filled Shandy's water bottle before she went back to help Jaren. The mercenary was weak, but not yet in the kind of pain that Ranira remembered seeing the other snake bite victim suffer. Still, she could not help eyeing him worriedly as they continued on their way.

Late in the afternoon, Arelnath began studying the sides of the road for a place to stop. They were not fortunate enough to find another spot as sheltered as the forest, and the sun was nearly down before Arelnath finally settled upon a brush-filled hollow between two low hills. Wearily, Ranira and the others followed Arelnath off the road and into the bushes. Crawling while dragging the litter was difficult, but at last they reached the center of the hollow, where they collapsed gratefully.

CHAPTER FOURTEEN

Ranira was the first to rouse herself. She sat up, groaning in the semidarkness, and winced as her hair tangled in the twiggy branches of the bushes above her. She worked it free, then moved to shake Mist and Arelnath out of their stupor. Shandy was asleep, curled protectively around the second chicken.

"Mist!" The woman stirred under Ranira's insistent proddings and started to sit up. Ranira held her back. "Watch out for the branches," she said.

"Branches? Oh, I see." Mist smiled ruefully. "I was more tired than I had thought."

"We are all tired," Arelnath's voice said behind Ranira. "Eat now. You will feel better afterward. Eat, and then cast your spells. There is not much time before dark. The Temple will attack as soon as they are able."

"It is not darkness that they wait for," Mist replied. In spite of her apparent certainty, the healer started crawling toward Shandy and the cold, rather dusty chicken beside him. "The priests of Chaldon will not attack until Kaldarin rises."

"How do you know?" Ranira asked nervously as Mist pulled the bird from Shandy's grasp and began dividing it. The boy stirred, but did not waken.

"The Temple waited until Kaldarin rose before they attacked us last night, though they felt my searching long before," Mist replied. She handed Ranira a piece of chicken. "Kaldarin's light strengthens Shadow-born, and the Temple

120

of Chaldon is focusing all its power through their god. They will not strike until that power is at its peak."

Ranira lost interest in the conversation; the day's walk had whetted her appetite to a razor sharpness, and she bit into the chicken hungrily. Mist did not attempt to reengage Ranira's attention. She, too, was more concerned with eating, at least for the moment, and the meal was finished in silence.

After she had eaten, Arelnath stretched herself on the ground beside Jaren, warming him with her own body heat. The brush-filled hollow was an almost perfect shelter against the night wind that was beginning to blow above them, but it was still far from warm. Ranira and Mist huddled together nearby, trying to find a way of being both comfortable and warm, while Mist tried to explain to Ranira what it was that her spells would do.

The attempted explanation did not help Ranira much. She was too tired to concentrate well, and she was growing increasingly doubtful about the proposed attempt to "hide" Mist from the Temple priests and their spells. Finally, Mist abandoned the pretense of conversation, and they sat in silence as the darkness deepened.

A dim pattern of shadows began to appear on the ground beneath the bushes. Mist stirred. "Elewyth has risen," she said. "Kaldarin will soon be up as well. If you are still willing, Ranira, it is time for us to try."

"I am ready," Ranira said, hoping that Mist would not see how uncertain she really was. Ranira could justify the healing spells, at least to herself. She had not, after all, ever asked Mist to remove the Temple's binding, though she had certainly been glad to be free of the priest's spells. But this was different. Willing participation in Mist's witchcraft seemed improper and unsettled Ranira, even though she knew now that the Temple of Chaldon was well-versed in the magic it professed to despise. Yet she owed the healer a debt for the spells of healing and unbinding, and she was determined to repay it.

Mist leaned closer, and her eyes searched Ranira's face. Satisfied, the woman nodded. "You will not have to do anything except be still, but you may find it easier if you are comfortable. I will begin as soon as you are prepared."

Ranira shifted a little and looked up. "I am ready," she said again. Would the woman never begin?

For a moment more, Mist looked at her. "Close your eyes, and try to relax," she said finally. "I think it will be easier for both of us."

Ranira obeyed. She heard Mist begin the chant. In her mind, she pictured the woman bending over the white stone as her voice wove a web of magic around them both. This time the chant was rhythmic but without distinguishable words. Ranira felt light-headed and lethargic at the same time, as if her mind were floating on a pool of thick honey. She felt something brush her face, light as a spider's web, and the touch brushed her mind as well, sending a pang through her entire body.

The spider-touch came again, but it was not really unpleasant, and Ranira was too relaxed to object. More of the gentle, invisible threads caressed her face, each finding its own anchor somewhere in her being. They fell like leaves around her mind, wrapping her in a cocoon of imaginary whispers.

A tremor ran through the web, disturbing her. Without thinking, she opened her eyes. At first the scene she saw made no sense to her bemused mind; then she blinked, and everything snapped back into its proper place. Mist was slumped beside her, partially supported by one of the bushes, her eyes closed and a half-smile on her lips. A faint silver-blue glow hung like a fog about the stone that dangled openly from the chain around her neck. Ranira reached for it like a child reaching for a glitter-toy.

A red flush stained the shadows on the ground, announcing Kaldarin's rising. Suddenly the world exploded in pain. This time Ranira felt more than a heavy blow; the spell was like a sword cutting into her head, but the slicing stroke did not stop. She heard voices crying out around her, then realized that one of the screams was her own. But she was too caught up in pain to care.

Somewhere under the flooding anguish she could feel Mist, writhing with her as the pain went on and on. 'But she's a witch and I'm not,' Ranira thought hazily. 'The Temple spell only works on witches, and I'm not a witch. Mist is a witch—and Arelnath—but not me!' Pain made it difficult to think, but the habit of denial was old and strong. Ranira clutched at the familiar rejection. 'I am not a witch,' she insisted in her mind. 'This should not be happening to me.'

The pain began to abate. Ranira fought desperately and instinctively to keep the ground she had gained. Suddenly the attack shifted; the memory of her parent's execution rose vividly before her, filling her with a different kind of pain and distracting her from her efforts. For a moment, she heard their cries once again, smelled the sickening odor of burning flesh, and felt the heat of the flames. Then she thrust the scene away, trying to force it out of her mind before it reached the moment that had haunted her dreams for so long.

She almost succeeded—almost, but not quite. As if she stood once more in the courtyard of the Temple, she saw two figures clearly through a sudden gap in the smoke and flames; she reached out for them. A wave of fear and agony and protest swept out from them and engulfed her, then ceased in a shock that was more painful than the emotional storm that had preceded it. She screamed as she felt again the deaths of the two people she had loved and trusted. With all her strength, she threw the memory out of her mind, pushing it blindly toward whatever was waiting outside.

Like a distant echo, Ranira felt a cry of anger and hurt that ended abruptly. With that, the pain, both emotional and physical, ceased. Uncertain whether the memory she had just relived was a product of the Temple attack or an unpleasant reaction of her own mind, she sagged against the base of a bush, ignoring the scratches that the twigs were inflicting. At least it was over. Her head hurt, she was drenched in sweat, and she felt exhausted. It was a moment before she realized that someone was speaking to her.

"What's the matter? Why was everyone yelling? Renra, are you all right?" Shandy was standing next to her, and she was surprised to see that the boy was in tears.

"I'm all right now," she said, trying to sound reassuring. Her voice creaked as if it had not been used in days. She decided to try again. "It is over now, Shandy. But I am hungry again. Is there anything left to eat?"

Shandy nodded eagerly and scuttled off. Ranira sighed and

put up a hand to straighten her veil. Only then did she realize that she was holding something. Puzzled, she lowered her hand without touching the veil, and opened it.

A dim glow hung like mist or fog around the white stone. She dropped it as if it were a Temple snake, then scrabbled desperately after the stone, afraid she would lose it in the leaves. She retrieved it easily and held it gingerly for a moment, wondering how Mist's gem had come into her hand. Automatically she turned to look for Mist.

The healer was lying unconscious beside her, one arm outstretched as if in protest. A thread of blood traced a line from the corner of her mouth to the ground. Ranira would have believed the woman dead if she had not seen the folds of Mist's robe slowly shifting in the moonlight as her breath came and went.

She stretched a hand toward Mist, then paused. The last time the Temple attacked, Mist had gone into some sort of trance, and Arelnath had not tried to rouse her. This did not look much like a voluntary trance, but Ranira hesitated. Perhaps Mist should be left alone now as well. Still undecided, she turned to look for Arelnath.

The Cilhar woman was sprawled across Jaren, but even as Ranira watched, she began to stir. Ranira was starting to crawl toward her, when Shandy reappeared. "There's a little of the last chicken, and I found a bush with redberries on it. What are you doing with that thing?" the boy said, frowning disapprovingly at the dimly glowing white stone.

"Waiting for Mist to wake up," Ranira said. "Stay here a moment, Shandy. I want to talk to Arelnath."

"That thing's magic," Shandy said, ignoring Ranira's instructions. "You should throw it away. Magic is dangerous."

"Magic is dangerous? Oh, Shandy," she laughed—a little hysterically.

"What is all the amusement about?" a weak voice said from behind Shandy. "I could use a laugh right now. Oh, my head."

Ranira stopped laughing and pushed past Shandy to where Arelnath was shakily sitting up. "On second thought, don't tell me," the woman said as Ranira reached her. "If I laugh now, my head will probably explode. You seem to have come through all right," she observed a little enviously. "How is Mist?"

"She is alive, but she is unconscious again," Ranira replied. "I didn't want to try waking her, because I wasn't sure whether she was doing it on purpose or not."

"On purpose?" Arelnath shook her head, then winced. "Oh, you mean the life-trance. Just a moment, and I will see." She started to crawl in Mist's direction. Ranira was appalled to see how weak she seemed. Ranira slid around to touch Shandy's shoulder as Arelnath bent over Mist.

"Were there more of the redberries?" Ranira asked in a low voice.

"Lots," Shandy said. He looked over at Arelnath, who was too preoccupied with her companion to notice. "You sure you want me to get more for them?"

"Shandy!" Ranira was shocked. "They have helped us over and over. We never would have gotten out of Drinn if Mist hadn't healed my leg and then held the snakes off while Jaren and Arelnath towed us through the river."

"And Jaren got bit by a snake, and Mist was too sick to walk afterward," Shandy said. "They're witches, and Chaldon doesn't like witches."

"Well, I do not like Chaldon," Ranira snapped. "Or his Temple. What is the matter with you, Shandy? You act as if you would be glad to see the Temple guards catch us all."

"Not *you*, Renra!" Shandy said, horrified. "Just the witches. Witches are bad luck."

"Mist and Arelnath say I'm a witch, too," Ranira said angrily. "I suppose if they turn out to be right, you will give us all to the Temple and go off to enjoy yourself somewhere while they burn us. There is probably a big reward."

"Ah, Renra," Shandy said in genuine distress. "I wouldn't do that. Anyway, you aren't any witch. They're wrong."

"Maybe." Ranira was beginning to wonder, but this was hardly the time to explain to Shandy. She fingered the white stone absently as she looked at him. "Letting them starve would be just as bad. Maybe worse. You wouldn't have to watch if you turned them over to the Temple."

"I told you I wouldn't do that!" Shandy said sullenly. "I don't blab to the Temple. I didn't mean to starve them either. I brought the chickens back, didn't I?"

"You don't think about what you are saying enough," Ranira told him. "Go get the redberries. Or if you don't want to, tell me where they are and I'll get them."

"Ah, Renra," Shandy said disgustedly. "I'll go." Ranira thought she heard him mutter something about magic as he turned away, but she was not certain, so she let him go without saying anything more. She watched until he disappeared among the bushes, then turned back to Arelnath and Mist.

Arelnath was watching her. "Problems?" she asked as Ranira reached her side.

Ranira sighed. "I don't think Shandy likes you very much. I don't know why. He wasn't acting like this in Drinn."

"Drinn was his home," Arelnath said. "There he was our guide. We could not have remained hidden for an entire day without his help, and he knew it. Now he feels insecure, for he is no longer necessary. Is it any wonder he resents us?"

Ranira said nothing. Arelnath's analysis was uncomfortably close to what she herself had been thinking, and she had the uneasy feeling that the other woman knew it. She almost missed Arelnath's next sentence.

"I think, too, that Shandy is jealous of us," Arelnath went on.

"Jealous?" Ranira frowned. "Why should he be jealous?"

"Shandy sees you worrying about Mist and helping us," Arelnath replied. "You were a special friend to him in Drinn, were you not? It is not surprising that he feels threatened, when his best and only friend turns away from him to strangers. And witches as well—which makes it worse."

"I will have to talk to him," Ranira said. She was surprised by Arelnath's explanation, but she could see how it fit Shandy's behavior. 'He should know better,' she thought. Did he think she was going to forget two years of friendship just because the three foreigners had helped her? "How is Mist?" she asked.

"Badly hurt, but alive," Arelnath replied. "Your help was at least that much use. I think we should try to wake her; this is no willing trance."

"Will this help any?" Ranira asked, holding out the white stone. Its steady, unexplained glow made her uneasy. She was suddenly anxious to be rid of it.

"Mist's moonstone! What are you doing with that?" Without waiting for an answer, she took the stone from Ranira's hand and frowned at it. There was no trace of the chain that had suspended it from Mist's neck. Arelnath threw a puzzled glance at Ranira, then ran her hand around Mist's neck. Almost at once she lifted the glinting, threadlike chain from the folds of Mist's gown.

The puzzled expression on Arelnath's face deepened. She brought the dimly glowing stone close to the chain, and to Ranira's eyes the two seemed to leap out of Arelnath's hands. There was a barely audible click as chain and stone met. Then the moonstone was dangling from the chain once more. Arelnath released her hold on the chain, and the necklace slid out of sight again.

"That should help a little," Arelnath said. She reached under Mist's body and winced as she tried to move the other woman. Ranira hurried to help, glad to be of some use. Between the two of them, they succeeded in bringing Mist back to consciousness, but only just. The healer was disoriented and spoke only a few words, which made no sense at all to Ranira. They managed to feed her a few of Shandy's redberries before she slipped into unconsciousness again, but they could not rouse her a second time.

Arelnath abandoned her efforts to reawaken Mist just as Shandy returned. She accepted the boy's grudging offer of the redberries he had collected, then lay down beside Jaren once more and quickly fell asleep. Ranira, still munching redberries, was surprised and disturbed; Arelnath was not a consistently pleasant companion, but she had always seemed energetic. The Temple attack must have been more wearing than Ranira had supposed.

A snore from beside Ranira broke in on her thoughts—Shandy, too, had fallen asleep again. There would be no talking to the boy tonight. She might as well go to sleep herself. Feeling singularly dissatisfied, she finished the berries and curled up on the ground next to him.

CHAPTER FIFTEEN

Ranira was awakened by cold sunlight sifting through the bushes. She shivered as the last shreds of the nightmare evaporated and the movement brought her fully awake. She sighed and relaxed. At least this time the dream—a black-clad man with dagger in hand, chasing her while Gadrath watched—had not been vivid enough to make her scream and disturb the others. A strand of hair tickled her nose as she sat up—her braid needed to be remade. She put the dream out of her mind and looked around.

Arelnath was already awake, sitting beside Jaren and absently chewing redberries. The cause of her abstractedness was not immediately obvious, and Ranira hesitated to break the silence. She shifted uneasily. The faint rustle of movement brought Arelnath's head around.

"He is worse again," Arelnath said without preamble. "I do not think he will last four days. It has only been one and a half since he was bitten."

"It is the cold, and the traveling," Ranira said. "It weakens him and makes the poison act more quickly. If we could find a place to stay . . ."

"With Temple guards chasing us? It would be death for us all if we stayed in one spot for more than a night."

A rustle in the bushes beside Arelnath announced Shandy's arrival. "Renra! I thought you'd wake up soon. I brought you some more berries."

"Thank you, Shandy," Ranira said as she accepted the berries. She turned back to Arelnath. "Why are you so sure the Temple has sent someone after us? We haven't seen anyone since we left Drinn. Perhaps the High Priest will not let the guards leave the city, even to look for us. After all, it is Festival week.''

''Ah, Renra,'' Shandy said before Arelnath could answer. ''The Temple chases everybody. You know that.''

Arelnath laughed and shook her head. ''I must agree with Shandy. Do you think the Temple of Chaldon will take the chance that we might get a warning to the people of the Third Moon? No, they will follow us, and soon. I am surprised we have seen none of them already. They have been relying too much on their spells, I think.''

''You may be right, Arelnath.'' Though Mist's voice was hardly more than a whisper, both Arelnath and Ranira heard it clearly. Their heads snapped in her direction; Ranira's hit the low arc of the bushes, and she winced. Mist smiled. ''I owe you thanks for my life, child,'' she said to Ranira. ''And to you, Arelnath.''

''I do what my oath demands,'' Arelnath said, her lips tightening. ''If you owe me a life, it is Jaren's.''

''I can do nothing for him now,'' Mist said with a sigh. ''Even with Ranira's help and protection, I was badly drained when the Temple attacked us last night.''

''Protection? What do you mean?'' Ranira said. ''I did not do anything. You told me *you* would work the spells!''

Mist's face clouded. ''You did not contribute to my spells, if that is what you fear. I doubt that you could. You have a block against magic the like of which I have never seen. It saved us both last night, but I fear you may never be able to use your power freely because of it—it is too much a part of you.''

''But I am not a witch,'' Ranira said automatically. She saw Shandy nod his agreement, but his mouth was too full of berries for him to speak.

''That is what I mean,'' Mist said, smiling ruefully. ''You are too good at denying your abilities. It is a pity, for you have great potential.''

''Renra's not a witch!'' Shandy said loudly. Immediately, he choked on a too-hastily swallowed redberry. Ranira pounded his back.

Arelnath was watching Mist narrowly. "If Ranira can block magic so well, why are you so wearied?" she asked. "I thought you were not going to fight the Temple, but hide from it."

A puzzled look crossed the healer's face as she struggled to a sitting position. "I do not know," she said. "And I did not try to oppose the Temple spell; Ranira's block did that. It is almost as if my own power were working against me. I have not felt like this since . . ." Mist stopped short, and her face went white. Ranira looked at her curiously, wondering what memory could have such a profound effect on the ordinarily calm healer, but Mist did not seem inclined to finish the sentence.

"Well, I hope Ranira's block is strong enough to protect you when the Temple strikes again tonight," Arelnath said, ignoring Mist's last comment after one penetrating look at the other woman's face. "I do not think we will get very far today."

"We may not have to," Mist replied carefully. "I am not certain, but I think the Temple priests believe we are dead. Did you not notice how suddenly the attack ceased?"

"Dead? Their spell was strong, but they could hardly be sure of a killing blow if they did not even know where we were."

Mist glanced at Ranira, who returned the look with a puzzled frown. The healer hesitated, then said, "Any magician who would cast a spell over a long distance must have a way to know when the spell has succeeded, or he might continue to use his power when it was no longer necessary. The Temple of Chaldon is no exception. The priests knew their spell would be painful. They designed it so that they would sense the death-agonies of anyone of power and skill who was caught in it. Ranira accidentally sent out exactly the feelings the Temple hoped to find, and they were deceived, at least enough to stop their attack. We will know tonight whether they are certain of our deaths."

"I would rather be certain now," Arelnath said. "How could Ranira convince the Temple of Chaldon that it was killing magicians?"

Comprehension hit Ranira like a blow. "My parents," she

said in a strangled voice. ''The Temple felt my parents die, as I did.''

For once Shandy had nothing to say; Arelnath, too, was silent. Mist looked at Ranira. ''I am sorry,'' she said. ''I had no wish to cause you pain.''

Ranira started to reply, then stopped and swallowed hard. ''Mist,'' she said in a voice she hardly recognized as her own, ''tell me truly. Could the memory of watching someone die have fooled the Temple priests?''

Slowly Mist shook her head. ''A memory of another's pain, however vivid, would not be strong enough to convince a sorcerer that he had successfully killed,'' she said reluctantly. ''The sensation of death is unmistakable.''

''Then how . . .'' Arelnath looked at Ranira and stopped in mid-sentence. Ranira ignored her.

''And so, the Temple was deceived because I felt my parents' deaths with them,'' Ranira said, still concentrating on Mist. ''I lived it anew instead of simply remembering. But an ordinary person could not have done that, could they? It would take someone who is a . . . who has power.''

''Yes.'' Mist seemed to be waiting. Ranira went on.

''The Temple of Chaldon was watching for the deaths of those 'of power and skill.' Could they have been misled by the deaths of two ordinary people, even if such deaths were relived by a person with power?''

Again Mist shook her head. Ranira felt the blood drain from her face, and she had to force herself to speak, to ask the last question, even though she knew with certainty what the answer would be. ''The priests of Chaldon were trying to kill witches. If my memories deceived them, then my parents must have been witches. Am I not right?''

Even more slowly than before, Mist nodded. ''I am sorry,'' she said again. ''I know how you feel about magic.''

Ranira closed her eyes and leaned back against a bush, feeling her world crumbling for the third or fourth time in as many days. The successive shocks were too much to absorb in so short a time: Gadrath's proposition, Lykken's death, certain death as the Bride of Chaldon and then impossible escape, leaving Drinn, and, finally, Arelnath's claim now that she, Ranira, was a witch. Ranira wanted to be left alone, to think—but that was not possible. Someone was tugging at her sleeve. She opened her eyes.

"Renra?" Shandy said almost plaintively. "Does that mean you really are a witch?" His eyes begged her to deny it, but Ranira nodded jerkily. She could no longer refuse to accept the truth of the accusation, though it upset the very foundations of her life. If her parents had been witches, then so was she. Shandy looked at her in distress. "But the Temple burns witches."

"If they caught us, we would all burn anyway," Ranira said wearily. "What difference does it make?" The boy did not answer.

Arelnath cleared her throat, and Ranira's head turned. "We had better start moving," the Cilhar woman said. "I am sorry, too, Ranira, but I do not think that memories will confuse the Temple of Chaldon for long. If we hope to survive this night, we must be farther from Drinn."

"I think the Temple will prefer to save its power to attack the Island of the Moon," Mist said. "It is growing too close to the Night of Two Moons for them to risk wasting their power. Even with such a great number to draw upon, the priests will need as much as they can manage to destroy the island."

"If they do not send spells after us, they will send men," Arelnath said impatiently. "In either case, it is safer for us to move—the farther, the better. With Jaren to carry, we will not be able to travel fast, so we must start as soon as we can. We have wasted enough time already."

Without waiting to see what the others would do, Arelnath turned and began tugging at Jaren's litter. Mist sighed and went to help her pull the stretcher over the rough, twig-strewn ground. It soon became obvious that it would take them far longer to maneuver Jaren's litter out of the brush-filled hollow than it had taken to move him in. Ranira tried to help the other two women as much as she was able, but in the confusing tangle of bushes it was hard for more than one person at a time to move the litter effectively. For three people it was next to impossible. When they finally reached the road once more, Ranira felt as tired as if she had spent a day scrubbing floors for her bondholder.

None of the others seemed to feel much like continuing at once, either. Arelnath stopped as soon as Jaren's litter was clear of the bushes and stood up, panting. Mist sank down beside the road in undisguised relief, while Shandy looked around uncertainly. Ranira sighed and sat down abruptly, trying to relax before she had to begin walking again. her muscles were sorer than she had thought when she first awakened; she had not noticed the stiffness until she tried to move.

It was Arelnath who finally got them moving once more. She and Ranira each took one end of the litter. The healer was clearly exhausted, but she forced herself to continue moving. Several times Ranira noticed Arelnath watching Mist with thinly veiled concern, for, though Mist did not complain, she stumbled repeatedly, and there were new lines of tiredness on her face.

Jaren himself was yet another handicap. The poison working in him was starting to show its presence more forcibly. He had begun to moan and thrash about, and several times he nearly fell from the litter. At last Arelnath stopped and set the litter down in the center of the road. While the others rested briefly, she sliced a strip from the hem of Ranira's robe and with it tied Jaren to the wooden poles that made the framework of the stretcher. It was an awkward arrangement at best, but it kept him from falling during the periods of delirium.

Jaren's brief spells of lucidity were almost worse for his companions than the times when his mind wandered, for when he could think clearly, Jaren also felt the pain of the slowly working poison more acutely. He did not scream or cry out, as the nameless victim at the Inn of Nine Doors had done, but his grimly determined efforts to remain silent were painful to observe.

The strain of continued flight had taken its toll on them all. Ranira was grateful when Arelnath called a halt at midmorning. "There it is," the warrior said with satisfaction as she and Ranira set down the litter. "We will have to turn off the road soon, but we are much closer than I had expected."

"What? What do you mean, 'closer'?" Ranira looked

around nervously. Rolling fields stretched away on either side of them, giving her a feeling of exposure.

"Karadreme Forest," Arelnath replied, waving a hand toward the northeast, where a row of treetops made a dark line between the brown fields and the grey sky. "Venran's caravan is to meet us there in two days." The Cilhar woman smiled briefly. "When he sees you and Shandy, he will probably try to double the price he wants for picking us up there."

Ranira's shoulders twitched. She looked around again. "How long will it take for us to get there?" she asked. "I do not like these open fields."

"The forest is closer than it looks. But we are traveling more slowly than I had hoped to. Another hour or two, I think."

"Then can we stop?" Shandy asked.

"When we get to the forest, we can rest for a while. We will have to go on to join Venran eventually, but the meeting place is not more than half a day's travel into the Karadreme."

"Can we go on now?" Ranira asked. Arelnath looked surprised, but she nodded. She bent to hoist the litter once more, then paused and looked over at Mist.

"Are you ready to start walking again?" Arelnath asked.

Mist nodded. "If it is only for another hour, I can manage. Do not hold back because of me."

Arelnath nodded agreement, but Ranira saw the little crease that formed between the other woman's eyebrows as she turned back to lift the stretcher poles. Ranira was not surprised to find Arelnath setting an even slower pace than she had that morning.

They stayed on the road as long as they were able. When Arelnath finally turned to cut across the fields toward the forest, they were able to go almost directly north. The Cilhar woman had been right in saying that the forest was closer than it looked, but by the time they reached it, they were all glad to stop once more. Jaren moaned as they set the litter down. Arelnath hurried to untie him from the frame.

Mist moved to help, but Arelnath waved her away. With

surprising gentleness, Arelnath laid back the layers of cloth that surrounded Jaren's injured leg. Ranira recoiled from the sight. The ankle was black and swollen to twice its normal size. Blue-black streaks ran up the leg halfway to the knee, and the skin that showed between them was an angry red. Arelnath looked up, and her eyes sought Mist. "If you do not help him soon, he will lose the leg," she said grimly.

Mist leaned forward to examine Jaren's leg more closely. "You are right," she said quietly. Ranira was surprised at the healer's calm. Then Mist's eyes moved toward the south, and Ranira saw the tension in the motion. "You are right," Mist said again. "Jaren will lose his leg, and perhaps his life, if I do nothing for him. Those on the island will die just as surely if I cannot warn them before both moons are full and the Temple of Chaldon attacks. Yet, I cannot do both; I fear that I have not even strength enough for one." She bowed her head. For a moment there was silence.

Arelnath cleared her throat. "I have helped you before," the woman said when Mist looked up. "Whatever assistance I can give is yours. I do not think we can reach the Temple of the Third Moon where we failed before, but if there is any chance that we can do so, we must try."

Indecision wrenched at Mist's face. "I do not know," she said, looking down at Jaren. "Even without the barrier, it is so far. . . . And I am tired. I may not be able to try healing afterward, even with your assistance."

Unexpectedly, Jaren's eyes opened. "Mist," he said in a strained voice. Mist bent over him, and he blinked up at her face for a moment. "Try," he said clearly. His eyes sought Arelnath, and he spoke briefly in a language foreign to Ranira.

Arelnath nodded. From her belt, she drew the Temple dagger. She stepped to Jaren's side and bent swiftly to place it in his hand. As his fingers closed around the hilt, she murmured something in the same tongue that Jaren had spoken. Jaren smiled and let hand and dagger fall to his side. His eyes closed. Arelnath looked up into Ranira's uncomprehending stare.

"He has the right to hold a weapon so long as he is able,"

Arelnath said a little defensively. "It is his own choice when and how to use it."

Ranira was aghast as the implications of Arelnath's statement penetrated. "You couldn't let him . . ." she started to protest, but stopped in mid-sentence, silenced by the look on Arelnath's face.

"It is his choice," Arelnath repeated. She turned away, leaving Ranira standing with a hollow feeling in her chest. She did not want to believe Arelnath's unspoken assertion that Jaren might choose to kill himself, and she resented the implication that Arelnath would allow it. She stared angrily at the Cilhar woman's back, trying to find words to express her indignation. Unconscious of her stare, Arelnath dropped to the ground beside Jaren and began absently running one finger along the blade of the knife he held.

The action startled Ranira. Arelnath looked up. For the briefest instant, Ranira saw an expression of hurt and doubt and fear for Jaren's life. Then the woman's habitual self-discipline returned, erasing all trace of emotion except the deepening lines of strain and tiredness.

Ranira's anger evaporated in sympathy. Whatever code the Cilhar woman lived by was a harsh one, she thought, to demand such control. Ranira was sure that she could never match Arelnath's conduct—if Shandy had been bitten, instead of Jaren, she knew she would not have been able to accept his death, much less offer him an opportunity to cause it himself. No, she would try everything she could to keep him alive, and Shandy was only her friend, not her swordmate, as Jaren was to Arelnath.

Breath stopped. Then Ranira let out a slow, shaken sigh of realization. Jaren was *her* friend, too. In addition, she owed him a debt; he had saved her life more than once. She was bound to help Jaren just as she felt bound to help Shandy. And, she realized with a sick feeling, there was at least one thing she had to offer that might be of some use. She was a witch, she had admitted it to Shandy. Now she had to admit it to herself.

Before she could think too much more about it and perhaps change her mind, Ranira walked over to Mist and touched her shoulder. "Could you . . . ." She hesitated, then said with difficulty, "Would you be able to do both—I mean, heal Jaren and reach your island, if I helped?"

Mist looked at her thoughtfully. "It is possible. You have a great deal of power, and you have not tired yourself by using it, as Arelnath and I have done. But are you sure you really wish to offer this? You have a strong block against magic; at best, it will be difficult for you."

Ranira swallowed hard and nodded miserably.

"Renra! You're not going to help witches!" Shandy was appalled.

"I am as much a witch as Mist or Arelnath," Ranira said. She faltered, then continued with growing strength and resentment, "Furthermore, I have been helping witches for almost four days, and so have you, Shandy! How much difference does it make to work magic instead of just watching it?"

"Ah, Renra," Shandy mumbled. "I didn't mean . . ."

"And I am tired of the way you have been acting," she went on, disregarding the boy's attempted interruption. "You have been giving me advice and orders ever since we left Drinn as if I were your sister or your cousin. Well, I am not either, so stop acting as if I were!"

"But Renra!" Shandy was visibly upset. "You don't have any family to take care of you. And magic is dangerous. Templemen catch people who do magic. And you never pay any attention to me, anyway," he finished sullenly.

As she realized the truth of this statement, Ranira's anger faded. "I am sorry, Shandy," she apologized. "I am tired, and—and too many things have been happening."

"We are all tired," Arelnath put in. "The sooner we finish, the sooner we can rest. If you are ready, Ranira, perhaps we should begin."

"Yes," Mist said before Shandy could voice another objection. "It will be better for all of us if we know at once whether this will succeed or not. Come here, child."

Slowly, Ranira seated herself beside Mist. For an instant, she regretted her impulsive offer, but a quick look in Jaren's direction was enough to harden her resolve. Silently, Ranira offered Mist one of her hands, as she had seen Arelnath do.

She was a little surprised when Mist clasped it without comment or explanation. Perhaps the healer felt that Ranira had seen enough magic to understand what was required of her. Ranira was not so confident. She glanced nervously at Arelnath, who smiled reassuringly as she coiled down on the other side of Mist.

Mist began to chant. Almost at once Ranira felt warm. 'I won't give up,' she told herself firmly. Flames leapt up around her. Ranira tried desperately to ignore them. The heat grew more intense. Mist's voice was lost in the crackling sound of the fire, but she did not seem to be aware of the flames. Ranira tried to look for Jaren, but he too was hidden by the blaze. The fire crept closer. Ranira closed her eyes in an attempt to subdue the fear that almost overwhelmed her.

The heat increased again, and pain shot through Ranira as the flames reached her. She cried out. Suddenly she felt a sharp jerk, and then a delicious coolness ran over her face. She opened her eyes on Arelnath.

"That was the last of our water," the warrior commented, watching it seep into the ground. Her eyes met Ranira's. "I owe you an apology," she went on a little stiffly. "I did not really believe your use of magic was so restricted. I am sorry I doubted you."

Ranira frowned in puzzlement. Arelnath gestured at her hands. Ranira looked down, then gave an exclamation of dismay—the backs of her hands were red and covered with tiny blisters as if they had been held in a fire. She looked up in sudden comprehension. "The flames—they were real!"

"Real enough to harm you, though no one else was in danger," Mist said.

"How could a fire burn me and no one else?" Ranira asked. "You were holding onto my hand. Your fingers must be burnt as well."

Without comment, Mist spread her hands before Ranira. They were scratched and dirty from traveling, but there was no sign of a burn. "Your mind works against itself," Mist said after a moment. "A part of you is determined never to use the powers of magic you possess, and it is strong enough to create a flame that only you can see. You are lucky that Arelnath realized what was happening. It is possible that you could have burned to death if you had persisted.''

"I *told* you magic is dangerous," Shandy put in. "You should listen to me, Renra!"

Ranira smiled shakily behind her veil. "Well, it didn't work, and I don't think I had better try it again, so you have your way at least that much, Shandy." Her smile vanished quickly. "But how will you reach the island now? And Jaren?" she asked, turning to Mist.

"Arelnath and I will try alone," Mist said, glancing quickly in the Cilhar woman's direction for confirmation. "If we succeed, they may be able to help us a little with Jaren, even at this distance. Your assistance was not totally wasted," she added. "I managed to tap a little of your power; it may make the difference between success and failure for us."

Privately, Ranira thought that Mist was only trying to be kind, but even so, she found the words reassuring. She watched with mixed emotions as Mist settled herself more comfortably on the ground beside Jaren. Arelnath joined Mist almost immediately, and once again the two clasped hands. Ranira looked on with ambivalence—and Shandy with undisguised disapproval—as Mist began the murmuring chant that would work the spell.

The chanting ceased almost as soon as it began, and Mist's shoulders slumped as her hand slid out of Arelnath's. "The Temple of Chaldon is still blocking magic," she said dully. "I dare not attempt to break through unless I am sure of success, for the Temple priests would detect it and realize that we are still alive."

"What about Jaren, then?" Ranira asked anxiously.

"I will be ready to try healing him in a moment or two," Mist said. She looked at Arelnath. "I owe you that, whatever it costs me."'

"What good will it do me or Jaren if you kill yourself attempting something beyond your strength?" Arelnath asked. "We are both weakened, and poison is difficult to heal."

"I will not fail both my home and you!" Mist blazed.

"I cannot prevent you from trying," Arelnath said. "Indeed, I do not wish to do so, for Jaren's sake. However unwise I believe this to be, I will aid you if I can."

Mist shook her head. "Healing is not like other magic. It requires too much attention; I will have none to spare for tapping your strength. A healer can link only with another healer when she is trying to cure wounds or disease. I am sorry."

"But alone you have no hope of healing him!" Arelnath replied with deep concern. "You will certainly overreach yourself."

It was Mist's turn to hesitate. "I cannot let Jaren die," she said finally.

"Jaren is not dying yet," Arelnath pointed out. "He has another day, at least, before the poison claims him."

"I cannot watch him in pain any longer. And if I do nothing, he will surely lose the leg. I can wait no longer; it betrays my calling, and I swore I would never again . . ." She stopped short and calmed herself with evident difficulty. "I *will* do this," she said at last.

"For yourself or for Jaren?" Arelnath asked.

Mist did not answer. The healer's right hand rose to clasp the white stone she wore, and she shifted her position so that she was closer to Jaren's injured leg. Ranira watched without speaking as Mist extended one hand to hover above the swollen ankle. Slowly, she began to chant.

Orange light flared about Mist's arm from elbow to fingertips. Sparks fell from her hand onto Jaren's leg. She cried out in pain, and her hand jerked away even as Jaren gave a low moan. The abrupt motion disoriented the healer, and she sprawled backward on the ground. Ranira went to her aid at once, while Arelnath stooped beside Jaren. "What happened?" Arelnath demanded, her face white.

"It is not possible!" Mist said. She paused, breathing hard as if she had been running. "It is like Saranith again—Saranith, where I killed to save a city and nearly died of it!"

Ranira's mouth fell open. She looked quickly from the clouded pain on Mist's face to the dawning comprehension on Arelnath's. "But, what happened?" Ranira asked, repeating Arelnath's question when no further explanation was forthcoming. "And what does Saranith have to do with it?"

It was Arelnath who answered her. "Healing requires talent as well as power. Think of it as a special channel through which power flows. A healer can twist her talents to harm instead of heal, but to do so she must twist the part of herself that channels the power. It is dangerous as well as difficult to do; healers have died when they failed to control the new directions their power took. And once the harm has been done, the flow of power must be bent back into its normal paths or it will kill the healer as surely as the uncontrolled energy could. Mist was lucky at Saranith—she survived."

"Enough!" said Mist. "That I survived is my punishment, not my good fortune. I had no wish to kill. I will not do so again."

"I thought witches always kill people," Shandy said skeptically. "So how come you're so mad about it?"

"I failed my calling and my vows," Mist said bitterly. "But I have not harmed anyone here. It is the old ghosts who haunt me still."

"You brood too much," Arelnath said. "The Temple of the Third Moon did not think you a failure, else they would not have asked you to come to the Empire of Chaldon for them."

Mist gestured ambiguously with her good hand. Shandy looked up. "What was he like?" the boy demanded abruptly.

"Who?" Mist asked, bewildered.

"The guy you witch-killed. What was he like?"

"He was an evil almost as great as your Shadow-god," Mist replied. "He would have enslaved an entire city if I had not—stopped him."

"And you feel *bad* about it?" Shandy said incredulously. Mist nodded. Shandy eyed her warily. Finally convinced that Mist was telling the truth, the boy shook his head. "That's dumb," he declared flatly.

Mist reddened. Arelnath laughed shortly. "You see, Mist? Not everyone thinks your crime so heinous. And I doubt that such old events could affect your abilities now. You were able to heal in Drinn, remember. No, you must look elsewhere for the cause of this."

"I think that I can offer some explanation," a strange

voice said. "Unfortunately, it will do you very little good."

All eyes turned in the direction of the sound. Ranira gasped in dismay when she saw the man standing on the other side of Jaren's unconscious body. His black hair and brown eyes were not unusual, but Ranira recognized his face at once. He was the man she had seen in her nightmare, chasing her. Now he stood only a few feet away, with a drawn sword in one hand and a dagger in the other. Ranira could make out beneath the peasant cloak he wore the black uniform of a Temple Watchman.

CHAPTER SIXTEEN

Arelnath started to draw her sword, but as she moved, the man lowered the point of his own weapon to Jaren's throat. Arelnath froze. "I am glad you will be reasonable," the man said. "From what I have heard of your conversation, this person means somewhat more to you than casual acquaintanceship. I would be distressed were I forced to kill him too soon."

Ranira made an involuntary noise of protest. The Templeman nodded respectfully in her direction, without taking either his eyes from Arelnath or his swordpoint from Jaren's throat. "I am most pleased to have found you, Chosen One," he said. "You and your companions have made my fortune today. No, you will not touch that weapon again," he went on, still watching Arelnath. "Unbuckle the entire belt and throw it over there."

Her face a mask of rage, Arelnath complied. The Templeman smiled. "Thank you. Now, I am afraid I must cause you some little discomfort. It is only temporary, I assure you. Unlike this one, you are much more valuable alive." He nudged Jaren's body with his foot, then looked down, startled.

As the Templeman's eyes left her face, Arelnath leapt. Ranira saw a flash of satisfaction cross the face of the man in black as his arm, holding the dagger, came down. Arelnath saw the trap too late. Even so, she managed to twist in midair and nearly avoided the blow. But she was tired, and her

144

reflexes were slow. Stunned, she fell across Jaren's body. The man in black struck a second time. Ranira hardly had time to cry protest, and none at all to act, before Arelnath collapsed soundlessly.

The Templeman stood looking at Arelnath, panting slightly. Ranira thought longingly of the dagger she carried hidden beneath her robe, but she could not reach it easily. Furthermore, she knew that she could not hope to succeed in a direct attack on a trained fighter. Her only chance lay in surprise, but she was not close enough to the man in black to attack without giving him more than enough warning of her intention. The Templeman looked up and met her eyes.

"I regret that I have distressed you, Chosen One," he said with polite deference. "But I am afraid I had no choice. This lady was far more of a threat to me than are the rest of you." He sheathed his sword as he spoke and shifted the dagger from one hand to the other. The blade of the dagger flashed as he took the hilt in his right hand.

Suddenly Ranira realized that the man had been holding the weapon by its blade. Her eyes flew to Arelnath. There was no sign of blood on her clothing. Ranira strained to see whether she was breathing. The distance was too great. "Is she alive?" Ranira demanded.

"Of course." The Templeman sounded surprised, even offended. "Did I not say she was more valuable to me alive than dead? However, I have a few more things to do before she recovers. You will, therefore, please oblige me by backing up three paces and seating yourselves close together. It will be much more comfortable for you, and there will be far less chance for you to attempt to give me any unpleasant surprises."

The man watched, dagger poised, as they complied, then he nodded. "Again, I thank you. A lone man cannot take chances." He placed two fingers in his mouth and whistled piercingly.

Before Ranira could wonder at the unexpectedness of the gesture, a chestnut horse appeared walking through the trees behind the Templeman. It stopped when it reached his side. He took a coil of rope from the saddle and tied Arelnath's hands firmly behind her. Ranira watched in frustration, but there was nothing she could do. Beside her, Shandy shifted restlessly. Ranira put out a warning hand.

Small as it was, the gesture made the Templeman look up. "You are wise, Chosen One," he said as he returned to his task. "The boy could do nothing against me, and I would dislike having to kill him if he tried to escape."

"I killed a Templeman once already," Shandy said in half-sullen defiance. "You're not so smart."

The Watchman finished tying Arelnath and rolled her unconscious body off Jaren. He sat back on his heels with a smile. "That may be, but I would still not advise you to try attacking me." He looked at the boy with a slight air of puzzlement. "The Chosen One I know, and these three foreigners, but you are unexpected. How do you come to be in such company?"

"My name is *Ranira*," Ranira said, nudging Shandy to keep him from making any more exaggerated claims. "Why are you playing games with us? Who are you?"

"I am not playing games," the man said. "Still, I admit I have been remiss; it is only courtesy that I introduce myself." He rose to his feet and bowed gracefully. "I am Erenal, one of the special servants of the new High Priest of Chaldon."

"The *new* High Priest?"

"Yes, I am afraid you killed the old one last night with some sort of spell," Erenal said. He did not seem very concerned about it. "It was very convenient for Gadrath; he has been waiting for this for a long time."

Mist gasped. "Then, that is why . . ." She stopped short, but Erenal nodded as he reseated himself.

"I told you I might shed some light on your . . . difficulties," he said. "I am afraid I overheard a good deal of your conversation. You must forgive me. Magic is so interesting, and in Drinn there is little opportunity to indulge such interests."

"Gadrath is the new High Priest?" Ranira interrupted. "Then you are one of *his* 'special servants'!"

"I cannot deny it," Erenal said. An expression of genuine distress crossed his face as Ranira shrank back. "Please, Chosen One. You have nothing to fear from me."

"Nothing to fear!" Ranira replied indignantly. "Do you know what happens to the Bride of Chaldon?"

"To be the Bride does not seem to me a pleasant thing," Erenal admitted. "But I do not know for certain that Gadrath intends you to play that role."

"He chose me himself, because I insulted him in public," Ranira said scornfully. "He won't change his mind. And even if he is High Priest now, he couldn't possibly stop it, since it has been announced through all of Drinn."

Erenal smiled. "Gadrath has many ways of keeping the people he finds useful safe," he said. "He will not fail to protect you if that is what he wishes."

"What possible use could Gadrath have for me?" Ranira demanded in exasperation. Then she remembered the way Gadrath had accosted her in the square, and she bit her lip, glad that Erenal and Mist could not see her face behind the veil. There was at least one use the new High Priest might wish to make of her, though she had difficulty believing that Gadrath would go to the trouble of deceiving all of Drinn just for that.

"You are a witch," Erenal said, seeming not to notice Ranira's hesitation. "The High Master . . . that is, the Highest Born collects witches. It is one of the duties I and the others in his special service perform." The Templeman smiled. "He rewards us well, and there is a bonus for these three. Gadrath must want you badly indeed. He sent a messenger-bird to me nearly two days ago, as soon as he was certain you were not in Drinn. It is a good thing I was not in the city. The old High Priest would not allow the Festival rules to be broken in order to send people after you. Gadrath was most annoyed, but as you see, things have turned out well for me. Gadrath may even raise the payment when he learns that there are at least three witches among you."

"And what use does Gadrath have for witches?" Mist asked. "I did not think such people were popular in Drinn. Indeed, does not the Temple of Chaldon burn witches?"

"The Temple certainly would, if it could catch any," Erenal said. "But the Highest Born has been very clever. I do not think many real witches have burned since he first came to power over the Eyes of Chaldon."

"That is not true!" Ranira cried. "The Temple burned seven people in the past year alone, two of them in Drinn itself!"

Erenal shrugged. "They were not witches. I told you, Gadrath has ways of protecting those he wishes to use."

"You mean he replaces the captured witches with other innocent people," Mist said. She looked ill. "And you help him?"

"I find witches for him," Erenal corrected. "If I am good enough, the other branches of the Temple do not even realize that the people I find . . ." Arelnath groaned, and Erenal broke off to look at her. Satisfied that she was merely recovering consciousness, he turned back to Mist. "If I reach a witch before the other Templemen, there is no need for a replacement in the flames. The witch simply disappears."

"What does Gadrath do with all these witches?" Ranira asked in a hard voice. Her right hand itched to reach for the dagger inside her robe, but she held herself back. She would not risk betraying the presence of the weapon before she had a chance to use it.

"For many years, Gadrath has been trying to build up a source of power independent of the Temple of Chaldon," Erenal explained. "The witches are that source. You will be well-treated."

"I have had experience with Gadrath's version of good treatment," Ranira spat, remembering the drugged wine. "Do not try to tell me he will behave any differently because he knows I am a witch!"

Erenal started to answer, but at that moment Arelnath groaned again, shifted, and opened her eyes. She glared into the Templeman's unwavering gaze. "You are good, Templeman," she snarled. "But if I had been less tired, you would be dead."

"I am aware of that," Erenal said, unperturbed. "I must apologize for the inconvenience and discomfort I have caused you, but you must admit that from my point of view it was necessary." He bowed politely without rising. Arelnath's face was a study in surprise. Under other circumstances Ranira would have laughed.

"You are a courteous and well-spoken man," Mist said thoughtfully, drawing part of Erenal's attention away from Arelnath. "You do not seem to relish the suffering you cause. Why . . ."

"I must beg to contradict you," Erenal interrupted. "I cause no suffering. I prevent it. The witches I find are safe from the fire, and they are given comforts the like of which most of them have never seen."

Ranira snorted. She started to reply, but Mist's warning touch on her arm restrained her. Ranira choked back her angry retort. After a moment, Mist went on, "By taking us to Gadrath you will be the cause of more suffering than you can realize. Do you not know what your Temple plans to do? On the Night of Two Moons they will attack my homeland through their rituals. My people will die if I cannot warn them in time."

Erenal looked interested, even slightly sympathetic, but all he said was, "I do not see how I can be the cause of something I am not even aware is happening."

"You could prevent this," Mist said. "Is it so much to ask?"

"To assist you in your escape?" Mist nodded. Erenal watched her for a moment. "And if your home is warned, what will your people do?"

"If they are warned, they can defend themselves," Mist replied. "Chaldon and the Temple priests will not be able to harm them." She spoke confidently, but Erenal shook his head.

"Your people will not be content to simply resist," Erenal said. "If they have such abilities, they have the power to attack in their turn. You propose only that I choose whether the deaths on the Night of Two Moons will be among your people alone, or among mine as well."

"There need be no deaths at all," Mist insisted. "The Island of the Moon is not interested in killing."

"And what are your chances of success?" Erenal asked. "You have little more than two days before the Night of Two Moons. I am not the only person searching for you now, and you have not come so far that Gadrath cannot reach you if he chooses to ride out of Drinn."

"Without your help we have little hope of success," Mist admitted. "With it—I do not know. It is possible."

"I am sympathetic," Erenal said. "But even you yourself sound unsure. And if I betrayed my own people to help you, how could you trust me to keep my bargain? No, I am afraid I must take you to Gadrath, as I intended."

Mist was silent. Ranira looked toward Arelnath and was surprised to see an expression of near-approval on the woman's face. As she puzzled over Arelnath's acceptance of Erenal's decision, the Templeman sighed. "But enough talk. Though this conversation is interesting, I think it is time to be moving." He looked from Arelnath to Jaren and paused, considering. "The sick one I can carry in front of me, but I do not wish to overburden my horse with three riders. May I have your oath?" he asked, turning to Arelnath.

"No." The quiet word was more emphatic than Arelnath's earlier anger. "My oath is given."

Erenal nodded without surprise. "Then, I fear I must tie you to the saddle. It is undignified, but I will try to see that it is not uncomfortable." He rose, still holding his dagger in one hand, and stepped back to stand beside the chestnut. As he retrieved a second coil of rope and secured one end to the saddle, Ranira realized what he planned to do. She had seen witches dragged through Drinn behind mounted Templemen, stumbling along at the end of a rope behind the faster-moving horses. Erenal looked up and read the expression in her eyes correctly.

"I have said I will try to cause your friends no discomfort," he said almost gently. "I will ride no faster than I have to."

Ranira swallowed hard and nodded. She understood all too well—Arelnath and Jaren were to be held hostage for the good behavior of the others. So long as they followed Erenal without causing trouble or attempting to escape, he would travel slowly. If one of them ran, he would gallop until he caught the fugitive, without worrying about dragging Arelnath along behind him.

Erenal turned his attention back to Arelnath, studying her for a moment. "Roll onto your stomach, please," he said. Arelnath looked at him. Erenal gestured toward Jaren with his knife. "Please, do not be foolish," he said. Arelnath's eyes glittered angrily, but she complied. Erenal did not approach her until she had stopped moving. Then he stepped forward and quickly knotted the other end of the rope around Arelnath's arms, twisting it between the bonds that already held her hands.

The Templeman tested the knots briefly and stepped back. "I would offer to help you to your feet, but I am sure it would not be wise," he said as Arelnath rolled onto her back.

Arelnath chuckled. "You are correct," she said. In one fluid motion she was on her feet. Without pausing to check her balance, her weight shifted. One foot lashed out. The knife in Erenal's hand flew into the trees. But Arelnath had no time to take advantage of her opportunity. Even as she moved, the chestnut horse neighed and reared. The motion pulled taut the rope which connected Arelnath with the saddle, and the jerk sent her sprawling heavily.

A second knife appeared as if by magic in Erenal's hand, but he made no move to throw it. "That also was not wise," he said as Arelnath tried to regain her feet. The horse moved, pulling her off balance again. "As you can see, my horse is well-trained."

Without hurrying, Erenal crossed in front of the horse to the spot where his dagger had landed. The second blade disappeared as he retrieved the first, and he returned to stand beside the horse's head. As soon as he touched the bridle, the chestnut stood motionless. Once the horse was quiet, Arelnath was easily able to stand. She made no further attempt to attack Erenal, though she watched him narrowly.

The Templeman nodded his approval and turned his attention to Jaren. "Now, if you will tell me what malady troubles your friend, I may be able to make him more comfortable until we reach Drinn and one of Gadrath's leeches can see to him."

Ranira thought she saw Jaren's eyelids flicker as Erenal spoke, but she could not be sure. She hoped he was not going to start hallucinating again. If he began tossing around, Erenal might kill him before she had time to explain. She looked up. "A Temple snake bit him two days ago. Do you really think you will be able to reach Drinn with him alive?"

Erenal recoiled slightly, staring down at Jaren. "Two days? And you have carried him this far? Why? He cannot survive much longer, that is plain."

Arelnath's face darkened. "Would you leave a friend to die if you had hope of saving him?"

"Save a victim of the river-snakes?" the Templeman replied skeptically. "I think you would be kinder to grant him a quick death. No one can heal the bite of those snakes."

"I doubt that Drinn has any healers left who could," Mist said bitterly. "It is one of the drawbacks of burning witches—you cannot use the talents of a dead man."

"You can heal him?" Erenal looked at Mist skeptically. Mist nodded. Erenal's eyes narrowed, watching Jaren. A moment later, he looked up and shook his head.

"I cannot allow you to use your magic, even if it may cure your friend," he said regretfully. "How am I to know what spells you weave? And it is needless cruelty to drape him across my horse and carry him to Drinn. He will be dead long before we reach the city." He looked down at his dagger for a moment, then stepped to Jaren's side. "I am sorry, but there is only one thing I can do. He will feel nothing, I promise you." He knelt and raised his hand for the death blow.

CHAPTER SEVENTEEN

Ranira cried out as she realized Erenal's intent. She threw herself forward, knowing sickly that she could not reach Jaren in time. She saw Arelnath begin to move as well, and she heard Mist cry something from behind her. Erenal did not seem to notice any of them. His hand was steady as the dagger came down—and embedded itself in bare ground. A look of surprise, almost wonder, touched the Templeman's face and froze there.

Slowly, he toppled backward. Ranira saw the hilt of a Temple dagger protruding from his chest, and saw Jaren beside him, hand still outstretched from the unexpected blow. Her mind refused to find sense in the abrupt reversal of events. Then her eyes met Jaren's. They were clear and unclouded by the effects of the poison. Ranira's brain began to function again. "Shandy, get Arelnath!" she called over her shoulder. Without waiting to see whether the boy obeyed, she threw herself down beside Jaren.

Jaren's eyes closed as Ranira reached his side. He sank to the ground beside the Templeman he had killed. Ranira's hand shook as she touched Jaren's shoulder—she still could not believe he was unwounded. How could a man half-dead of snakebite dodge a Templeman and then kill him?

"I am Cilhar," Jaren said quietly, as if it explained everything. Ranira blushed as she realized she had spoken aloud, but Jaren's eyes were still closed and he could not see her embarrassment. Ranira wondered if she should try to move him. She looked toward Mist for guidance.

A low snort from just in front of her distracted Ranira. She turned, then jerked back in surprise. The chestnut horse stood practically on top of her, investigating Erenal's body with his nose. Ranira had barely time to register the horse's presence before the animal reared and sent a high-pitched whinny ringing through the woods.

Ranira fell backward. The horse reared again above its master's body, and then bolted. Ranira scrambled to her feet as she realized that Arelnath was still tied to the horse's saddle. She was too late. The rope pulled tight, jerking Arelnath off her feet and revealing Shandy standing behind her with a look of dismay on his face. "The knots were too tight!" he wailed. "I didn't have time!"

Ranira ignored him. She ran forward, hoping to stop the horse, but it swerved away from her. She continued to run. The horse was headed into the forest where the trees grew more closely. She hoped it would have to slow down once it had to begin weaving in and out among the trees. As she ran she groped blindly for her dagger.

Suddenly the horse slowed and stopped, shaking its head. Ranira forced her legs to keep moving. The ground was uneven. She stumbled and half-fell forward. She flung out her free hand and found herself gripping the rope that stretched between the horse and Arelnath. Ranira abandoned any attempt to keep her feet and began sawing at the rope.

The chestnut reared as it felt the additional weight pulling at its saddle. Ranira clung grimly to the rope, afraid that if she let go she would never get close enough to catch it again. The rough, twisted fibers stung her blistered hands painfully, but she ignored them. As the chestnut came down, she hacked at the rope again. The fibers parted reluctantly, a little at a time. The horse reared once more and started to move. Ranira threw her weight onto the knife as she felt the rope slipping from her grasp.

The rope parted at last. With a sound like a scream, the chestnut sprang forward and vanished among the trees. Ranira lay panting on the ground, watching. Slowly her breath began to come back to her, and she climbed to her feet. She left the Temple dagger lying where she had dropped it and turned to Arelnath.

"Are you all . . ." Ranira stopped. The Cilhar woman's face was twisted with pain. Ranira dropped to her knees and reached for the ropes that encircled Arelnath's arms. As she started to tug at the knots, Arelnath gasped in pain. Ranira stopped fumbling with the rope and bent to examine the other woman more closely. Both of Arelnath's shoulders were bent at an unnatural angle.

Ranira sat back. Should she continue trying to untie the knots, or would it harm Arelnath even more? Her dilemma ended when Arelnath blinked painfully up at her and said through clenched teeth, "Untie me! Hurry!" Ranira obeyed. The knots were stubbornly tight, and every pull made Arelnath shudder in pain. At last the bonds fell away. As her arms changed position, Arelnath gasped and fainted.

Ranira hesitated. Not knowing what else to do, she brushed the limp pieces of rope away from Arelnath's hands and waited. After a moment, Arelnath stirred and winced. Her eyes opened. "Remind me to be more careful about moving. Can you help me?"

Ranira nodded uncertainly and reached out. "Not the arms!" Arelnath nearly screamed as Ranira touched her.

"I am sorry," Ranira said. "I didn't realize."

"Sorry? What are you trying to do, cripple me? Don't you know a dislocated shoulder when you see one?"

"Dislocated shoulder?"

"No, I suppose you wouldn't, at that." The anger drained out of Arelnath in a visible relaxation, leaving only a stubborn resistance to pain. "Go and get Mist. She'll know what to do. Go! I don't want to lie here forever."

Ranira rose to her feet, automatically dusting the front of her robe as she looked around. She was surprised to see how far they had come; she could barely see the others. She shouted "Mist!"

The voice that answered was Shandy's. "Renra! C'mere!"

Ranira picked up her dagger and plodded back toward the edge of the forest where she had left Mist and Shandy. The trees kept her from seeing either of the two clearly until she had almost reached them. Then she stopped short. "Shandy, what happened?"

Shandy looked up from beside Mist. "Renra, do something with Mist. I don't know anything about sick witches."

"What happened?" Ranira asked again. She walked over and knelt beside Shandy. Mist lay half-curled around herself, showing no signs of consciousness.

"I don't know what happened. I think she was trying to do some more magic," Shandy said disapprovingly. "She yelled something weird when that horse took off with Arelnath, and then she just sat there for a while with her eyes closed. And then she said 'I can't hold him,' or something like that, and fell over. I don't like magic."

"I know," Ranira said crossly. She looked at Mist again. "We have to wake her up somehow, Shandy. Arelnath did something to her shoulders, and she can't move. She says Mist knows what to do about it." She reached out to shake Mist, but recoiled as her hand touched the other woman's shoulder. "Shandy! She feels like she's frozen!"

"It's not that cold," Shandy said scornfully, "and she was fine a minute ago."

"Well, she isn't now," Ranira snapped. She looked around desperately for something to cover the healer with. Whatever the reason for the sudden chill in Mist's flesh, Ranira was certain that the woman would die soon if nothing were done to stop the growing iciness. "Shandy, can you start a fire?"

"Arelnath's got the firebox," Shandy said. "And there's no wood."

"There's plenty of wood. You're in the middle of a forest, aren't you? Arelnath is over that way. Get the firebox and tell her what's happened. Hurry!"

As Shandy plunged into the trees, Ranira grabbed one of Mist's hands and began rubbing the wrist. There was no response; if anything, the hand seemed to grow colder. She pulled at Mist's arm. The tug moved the folds of Mist's robe, and Ranira saw the moonstone dangling from the chain at Mist's neck. It was glowing faintly, but even as she watched, the light dimmed.

Ranira hesitated. She knew nothing about her own magical abilities, much less Mist's, and Arelnath had treated that stone with respect. An idea began to grow in her, and her eyes widened. "No," she whispered. But the stone's light was failing visibly and there was nothing else she could do. Ranira stretched herself on the ground beside Mist, holding the other woman's body close to her own. Then she gritted her teeth and took the white stone in her hand.

Nothing happened. Ranira blinked and clenched her hand around the stone. "Do something, curse you!" she muttered. She closed her eyes. Deliberately, she called up memories of Mist working magic, trying to force her own power into action. For a moment, she thought nothing was going to happen. Then she became aware of a slow, growing warmth in the palm of her right hand.

Simultaneously, Ranira felt the heat of a fire, the invisible flames that warned her away from magic. This time she welcomed them, gripping Mist closer in hopes that some of the warmth would penetrate the other woman's iciness. Fire began to leap around Ranira. She could see it even through her closed eyelids. She clenched her teeth and held Mist tighter. Fear rose in her as she saw the fire come closer; it was moving faster than she remembered.

The heat intensified. Suddenly, Ranira realized that her right hand did not feel abnormally warm. Without knowing why, she shoved the hand closer to Mist's face and opened her fingers. By now she could see nothing except flames, but she knew by the sudden wash of pain that the white moonstone had dropped free. Then the fire reached her.

Instinctively, Ranira jerked back, but she had nowhere to go. Pain flashed through every nerve of her body. She screamed. Her purpose was forgotten. She tried to reject the power that had brought the flames, so that the burning would stop. But she had called up her power for the very sake of that fire, and it was too late to change her mind.

She screamed again. Her eyes flew open, but she was blinded by the light of the flames. She could not even tell whether she still lay beside Mist or not; she was no longer conscious of anything but pain. For an eternity, she hung suspended in a maze of fire. Then, unexpectedly, the flames began to die. As they faded, the pain ebbed to a dull, constant ache. Her eyes began to clear.

The first thing Ranira saw was Mist, seated on the ground next to her with the moonstone cupped in one hand, watching her anxiously. "It worked," Ranira croaked.

Mist smiled, but her eyes were stern. "Yes, and I thank you. But you must not try such a thing again! Without training in the use of magic, it is far too dangerous."

Ranira started to shrug. Pain stabbed from her shoulder as her burns rubbed against the coarse cloth of the pilgrim's robe. Ranira decided that it would be much better not to move. "I see what you mean. Can you do anything about it?"

"No more than I have already done," Mist replied. "You are lucky to be alive. If that storm of power had not wakened me, you could have burnt to death."

"Storm of power?" Ranira said, puzzled. "All I saw were flames."

"Did you think your fires came from ordinary flints?" Mist chided gently. "No one but you can see them. The fire is a token of your power, which your mind is forcing against you to keep you from learning to be a witch. It is a good thing I knew that your block behaves that way, or I doubt I could have reacted quickly enough to save you."

"*You* stopped the flames?" Ranira asked, remembering how abruptly the heat had begun to die.

"Whatever you saw, I stopped," Mist said. "I also managed to take in enough power to refresh myself somewhat. But how badly are you hurt?"

Ranira shifted an arm experimentally. The movement hurt, but not as much as she had expected. Evidently, the burns were not as bad as Mist had feared. Ranira puzzled for a moment: If the flames were real enough to burn her, why had they not hurt her more severely? She did not know how long she had spent surounded by the fires that only she could see, but it had certainly seemed like a long, long time. Ranira looked at Mist. "Not too badly, I think. It is uncomfortable to move, but that is mostly because this robe is so prickly." She noticed as she spoke that the fire had not touched her garments—only her flesh had been burned.

Mist nodded, but insisted on examining Ranira more closely anyway. A narrow line appeared between her eyebrows as she worked. "You are very lucky indeed," she said finally. "You will find it painful to move for a few days, but the burns are no worse than you would get from the sun at midsummer."

The puzzled line did not disappear, though, and after a moment's hesitation, Mist went on, "What were you trying to do, that you would take such a chance? Why would you turn to magic when you knew something like this would happen?"

"I was trying to get the fire to come," Ranira confessed. "I didn't have any other way to make you warmer. I was afraid you would die if you didn't wake up."

Mist looked at her, aghast. "What a chance to take! And for nothing. I can no more feel your fires than I can see them."

"Well, it worked anyway, didn't it?" Ranira said. "What else was I supposed to do? What happened to you?"

"I overextended myself, just as Arelnath feared I would," Mist admitted. "I drained myself, first by trying to contact the Temple of the Third Moon, and then with Jaren. . . . But I could not let Arelnath die in such a way without trying to do something, and the spell for controlling animals is a simple one. So, I tried to hold the horse in its place, but it was stronger than I had thought, and I did not realize how much of my power I had used up. I could not hold it long enough." Her head bowed.

"Yes, you could. You did," Ranira said. She extended her arm, forgetting her burns, and winced as her sleeve scraped her skin. "Arelnath is over in the woods a little way. I cut her free before the horse got away, but she couldn't move because of her shoulders."

Mist's head came up. "Where is she?"

"That way," Ranira said. "I told Shandy to go to her." She quickly outlined what had happened, ending with, "She said you could do something about her shoulders."

Mist hesitated. ''I will do what I can. This way? Thank you, Ranira.'' The healer rose and, following Ranira's directions, quickly vanished among the trees.

CHAPTER EIGHTEEN

Ranira lay where she was for a moment, then sat up cautiously, wincing as the pilgrim's robe shifted across her back and shoulders. Mist was right, though—the pain was no worse than that of skin reddened by working in the midsummer sun all day. Somehow, thinking of it that way helped. Ranira was much more comfortable with a sunburn in midwinter than she was with a magic fire that burned whenever she thought about spells.

As she rose to her feet, she heard people approaching. A moment later, Shandy burst through the trees. He was followed at a more sedate pace by Mist, who had one supporting arm about Arelnath.

"Renra, you wouldn't believe it!" Shandy said excitedly as he skidded to a stop in front of Ranira. "Arelnath was lying there, and Mist grabbed her arm and *twisted*, and it went pop! And then she grabbed the *other* arm, and . . ."

"I don't think I want to hear any more about it," Ranira said, looking toward Arelnath. The Cilhar woman was pale, and she seemed to be avoiding any movement of her arms.

"But it was real strange," Shandy insisted.

Arelnath, with Mist's help, was seating herself at the base of a nearby tree. She looked up at Shandy's comment. "Strange or not, you will refrain from discussing the matter further," she said. "Or you will regret it greatly in a few days when my arms are healed."

Shandy subsided into resentful mutterings. Ranira looked from Arelnath to Mist and back. "In a few days? Can't you heal her now?"

"Do you remember what Arelnath told you of a healer who kills?" Mist asked tiredly. "I was in your mind when the High Priest died. I have been part of a killing, and it has warped my healing talent. You saw what happened when I tried to heal Jaren."

"I should have guessed it, but none of us knew of the priest's death then," Arelnath said. She turned to Mist. "You will certainly be able to rechannel the power now that you know what is wrong, won't you?"

"I think so," Mist replied. "Thanks to Ranira, I am not so drained as I was, but even so, it will be a long, difficult job. I must begin soon, or I will not have strength to complete it."

"Then do so!" Arelnath snapped. "The sooner you begin, the better your chances." Mist looked at Arelnath in surprise. Arelnath glared back for a moment; then her expression softened. "I have no more power to give you," the Cilhar woman went on more gently. "Nor can you ask Ranira to live through her nightmares again just to renew you. And you cannot just let yourself die."

"Die?" Ranira asked, but Arelnath motioned her to silence. Arelnath's eyes were on Mist. Ranira could see the tension in her. Slowly Mist nodded.

"You are right," the healer said. "There is no reason for me to delay." She glanced around and seated herself, shifting her position carefully until she was braced firmly against a tree. Arelnath watched intently until Mist looked up once more.

"I will begin now," Mist said. Her eyes flickered across each of them in turn. "Do not try to rouse me, whatever happens. This will take much of the night, and perhaps longer, so do not be disturbed by the length of time. Do you understand?" She held their eyes with her own until each of them nodded.

With a deep breath that was almost a sigh, Mist settled back against the tree. She lifted the white stone in one hand, cupping it so that she held it less than a hand's breadth from her own face. Her eyes unfocused, and her breathing slowed. Ranira could see no other outward change in the healer; but for her open eyes and raised hand, Mist might have been asleep.

Arelnath relaxed. "Good. I was afraid she was going to delay until she was too weak to succeed. Now there is at least a chance."

"What do you mean?" Ranira demanded.

"I think you know some of it already," Arelnath said. "When a healer's power is twisted, it begins to eat away at her—slowly if it is seldom used, rapidly if the healer attempts to cure. Eventually, if the healer waits too long to channel the power back into its proper path, the uncontrolled power will kill her. And the process of rechanneling is not easy; that, too, can be fatal. Especially if the healer is already weak."

"But why would Mist wait if she knew it would make things harder?" Ranira said.

A thin smile touched Arelnath's face briefly. "Mist is a very good and gentle person who happens to think that killing is a misuse of her talent and a betrayal of her calling. I think I know her better than you. I was at Saranith when she killed Dal Mirren. If ever a man deserved death, it was he, but Mist could never accept that. She was ill for weeks afterward, in spite of all that her comrades of the Third Moon could do for her. They said the sickness was caused more by remorse than by the effects of the killing."

Arelnath sighed. "Mist has never forgiven herself for her 'betrayal.' She still thinks she should have died at Saranith to atone for Dal Mirren's death at her hands. Now she has done it again; unwittingly, perhaps, but she was enough a part of this killing that her healing talent was warped by it. What would be easier than waiting until it was too late to move her power back into safe paths? She would have the death she feels she deserves, with no suggestion of blame attached to it."

"She wouldn't!" Ranira said. "Mist would never do such a thing! Even if you are right about the way she feels, it would be just as bad for her to kill herself as it would be for her to kill someone else."

"Perhaps." Arelnath shrugged. "But Mist would not see it as killing herself. From her point of view, it would be only justice if her healing talent twisted to kill her."

Ranira could not think of anything to say. She looked at

Mist uneasily. It was hard to believe Arelnath's words, but she could think of no way to refute them. She did not know what codes of honor governed a foreign witch. She felt a pang of guilt herself; if she had not reacted so strongly to the memories that the Temple attack had roused, perhaps the High Priest would not have died and Mist's power would not have become so dangerously twisted.

Another thought struck her, and she turned back to Arelnath. "What happens if the Temple of Chaldon tries to attack us again tonight?"

"We die." Arelnath grinned wolfishly, without humor. "There is nothing you can do about it, though. Without Mist to cast the spells, you cannot link with either of us, and in any case, I doubt that your Temple priests would be fooled twice by the same trick. I think you are likely to survive, but I would not wish to be in your position then, either."

After a moment's thought, Ranira had to agree. If Mist and Arelnath were both killed, she would be left with Jaren, who would soon be dead himself, and Shandy, who knew no more than she of the world beyond Drinn. Furthermore, Gadrath had already sent people out to search for them. With nowhere to go, she and Shandy would not be able to evade them for long. Ranira shivered and tried to turn her thoughts away from that unpleasant picture.

A shout close by broke in on Ranira's thoughts. She whirled. Shandy was on the ground, wrestling with Jaren. Ranira blinked in astonishment, then realized that Jaren was in convulsions. "Ren-ra!"

Ranira dove forward. She found herself holding a wildly jerking shoulder. For a few breathless moments she fought to keep the injured bodyguard from hurting either himself or Shandy in his violent spasms. Then Jaren went suddenly limp. Ranira sat up, panting.

Mist had not moved, but Arelnath was standing, watching them. Her face was white and set. "Is he dead?" she asked in a tight voice.

"No," Ranira said. She hesitated, wondering if she should try to reassure Arelnath. She could not think of anything comforting to say. "It is just the way the poison works," she offered finally.

"I see." Some of the color returned to Arelnath's face. Moving slowly and carefully, the Cilhar woman reseated herself. After a moment, she said in a more normal tone, "Before it is too dark to see, we should have enough wood here for a fire. I do not like the idea of spending a night without one, particularly in the Karadreme. I would help you if I could. . . ."

With a sense of shock, Ranira realized that it was nearly dusk. "Of course. Come on, Shandy." The boy muttered a little, but he fell into step with Ranira as she set off into Karadreme Forest.

The two had no difficulty finding wood—the storms of early winter had brought down a number of dead branches. The problem was finding wood that they could carry or drag back to Arelnath. Most of the branches were too long and heavy to move easily. It took several trips for Ranira and Shandy to collect a respectable pile of branches. The sun was setting by the time they finished.

Ranira dumped the last armload of wood on the pile and sat down beside it. Shandy curled into a ball beside her and fell asleep almost at once. Ranira envied him. She felt too tired to move, but she was still too tense to sleep. She looked toward Arelnath and noticed with suprise that the woman was nearly invisible in the growing darkness. Ranira realized that if she did not light the fire soon, they would have to spend the night in the dark; it would be nearly impossible to wield the flints properly unless she could see them.

Hastily, she got to her feet, her tiredness momentarily forgotten. She sorted through the topmost branches of the pile, choosing a few that were small enough to burn easily. She laid them out in a rough square, the way she did at the inn, then went to retrieve the firebox from Arelnath. As she bent to strike a spark from the flints, though, she hesitated.

"Arelnath, didn't Erenal say there were other people looking for us? What if someone sees the fire?" Ranira asked, a flint in each hand.

"Karadreme Forest has always been well-traveled, even the parts of it that lie within the Empire of Chaldreth," Arelnath said. "But you are right—we cannot risk another Templeman finding us." Arelnath made a noise of frustration. "You will have to make some sort of screen for it. We can't go through the night without warmth."

"How do I make a screen?" Ranira asked crossly. She was tired and hungry, and the prospect of additional work was distinctly unpleasant. "And what good will a fire do us if we put a screen all the way around it?"

"Just screen the side toward the edge of the forest," Arelnath said. "We'll have to take the chance that no one further into the Karadreme will see it. Blocking off the whole fire certainly won't do us any good. Use the poles from the litter, and that Templeman's cloak. He might as well be some good to us, for all the trouble he's caused."

Scowling, Ranira replaced the flints in the firebox and rose. She walked reluctantly over to the dead Templeman and stooped to unfasten his cloak. Stiffness made her fingers clumsy. She had to try twice for the iron clip that held the cloak. At last it opened. She yanked at the cloak. Erenal's body lurched sickeningly, but it did not roll completely off the cloak. Ranira swallowed hard and yanked again.

At last the cloak came free. Ranira shuddered and looked away from the body as she wrapped the cloth around her arm. She looked toward Arelnath and said, "I won't do anything like that again. Even if I freeze to death."

Arelnath's shrug was barely visible. "If it bothers you so much, drag the body into the trees where you won't have to see it. But you had better hurry with that screen. It is getting darker."

In indignant silence, Ranira dropped the cape and went to fetch the litter poles. It took some time to coax them into standing upright, but at last she succeeded. As she worked, she tried to decide whether it would be worse to have Erenal's body in plain sight on the opposite side of the fire all night, or to know that the body was close by but invisible among the dark trees. It was a difficult choice, but at last she decided to follow Arelnath's advice as soon as the fire was lit. That is, if she could get the fire lit; by now it was already dark.

She finished wedging the poles into place with a couple of small rocks and bent to pick up the cloak. As she lifted it, something heavy swung against her leg. Puzzled, she reached for the fold of cloth that had hit her. Almost immediately, she found the pocket slit. She groped for a moment, then gave a crow of joy as her hand felt the unmistakable shape of a bottle.

"What is it?" Arelnath's voice said. "Have you found something?"

"Water, I think. . . . No, wine!" Ranira called. "The Templeman had it in a cloak pocket."

"Good," Arelnath said. "We are all in need of it." Then she lapsed back into silence. Ranira set the bottle on the ground and hastily checked the cloak to see if there were any more pockets. There were. The third held a small packet of journey-loaf and a knife. Ranira removed both and set them beside the bottle. Then she turned and draped the cloak over the two poles.

The rickety supports swayed dangerously, but they held. She sighed in relief. She bent to retrieve her plunder, then hurried to the other side of the shield. Once again she dropped everything she carried. For a moment she groped for the firebox; she knew it was near the sticks she had laid out, but she could not seem to find it. Then her hand hit it.

She bent forward, pushing her face almost into the twigs in her effort to see them. When she thought she was sure where the tinder lay, she positioned her hands and struck a spark. The first spark failed to start the wood burning, but its brief light was enough to show Ranira where her hands should be. She directed the second spark with more confidence, and the tinder caught.

Ranira sat back in relief. She replaced the flints in the firebox once more, but she did not return the box to Arelnath until she was certain the fire would not die. Then she rose and walked over to Arelnath. The Cilhar woman seemed relaxed, and singularly at home.

"Arelnath," Ranira said as she tucked the firebox back into the pouch at Arelnath's belt, "how is it you know so much about Karadreme Forest? I never heard of it before, but you seem to know all about it."

"Hardly," Arelnath replied. "Karadreme Forest is too big for that. But I traveled as a guard with the Trader caravans when I was first learning my profession. The Traders know more of the Karadreme than anyone else. I learned a little; it reminds me of home."

"The forest reminds you of the Island of the Moon?" Ranira asked, surprised.

"Mother of Mountains, no!" Arelnath said. "I am no priestess; I have not the patience for it. I am a Cilhar, from the Mountains of Morravik. The Karadreme reminds me of the forests there."

"How do you know so much about Mist, then?" Ranira asked, bewildered. "I thought surely you were one of her people. You know magic, and you knew about Saranith. . . ."

"I studied magic for a few months when I was a child, but it did not suit me," Arelnath replied. "Most of the Cilhar are mercenaries—the Island of the Moon hires quite a number of us. You might say that our peoples are old friends, and so we are. I have known Mist for a long time, and so has Jaren." Arelnath's eyes flicked to the dark shape lying motionless near the fire, and she fell silent.

Ranira wanted to ask more, but she hesitated to disturb Arelnath in this mood. Instead, she returned to the fireside. She retrieved the flask of wine and the packet of journey-loaf, and moved back to Arelnath's side. In silence, they split the journey-loaf into five parts. Three of these Ranira rewrapped carefully and set aside for Mist, Shandy, and Jaren. The remaining journey-loaf she divided with Arelnath. Though Ranira was very hungry, she forced herself to set aside half of her own share as well. She knew she would be glad of it in the morning. But it was hard not to gobble it all up as fast as she could. Her restraint was rewarded with one of Arelnath's rare looks of approval.

When she finished her scanty meal, Ranira rose and went to Erenal's body. Reluctantly, she grabbed the man's arms and began dragging him into the trees. It was not as bad as she had feared, but she was glad when she could drop the body and return to the fire. Arelnath looked at her sharply. "Didn't he have a sword?"

"I didn't look," Ranira said as she seated herself and leaned back. "And I am not going to. Getting the cape was bad enough. If you want it, you can go for it yourself.'' A low chuckle was Arelnath's only reply. Ranira sat watching the fire, waiting. Not until Kaldarin was well above the horizon without bringing any sign of another attack from the Temple did she relax enough to sleep.

CHAPTER NINETEEN

The night was an uneasy one for everyone. Twice Ranira woke from vaguely menacing dreams to find Jaren in convulsions. She had to wake Shandy to help her deal with them. For Arelnath, it was harder yet; she could only watch Ranira and Shandy struggle with Jaren, unable to help. Only Mist sat silent and unmoving, totally unaware of what was happening around her.

Dawn came at last, reluctantly. It brought Ranira little relief. She felt nearly as tired as she did when she had sat down beside the fire the night before, and the grey light that filtered through the clouds did more to depress than to cheer her. A thin mist was rising in the forest, which only added to her discomfort.

Realizing that she could not sleep any more, Ranira sat up wearily, shook tendrils of dirty hair back from her face, and retied her veil. The fire was almost out, and as soon as she realized it she got up. She pulled the last few sticks from the depleted pile she and Shandy had collected. Carefully, she placed the wood on the remains of the fire and blew on the embers until the fire blazed up once more. It caught suddenly. Ranira toppled backward in her haste to get away, before her hair or veil began to burn as well.

"Take care!" a voice said behind her. "We are not so in need of warmth that you must risk yourself to provide it."

Ranira's head turned. Mist was watching her, smiling. The healer looked bedraggled but rested; the signs of strain had vanished. Ranira sat up, shivering. "You may not need a

170

fire, but I do," she said. She looked over her shoulder uneasily, and shivered again.

"What is it?" Mist asked. She looked around, and Ranira's eyes followed. Shandy and Arelnath were still sleeping; Jaren, too, lay motionless. "What do you see?"

"It is nothing," Ranira replied. She spoiled the assertion by shifting restlessly, but she could not bring herself to explain her vague dreams and even vaguer fears. "The forest makes me uncomfortable," she said at last.

Mist frowned. "The forest? But . . . ." She stopped in midsentence, her head cocked as if she were listening to something. Her frown deepened. "No, I think you are right," she said finally. "Something is very wrong with the Karadreme."

"What can go wrong with a forest?" Arelnath's voice broke in. "And I am glad to see you so well, Mist."

"Thank you," Mist replied absently. She was still listening. "I do not know," she said. She shook her head and looked at Arelnath. "There are a number of things that can be wrong with a forest, but after what the Temple of Chaldon has tried to do to us for the past few days, I am not inclined to probe deeply enough to find just which of them it is. It is enough to know that Ranira is right to be uneasy."

"If you cannot even decide what is wrong, there is certainly nothing we can do about it," Arelnath said. She started to stretch but winced as her shoulders changed position. "Ranira, where did you put the journey-loaf and wine?"

"Journey-loaf?" Mist said, her expression lightening. "How did you come by that?"

Ranira handed Mist one of the portions she had saved and started to explain. She was interrupted by a moan from Jaren. Ranira turned and saw the sick man beginning to twitch. She dropped the rest of the journey-loaf in Mist's lap and ran to Shandy. "Wake up! Wake up!" she said, shaking him. "It is Jaren again."

Shandy sat up groggily. Ranira ran back to Jaren. She threw herself down beside him and grabbed his shoulders, trying to keep them from thrashing. At first it was not too difficult, but the spasms grew quickly worse. Even after two full days of illness, he was still strong.

D.O.W —9

A hand touched Ranira's shoulder, and she heard a low singsong chanting above her. Jaren's convulsions ceased. The hand vanished, but the chanting continued. Ranira sat up, breathing hard. Mist stood above her, one hand extended over Jaren's head. Ranira smiled and sat back.

Arelnath appeared beside Ranira. "The leg!" she hissed in Ranira's ear. "Mist cannot heal it if she can't see it. Hurry!"

Ranira scrambled down to snatch at the cords that bound the bandage on Jaren's leg. As she pulled the brown pilgrim's robe away, she coughed and fell back from the sudden stench. Remembering what the leg had looked like before, she could not bring herself to look down at it now. She kept her eyes fixed on Mist's face instead.

Slowly, the healer bent forward. It seemed to take a long time for her outstretched hand to reach a position just above Jaren's wound. Her chant never faltered, and the remote expression on her face never changed. Suddenly the planes and angles of Mist's face stood out sharply. Ranira drew back, startled. Then she realized that the effect was caused by a blue glow coming from just in front of her, below her line of sight. She swallowed and looked down

Jaren's leg was bathed in a globe of light that washed all color from it. It was like looking at a stone model. Ranira could see how the swelling had spread, and there were a few darkened areas that might have been the dark streaks she remembered, but it did not disturb her. As she watched, the dark areas vanished and the swelling subsided. The chanting stopped. The glow vanished.

Mist straightened with a sigh. Ranira stared. Jaren's leg and ankle looked completely normal. His eyes opened. "Thank you," he said weakly. He smiled. "It took long enough. How long has it been, by the way?"

"Two days," said Arelnath shakily. "Mist . . ."

"I could only stop the poison," Mist said wearily. "I could not renew his strength; I have none of my own to spare. Time and rest will have to finish the work, but there is no need to fear for his life now. And there is another task I must do. Let me see your shoulders, Arelnath."

"If you are too tired to finish your work with Jaren, you are too tired to try to heal me," Arelnath said firmly. "Time and rest will take care of me as well."

"Don't be so stubborn, mihaya," Jaren said.

Grumbling a little, Arelnath capitulated. This time the healing did not take as long, nor did Ranira see any glow beneath Mist's hands. Even so, Mist's face was white when she finished, and she swayed on her feet. Arelnath turned quickly to catch her.

"You see?" Arelnath said. "You are not as strong as you seem to think. One night's rest cannot make up for the way you have been spending your power since we came to Drinn, and you did not even get to rest really. It took you all night to rechannel your healing, didn't it?"

"It is not that," Mist said, but she allowed Arelnath to help her back to sit against a tree.

"Then, what is it?" Arelnath demanded.

"Chaldon," Mist said. Her face was white. "But they could not be so foolish. They could not!"

"Who could not be foolish?" Arelnath asked, exasperated.

"The Temple of Chaldon," Mist said, looking up. "The priests. No one could be so foolish as to deliberately release a Shadow-born!"

"The Temple has done that?" Arelnath said. Her body went suddenly tense.

"Not yet," Mist said. "I can feel the strain on the binding, even from this distance, but Chaldon is not yet free. He is growing closer to it, though; his power is spreading into the land itself. I do not think the Temple of Chaldon intended this to happen. I cannot believe it, even of them."

"And Chaldon is interfering with your healing?" Ranira asked.

Mist nodded. "I had difficulty with Jaren's first wound when I tried to heal it in the dungeons of the House of Correction. I might have guessed about Chaldon then. Shadow-born resist healing. Where their power is strong, it is not possible to make a remedy for sickness or injury, at least not by magic."

"Can the Temple find us through Chaldon?" Arelnath said.

"No," said Mist after a moment's thought. "Even if their powers were controlling the Shadow-born, they would need a far more specific spell than this to find us."

Arelnath relaxed a little. "In that case, I am going to eat. There is nothing we can do about Chaldon now." She walked to the place where Mist had been sitting and retrieved two of the pieces of journey-loaf spread across the ground. Ranira and Shandy followed her example. Ranira also picked up Mist's portion and returned it to her. Arelnath had already given Jaren his share.

As soon as they had eaten, Arelnath insisted on starting off once more. "We are close enough to the place where we are to meet Venran and his people. We may as well get there and not risk missing him," she said. "If he knows there are Templemen looking for us, he may not want to wait long."

Although they no longer had to carry Jaren, their pace was at least as slow as it had been the day before. They were moving more cautiously now, watching carefully for signs of the other Templemen who might be searching Karadreme Forest for them.

Jaren's leg troubled him in spite of the healing, and he limped noticeably. Ranira saw Arelnath frown in his direction several times, but no one said anything. Mist appeared not to notice. She, too, was obviously tired, and Arelnath was not as strong as she pretended to be. Shandy and Ranira were also nearing exhaustion from the constant travel and lack of food. It took nearly the entire day to reach the clearing where the foreigners had agreed to meet the Trader caravan.

The clearing looked exactly like several others Ranira had seen during the course of their journey. She saw no sign of Traders. She said as much, but Arelnath did not seem disturbed.

"Venran agreed to meet us here no later than tomorrow," she said. "He is probably cutting it close because he found some place to turn coppers into gold and couldn't resist. He will be here, though, never doubt it."

"I do not doubt that Venran will arrive," Mist said, looking up. "It is his promptness that worries me."

"Venran knows that we will want to leave at once," Arelnath said. She sat on the ground and leaned against a tree. "He will not delay."

"I hope not," Mist said. She stared into the distance. "If

he does not come, I will have to try again to contact the island before the Temple of Chaldon strikes tomorrow night. But I would rather wait 'til Venran comes.''

"Why would Venran make a difference?" Ranira asked. "I thought he was a Trader, not a witch."

Mist smiled. "Most caravans travel with a magician if they can. Traders will do anything to protect their profits, even use magic in the Empire of Chaldreth."

"You cannot depend on that," Arelnath said. She sounded irritated. "He knew he would be picking us up. He's just as likely to save himself the cost of hiring someone to travel from Rathane to Drinn and count on you to provide whatever magic is needed between here and the Melyranne Sea."

"That does not really matter," Mist said. "He is coming from Rathane, where they make arranna. The stuff is a profitable drug; he is sure to have some. With it, I should be able to increase the strength of my spells enough to reach the island."

"Arranna!" Arelnath frowned.

"This is my choice, Arelnath. It is my home which is in danger. Arranna is not dangerous if it is used with care."

"You will not be careful this time!" Arelnath said angrily. "If a small dose will not let you reach the island, you will use a larger one. Can you deny it?"

"Would you have me let the entire Island of the Moon die because I value my mind above their lives?" Mist blazed. "*You* would not do such a thing, yet you urge *me* to."

"I have not told you to abandon your home," Arelnath retorted. "But you are too anxious for your judgment to be good."

Mist looked angrier than ever, but before she could reply, Jaren broke in. "Before you continue your disagreement, I would like to remind you both that there are Templemen in these woods—looking for us. I am sure they would be delighted to find us easily, but I would prefer to make it at least a little difficult for them. Did you not say something earlier about warding us while we wait for Venran?"

With a visible effort, Mist controlled herself. "I am sorry," she said in a quiet, strained voice. "I should have done that at once." She pulled herself to her feet and began circling the clearing, one hand touching the moonstone.

Ranira and the others sat in silence until Mist was finished. Arelnath frowned thoughtfully the entire time, and as soon as Mist reseated herself, the Cilhar woman spoke. ''I am sorry, Mist. I have no right to judge your choices.''

''It is not entirely your fault,'' Mist said tiredly. ''I told you that the Shadow-born is spreading his power into the land itself, and his influence is strong enough to affect us here. I should have recognized the cause of this at once. I think there will be a great deal of dissension among friends this night.''

''The Shadow-born is doing this?'' Arelnath frowned again. ''I did not think even he could reach us here without the power of Drinn behind him.''

''This spell is not aimed at us alone, and he cannot reach us directly,'' Mist replied. ''I do not think Chaldon is looking for us himself. Even if he is, the warding spells will help to hide us. No one must go beyond the edges of this clearing; the warding spells cannot stretch beyond that.

''And be particularly careful after dark,'' she added sternly. ''Chaldon is strongest then.''

CHAPTER TWENTY

Ranira and Shandy gathered wood while Arelnath and Jaren hunted for edible plants. None of them found much. The journey-loaf was long gone, so they had to be satisfied with a mouthful of wine each.

What little wood Ranira and Shandy had been able to find refused to light at all. "I do not understand it," Arelnath said after the fifth unsuccessful attempt to start a fire. "The wood is dry. It should not be this hard to light."

"This is more of the Shadow-born's work," Mist said. "It is not specifically directed at us, but I fear there will be worse to come. This will not be a pleasant night."

"I thought your warding spells would stop this," Arelnath said crossly.

"I am not skilled enough to deflect all of the Shadow-born's malice without his knowing, and I would prefer to avoid a direct confrontation if I can," Mist replied. "I would not be strong enough to defeat a Shadow-born even were I at the height of my abilities, which I am not. I can hide us from the eyes and ears of Templemen, and I can keep most of Chaldon's spells of dissent from affecting us, but no more."

"You have done far more than anyone could have expected," Arelnath said hastily. "I do not seek to criticize."

Mist laughed. "I did not imagine you did. We are all tired, cold, and hungry. It does not need a Shadow-born's interference to make tempers short at such a time."

"And have you any remedy for this condition, healer?"

Jaren asked politely. "Other than a hot meal, a large fire, and a soft bed, that is. I doubt we shall find any of those here."

"Unfortunately, those are the best remedies I know for this particular ailment," Mist said with a smile. "We will have to sit close together. If we cannot have a fire, it is the only way we can keep warm."

Arelnath sat back from the wood with a sigh. "Well, I don't think we are going to have a fire," she said. She rose to her feet and stretched briefly, then sat down beside the healer, adjusting her sword so she could reach it more easily. Jaren joined her, and Shandy followed a moment later. Ranira shifted but did not rise. She was willing to acknowledge her friendship with the three foreigners, but she was not quite ready to accept them as intimates, and no one in Drinn would approach a veiled woman so closely on any other terms. She remained where she was.

Arelnath looked crossly at Ranira. "Oh, come on. Do you want to wait until the fog soaks you? It will take you twice as long to get warm then." She waved at the cloudy wisps that were beginning to creep in and out among the trees. "You will be cold and damp enough by the end of the night."

Mist looked at Ranira and smiled encouragingly. "Come, child. I would hear more of the customs of Drinn. You need not fear to join us."

Ranira gave in, and seated herself among the others. They made a small, crowded ring on the ground. Arelnath draped Erenal's cloak over Mist; it was large enough to also partly cover Shandy and Jaren, who were sitting on either side of her. It also blocked some of the dampness that was beginning to penetrate their clothing.

"What is it you wish to know?" Ranira asked the healer.

"I am curious about the Midwinter Festival," Mist said. "Had we known more of it, we might not have been trapped so easily. What can you tell us?"

"The Midwinter Festival is old," Ranira replied. "Far older than the Empire of Chaldreth; maybe even older than Drinn." She paused uncertainly. "The Festival lasts seven days. No one can leave Drinn during that time, though anyone who lives within the boundaries of the Empire can come in. The first day there are no rituals, but for the last six

days everyone in the city must go to the Temple of Chaldon
for the rites."

"Is Midwinter Festival the same everywhere in the Empire
of Chaldreth?" Mist asked. Her eyes were intent.

"I think so. The Temple of Chaldon tries to get everyone
to come to Drinn for Festival at least once every ten years."

"So the entire Empire of Chaldreth is involved in this,"
Mist said half to herself.

Ranira looked at her in surprise. "Of course. The Temple
of Chaldon rules the Empire of Chaldreth. When there are
changes in the rites, all of the lesser Temples must follow the
rulings of the High Priest of the Temple in Drinn." She
hesitated for a moment. "All of the Temples offer sacrifices,
though there was a time when only the Temple in Drinn did
so. Drinn is still the only place which ever has a Bride of
Chaldon, and even in Drinn it is not a common thing."

"And is Drinn also the only city where no one is permitted
to leave during Festival?"

"I don't know. I have never been outside of Drinn for
Festival."

"I see." Mist looked a little disappointed. "Tell me what
you can of the rites in Drinn, then."

Ranira spent some time describing the rites of the Temple
of Chaldon to Mist. The healer questioned her closely, and
she did not always seem pleased with the answers Ranira
gave her. Eventually, Mist's curiosity was satisfied, and
Ranira was allowed to relax and attempt to sleep. This proved
much more difficult than the girl had expected. The fog had
thickened, making everyone feel just as damp and cold as
Arelnath had promised. Insects that should have been in the
middle of their winter rest appeared to bite and sting. Mist
explained that this, too, was the work of the Shadow-born.
The worst thing, for Ranira, was knowing that somewhere
above the clouds and fog Kaldarin and Elewyth were both
nearly full. Morning would bring the dawn of the last day of
Midwinter Festival, when she would have been sacrificed to
Chaldon as his Bride. Ranira shivered for most of the night,
starting at every sound. At any moment, she was sure, a
horde of Templemen would appear to drag her back to Drinn
to face Gadrath and the altar.

Finally, Ranira managed a fitful doze. Almost at once she awoke, screaming. She looked around dazedly for the dark shape that had been pursuing her, but there was only the fog and the concerned faces of her companions.

"What is it?" Arelnath demanded.

"Only a dream," Ranira said. Her voice was shaky; she tried again. "I am sorry I woke you all. It is bad enough trying to sleep out here without me making it worse, even if it has gotten warmer."

"Warmer?" Arelnath said. "It hasn't . . . ."

Mist's hand on Arelnath's arm stopped the Cilhar woman in midsentence. "I think you had better tell us what frightened you," Mist said. She looked at Ranira with a frown. "This is not the first time you have had such dreams, is it?"

"No," Ranira admitted, thinking of her earlier nightmares.

"How often have they come to you?"

"Only since I left Drinn," Ranira said after a moment's thought. "You remember the first one—you said it was a Temple binding in my mind." Her own words echoed around her, and Ranira looked at Mist in horror. "You said you had gotten rid of all the Temple spells! Didn't you?"

"Calm yourself, Ranira," Mist said. "I do not believe this is the work of the Temple of Chaldon. Tell me what you have dreamed since we left Drinn, and when, and perhaps then I can explain with some certainty."

Uneasily, Ranira recalled her dreams. The nightmares rose before her eyes with vivid clarity. She began describing them, and Mist listened closely. When Ranira finished, the healer nodded.

"It is as I suspected," she said. She looked closely at Ranira. "You are a Seer. It is a rare talent." Arelnath's low whistle of astonishment echoed Mist's words. Ranira looked from one to the other.

"Seer? What is that?" she asked. "And why hasn't this ever happened to me before?"

"A Seer is . . . one who sees, one who knows the truth of things which are happening elsewhere," Mist replied. "From what you describe, I fear the Temple of Chaldon is not finished with us. Have you never had true dreams before?''

True dreams? "Not until I left Drinn," Ranira said.

"Then something has wakened the talent in you since then." Mist thought for a moment. "I suspect it is the magic you have been exposed to in the past few days. The Temple of Chaldon began the process with their drugs and binding spells, and my healings and warding spells have continued it. Your barriers against magic must be beginning to weaken."

"But I don't want to be a witch," Ranira protested halfheartedly. She thought of the formless darkness that had chased her through her nightmares, and shuddered. "Can't you stop it somehow?"

"You can no more deny your talents than you can change the color of your eyes," Mist said. "But you can refuse to use them. It would be a pity if you did, but the choice is yours."

"I—I see." Ranira wrapped her arms around her knees and huddled into them.

After a moment, Mist sighed and turned toward Arelnath. "Try to sleep; it is not long until dawn."

"Someone must keep watch," the Cilhar woman reminded Mist. "You sleep."

"It is your watch? I had forgotten," Mist murmured. She shifted, settled back, and her breathing slowed.

Ranira stared unseeing into the darkness. Her thoughts were in turmoil. Magic seemed to be forcing its way into her life whether she willed it or not, and she was not sure whether she was glad or sorry. All her training revolted against her knowledge of what she was and could be, yet she could not deny her power or her dreams. How could she, when her own mind betrayed her as soon as she slept?

Indeed, how long had she been using her power without knowing it? Ranira thought back. She had known where Shandy would find the foreigners after he pulled her out of the river. And there were other things. . . . But did it matter? Outside the Empire of Chaldreth, it seemed, witches were not feared and hated and burned.

For the first time, Ranira wondered what would happen to

her if she actually managed to escape the Empire of Chaldreth completely. The thought was frightening; it refused to remain steady in her mind. Without intending to, her thoughts returned to the little circles of argument that were witchcraft and Drinn, magic and the Temple of Chaldon. She got very little sleep for the rest of the night.

When the grey morning dawned at last, it brought no comfort and no sign of the Traders. Mist began pacing restlessly, in spite of the chilling damp. Shortly after dawn, she announced her intention to go looking for Venran and his caravan. This declaration brought an immediate protest from Arelnath.

"None of us are strong enough to walk for very long," Arelnath said. "And we are not even sure where Venran's caravan is. If we hunt for him, we may miss him completely."

"Something may have happened to him that will keep him from getting here in time," Mist said. She glanced toward Ranira, who shifted uncomfortably.

"You will go out looking for Venran on the strength of Ranira's dreams?" Arelnath said. "You cannot be serious. You can't even be sure what they mean!"

Mist flushed, but she remained adamant. "What if Venran does not arrive before tonight? I must try to reach him before Chaldon strikes. If I wait, it may be too late."

"What if he arrives here as soon as we are gone? You cannot be sure he won't."

"You do not understand," Mist said softly. "I do not mean for you to come with me. You are correct; together we cannot move very rapidly. Alone, though, I have a much better chance of reaching him in time. And someone must stay here to explain to Venran if he arrives."

"You cannot go out into Karadreme Forest alone," Arelnath said firmly. "You will be lost as soon as you are out of sight. The Temple Speaker hired me to see that you return safely. I cannot let you do this."

"The Temple Speaker does not know that the priests of Chaldon are going to attack him tonight with the power of a Shadow-born and a city full of people!" Mist replied in exasperation. "What else can I do to warn him?"

Arelnath considered. "Then, I am coming with you. I have at least a chance of guessing which direction Venran will be traveling; I have worked with him before."

Mist shook her head. "You can tell me what you know. But you are not coming with me. We would go more slowly as two than I can travel alone. And you cannot leave the others alone here."

Ranira almost resented Mist's last words. Still, she had to admit that a boy, a former bondwoman with no fighting skills, and a weak and exhausted bodyguard would hardly be a match for another Templeman such as Erenal. "What if a Templeman finds you?" she asked the healer.

"I can weave spells enough to warn me if any such is near," Mist replied. "Please, do not delay me further. I should have left last night."

Arelnath shook her head. "And what of the spells that protect us here when you are gone? I have not the skill to maintain them alone. You are right that I cannot leave Jaren and these others alone, but I cannot leave you, either. Would you have me foresworn?"

There was a long pause. "I will leave you my moonstone," Mist said at last. "You can use it to trace me, if you need to. You have enough training for that, and I will set it to hold the protections until I return." Her hands reached up to lift the golden chain from about her neck. She looked at it for a moment, then held it out to Arelnath.

"This means a great deal to you," Arelnath said without touching the stone.

"Would it not mean much to you if it were your homeland the Temple planned to attack?" Mist thrust the stone toward Arelnath again. "Take it, and let me go."

Reluctantly, Arelnath's hand closed around the stone. "Do what you must, then," she said as Mist released the chain.

"Thank you," Mist said. "Will you do one more thing for me? You are the most likely of us to be able to guess where Venran would be. Give me the benefit of your guessing."

"Of course." Arelnath sat down and began drawing lines in the dirt in front of her with the Temple dagger. Mist bent over to watch. For a few moments the two conversed in low voices. Finally, Arelnath handed Mist the dagger. Mist straightened, thrusting the dagger awkwardly through her belt.

"Thank you," she said. "If Venran reaches you before I find him, tell him what has happened and ask him to link his sorcerers through the moonstone to try to warn the island. I do not think he will refuse."

Arelnath snorted. "He had better not. The Traders owe a lot to the Island of the Moon. Without it they would have to hire twice as many guards whenever they come near the Melyranne Sea." She added a phrase in an unfamiliar tongue. Mist nodded, and turned. In a few more minutes she was completely out of sight.

CHAPTER TWENTY-ONE

Ranira broke the silence. "I thought Mist needed that stone to do her spells," she said. "Is she going to be safe without it?"

"At least as safe as we are with it," Arelnath said, looking almost amused. "The moonstone is a source of power, but it is not the only one there is. Mist will manage." She fingered the stone for a moment, then hung the chain from her belt, just behind her sword. She settled herself on the ground next to Jaren and looked up at Ranira. "You might as well make yourself comfortable; I think we are going to have a rather long wait."

The morning passed slowly. The fog never completely dissipated. Grey tendrils continued to shift among the trees long after most of the air had cleared. The two Cilhar did not seem to be affected by the dreary atmosphere. They sat side by side, polishing the two Temple swords with scraps of clothing and conversing in low voices. Shandy spent most of the morning sleeping, which left Ranira with little to do besides think.

She was glad enough to do so. She was surprised to find how many of her fears and doubts of the three foreigners had proven baseless. The stories the Temple encouraged about foreigners were obviously a fraud, but Ranira was not certain why the Temple so earnestly discouraged contact with strangers. Perhaps it was because they feared what such knowledge might bring. She was even more surprised to realize how much her own future had become tied to her three new

185

friends. Their concerns had become hers, even before she had discovered that she, too, was a witch.

Idly, Ranira tried to picture herself back in Drinn. If she had not been unlucky enough to catch Gadrath's eye, some new innkeeper or merchant—possibly even a noble—would hold her bond now, and she would be working in his kitchens until the bond was paid. Then what? She realized that she had never had a clear idea what she would do when her bond was canceled and she was free again. With no relatives to go to and the reputation of a witch-child to live down, she would probably have ended up as one of the women in the shacks at the edge of Drinn, where the castoffs of the Temple priests went. She shuddered at the thought. The movement made her veil shift. She automatically put up a hand to straighten it, then paused.

Slowly, Ranira removed the veil and looked at it. It was dusty and streaked; a small twig was caught in the cord, and there was a tear at one side. It was a short veil, the kind foreign women wore in deference to the customs of Drinn. But Ranira was no longer in Drinn, and it would be death to return. How much a foreigner did she want to be?

Even more slowly than before, she crumpled the veil into a little ball and stuffed it into the pocket of the pilgrim's robe. She would become accustomed to not wearing it, she supposed. She was already growing used to the sight of Mist's unveiled face, and Arelnath's did not bother her at all. Even so, Ranira felt as if she were severing her last tie to Drinn. 'That is silly,' she told herself. 'I don't want any more ties to Drinn. If I had any, the Temple priests would use them to follow me and burn me for a witch.'

Ranira looked up. Arelnath was watching her, but all the woman said was, ''Good. You will not attract nearly as much attention outside the Empire.''

Shandy awoke near noon. He was loud in his disapproval of Ranira's unveiled condition, which only succeeded in making her more determined never to wear a veil again. Their argument was loud and long, and managed to release much of Ranira's tension. It was almost a relief to have someone to shout at. Finally, Arelnath and Jaren put a stop to it, pointing out that the two combatants were making enough noise to attract Templemen all the way from Drinn.

The truth behind this exaggeration silenced both Ranira and Shandy at once. Shandy retired to sulk beneath one of the trees. Ranira could not help wondering what this latest strain would do to her friendship with the boy. Her anger evaporated quickly, though she still resented Shandy's high-handed orders. She was somewhat relieved when she saw Jaren beckon to the boy and begin talking to him. Shandy's glower quickly vanished, and he sat down beside the blond man, listening intently.

Arelnath came over to Ranira a moment later, chuckling. "Jaren is telling him about our adventures," she said. "Only about a third of it is true, but it will keep Shandy busy for a while. He may even learn to be a little quieter with his criticisms, though that could be expecting a little too much."

"Shandy is all right," Ranira said. She groped for words to explain. "It is just that in Drinn the only way to stay out of the Watchmen's way is not to be noticed, and that means doing everything as they wish."

"I mean no insult to your friend," Arelnath replied. "He is young and has much to learn, that is all. I think he will do very well, once he has adjusted to the idea that very few people outside the Empire of Chaldreth would approve of some of your customs and beliefs."

"I think Shandy will learn quickly," Ranira said. She was a little surprised by Arelnath's understanding. She opened her mouth to continue, but was interrupted by a cry from Jaren.

Ranira turned. Jaren was on his feet, his sword moving rapidly as he beat back the strokes of the Templemen attacking him. More black-robed men appeared. Ranira had little time to wonder what had happened to Mist's warding spells. She drew her dagger and started forward.

A black robe blocked her way. Ranira struck out with the dagger. The metal rang as the guard blocked it with his sword. She struck again. She felt a dull shock as something hit her arm. Then her dagger met resistance, and she heard a cry of surprise. The dagger was wrenched from her numb fingers as the Templeman fell back. Beyond, she could see Jaren and Arelnath, their backs pressed against the same tree and their swords dancing among the Temple guards without pause. Two of the Templemen lay motionless in front of Jaren, and another was collapsing in front of Arelnath.

A hand grabbed Ranira's arm and swung her around. She struck out with her free hand. Behind her a voice cried, "Alive, you fools! I will have them alive!" Ranira struck again before her hand was caught and held. Only when she had ceased to struggle did she realize that her right arm hurt and that something wet was running across her hand. She looked down, then looked up again quickly. The Templeman's sword had put a large, slanting cut in her upper arm; it was not a pretty sight.

Ranira's captor tied her hands quickly and went to assist the Templeman she had wounded. The other guards were closing in on Arelnath and Jaren. Their numbers worked against them—there were too many Templemen to attack effectively at the same time. "Back. Ring them!" a voice commanded. Ranira craned her neck in an effort to see the speaker. It was Gadrath.

Her mouth went slack with astonishment. Gadrath was High Priest. How could he leave Drinn at the climax of Midwinter Festival? Unless Erenal had lied. . . . But no, Gadrath wore the smoky-black crystal pendant that symbolized the office of the High Priest. Ranira shivered.

The Temple guards began to move in response to Gadrath's order. The ring around Arelnath and Jaren widened until the Templemen were just out of sword's reach. Four of the Templemen lay sprawled on the ground in front of the two Cilhar. Another was struggling to his feet, one hand pressed to his side. Arelnath and Jaren made no attempt to stop him.

Gadrath moved forward, his eyes flickering across the clearing. "I see I will have to do this work myself. It is a pity that twelve of the finest guards of the Temple of Chaldon cannot subdue a man and a youth," he sneered. "But at least you have managed to capture the girl. Ah, but there are no longer so many of you. No doubt, that accounts for it." A small, cold smile settled on Gadrath's lips. "Let me show you how such as these ought to be dealt with."

Gadrath's right hand rose and clasped the pendant. Ranira shivered. The gesture was the same she had seen Mist use in spell-casting, but in the hands of the High Priest of Chaldon it seemed far more menacing. "By the power of Chaldon!" Gadrath said, and his left hand gestured.

A bright, blue-white light flared around Arelnath, momentarily blinding Ranira. When her eyes cleared, she saw Jaren and Arelnath frozen motionless in the center of the ring of Templemen. "Bind them," Gadrath ordered. His voice was triumphant, but his eyes watched Arelnath narrowly, and his hand still held the crystal pendant. Ranira was too relieved to care. She had been afraid that the spell holding Jaren and Arelnath was permanent, but Gadrath would have no need to bind them if the spell alone would keep them motionless.

A guard hurried forward with two pairs of iron cuffs, each linked by a short, strong chain. Warily, he approached Arelnath and Jaren. Neither moved. With growing confidence, the guard plucked the sword from Arelnath's hand and fastened the chains about her wrists. Grinning, he repeated the procedure with Jaren and swaggered back to join his fellows. Gadrath's smile widened; his right hand dropped to his side.

As Gadrath's hand left the crystal, the motionless figures came alive. The Templemen closed in once more. Ranira glanced quickly around the clearing. She saw no sign of Shandy. She was beginning to hope that the boy had escaped in the confusion. Then she saw the branches above Arelnath sway slightly, although there was no wind. Ranira looked away at once. If Shandy was hiding in the tree, she did not wish to draw the attention of a Templeman to him.

Gadrath was still watching Arelnath. "Search them," he said abruptly. "Especially the youth." He walked forward, then paused. His eyes narrowed. He held up a hand. The guards stopped in confusion. Gadrath bowed mockingly to Arelnath.

"Forgive me, *Lady*," he said. "I am not accustomed to women who dress as boys. No doubt you have some excellent reason."

"No doubt," Arelnath said dryly. The guard behind her jerked her arm, but Arelnath ignored him. She studied Gadrath for a moment, as he had studied her, then snorted and appeared to lose interest. Gadrath's lips tightened.

"Search them," the new High Priest said again. The guards surged forward once more. They had almost reached Arelnath when a loud crack above them drew their attention upward. A moment later, Shandy plummeted into their midst, still clutching the dead branch that had given under his weight.

Arelnath alone moved fast enough. She twisted sideways and held out her arms just in time to break Shandy's fall. The boy's weight knocked her to the ground, and for a moment all Ranira could see was a tangle of arms and legs.

"Ow! Leave me alone!" Shandy yelled. "No! I don't like witches. Let me up!" The boy struggled clear at last and jumped to his feet as Arelnath sat up. He backed away from her, fists clenched. "You stay away from me, you witch!"

Arelnath rose and began dusting herself off, moving awkwardly because of the iron cuffs. Shandy backed up another couple of steps and bumped into a Templeman. Shandy did not seem to notice; his eyes never left Arelnath. Ranira had never seen him look so frightened. She could not understand it. Shandy disapproved of the foreigners, but he had never been afraid of them. Gadrath's cool voice cut across her thoughts.

"An admirable demonstration," he said. "But I am afraid you will have to be more convincing if you hope to avoid the House of Correction."

Shandy looked down, but his posture did not change. Gadrath's lips curled faintly, and he turned away. "I believe you were preparing to search your prisoners," he said with exaggerated politeness to the guards. He nodded at Arelnath. "Take particular care with her. She should not have been able to resist Chaldon's power at all."

The Templemen hurried to obey, and a wave of horror swept Ranira. The moonstone! That must be what Gadrath wanted. The guards would surely find it. Ranira remembered Arelnath hanging the chain in plain sight on her belt. She did not know what would happen if the moonstone fell into the hands of the Temple of Chaldon, but it could hardly be good. She held her breath, ignoring the hands that patted at her robe, watching the group around Arelnath.

The guards finished, and one of them stepped forward to deposit their plunder in front of Gadrath. It was a small pile: Shandy's battered water bottle, Erenal's flash and knife, a few scraps of cloth, and the empty swordbelts Jaren had taken from the Templemen in Drinn. Ranira strained to see. No, the moonstone was not there. She was sure of it.

From the corner of her eye, she saw Shandy shift. She moved her head slightly to see what he was doing. The boy stood almost motionless, staring at Arelnath with a belligerent pout on his face. As Ranira watched, one grubby fist crept down and disappeared into a hole in his clothing that might once have been a pocket. Suddenly Ranira knew what Arelnath had done with the moonstone. No wonder Shandy was frightened! Between his fear of witchcraft and his fear of being caught with the stone, the boy was nearly panic-stricken.

Gadrath had finished examing the pile and was berating the guards. "Does any of this look like something capable of resisting a god?" he said scornfully. "Look again. You have missed something. No, just that one," he said as the guards started for Jaren and Ranira as well as Arelnath. "She is the only one who showed any sign of resistance."

Ranira wanted to sigh with relief, but she did not dare give any outward sign that might direct the Templemen to more fruitful areas. She kept her eyes turned away from Shandy, watching in silence as the Temple guards searched Arelnath once more. They were very thorough, but there was nothing for them to find.

At last Gadrath was forced to admit that Arelnath had no talisman which might have protected her, however briefly, from his spell. When he finished deriding his guards for their failure, he had the four travelers collected into one group. He looked at them for a moment. "Now, where is the other woman?"

"Other woman?" Arelnath said. "Aren't two enough for you?"

"You are foolish indeed to mock the High Priest of Chaldon," Gadrath said. "I mean the black-haired witch who accompanied you at the Inn of Nine Doors. Your mistress, I believe. Where is she?"

Arelnath shrugged. "She died two . . . no, three nights ago, just as Kaldarin rose."

"I do not believe you," Gadrath said. "Where is her body?"

"Why should we carry a corpse with us?" Jaren asked. "We left it in the clump of trees where we spent the night."

Gadrath smiled. He studied each of them in turn, then shook his head. "I still do not believe you. None of you have the ability to cast spells like the ones I neutralized to find you." He turned. "Guard. Send someone out to find the black-haired witch. She can't be far. She is probably heading for one of those people we stopped. She would not have gone off alone if she did not expect to find friends."

One of the guards stepped forward and bowed. "Sir, Revered Lord and Master, there are but eight of us left, and two of us are wounded. There are not enough men for a search of Karadreme Forest."

"What guards!" Gadrath said. "You cannot fight, you cannot think, and you cannot search. Very well. I will do your work once more." He clenched the pendant again and raised his other hand. Slowly he brought his arm down until it was parallel to the ground, pointing.

"That way," Gadrath said. His lips curved very slightly. "She is indeed the one I want. I can feel the spells she uses to warn herself. Take two men; that will be more than enough. Bring her back here. I will see that her spells cannot detect or harm you."

The chief of the Templemen bowed again. He turned and snapped an order. Two other guards stepped forward, and all three knelt before Gadrath. The High Priest moved a hand above them briefly. His other hand was still wrapped around the black crystal. A moment later the guards rose and left the clearing, moving rapidly in the direction Gadrath had chosen for them.

CHAPTER TWENTY-TWO

Numbly, Ranira watched the Templemen until they were out of sight. She tried to believe that they would lose their way in the forest, or that Mist would be able to hide somehow when they came near. Or perhaps Mist could reach the Trader caravan before the guards caught up with her. After all, it was midafternoon, and she had been gone since morning. Ranira glanced at Gadrath.

The High Priest stood looking after his men, his hand closed about his pendant, a confident smile on his face. After a moment, his grasp on the pendant loosened and his hand slid almost reluctantly away from it. Some trick of light made the smoky crystal seem darker than it had a moment before. It was an unpleasant reminder of the black jewels Jaren and Arelnath had smashed. Ranira's head began to swim. She looked away. As she did, she swayed and nearly fell.

"Unless you want her to bleed to death, someone had better see to that arm," Arelnath commented.

Arelnath's guard jerked at her chains to silence her, but not before Gadrath noticed the brief exchange. He turned and studied Ranira for a moment, then ordered one of the Templemen to see to her. Hands pulled the rough cloth of the pilgrim's robe away from Ranira's shoulder and placed a crude bandage over the wound, then tied Ranira's hands behind her once more. The guard seemed deliberately clumsy and the process was painful, but the pain helped Ranira's head to clear.

Gadrath watched until the guard had finished. His eyes

lingered deliberately on Ranira's unveiled face. Her hands moved automatically to hide herself, but the bonds on her wrists prevented it. Gadrath smiled. Angrily, Ranira lifted her chin and glared back at the High Priest.

"We meet again, my dear," Gadrath said at last with a mocking bow. "I must congratulate you. You are much more resourceful than I had expected."

"What do you want?" she demanded.

"There are things I need to know. You and your friends will tell me. Is that not simple?"

Arelnath snorted. Gadrath glanced at her, then looked back at Ranira. "I won't tell you anything," she said.

Gadrath smiled again. "I think you will, Chosen One. You really have no choice. And do not think to lie to me. I am High Priest now. I have powers you would not understand. I will know if you lie." Gadrath's right hand rose toward the crystal pendant. As he finished speaking, he looked down; his hand stopped moving abruptly, as if he had only just realized what he was doing. Ranira thought she saw fear move briefly across the High Priest's face before he looked up again.

"What spells has the foreign witch cast since the High Priest's death?" Gadrath asked abruptly.

"Spells?"

"There is no need to pretend," Gadrath said impatiently. "We know that the black-haired woman is a witch. What spells has she cast?"

Ranira stared at him in undisguised confusion. She had expected to be asked about Mist's purpose in Drinn, about their escape from the city, about where they were going and why, but she had not expected to be asked about magic.

Gadrath frowned, evidently misinterpreting Ranira's silence. "Will you destroy all Drinn for spite? Answer me!"

"No," Ranira said. "Why should I help you?"

"You are a child of Drinn. Surely you have felt Chaldon's restlessness these past few nights. The foreign witch's spells have disturbed him. If he is not returned to his sleep, he will make a ruin of the city." Gadrath paused, watching Ranira narrowly, then continued persuasively. "There is a place for you in Drinn, a place of honor if you will tell me what the witch has done so that I may correct it.''

For a moment, Ranira hesitated. She did not trust Gadrath, but the proposal he made was tempting. Drinn was the only home she had ever known. She looked at Arelnath in silent appeal for guidance. Arelnath raised an eyebrow and shrugged. The gesture said as clearly as words, ''This is your decision.'' For a moment, Ranira was angry. She looked back at Gadrath. He was watching her avidly. Her anger faded into cold assurance.

''I am no longer of Drinn,'' Ranira said. ''And I don't want your place of honor. I don't trust you. Even if I could, I wouldn't tell you anything.''

''Well struck, little sister,'' Jaren whispered.

Gadrath's face stiffened. ''You are of Drinn whether you know it or not, and when Chaldon wakes, you will share Drinn's fate! Think on that, and tell me—what has the witch done?''

''I don't believe you!'' Ranira cried. ''You don't care about Drinn. You're just afraid of what will happen to you if Chaldon wakes.''

''I see I must be more convincing. Chaldon is restless; perhaps a Bride would quiet him. After all, Midwinter Festival is not yet over, and I am High Priest. Shall I complete the rituals now, Chosen One?''

''No!''

''Then you had best tell me what I wish to know, or you will resume your exalted position at once.'' Gadrath's smile was cold and contemptuous. ''Do you understand, my dear?''

Ranira froze. She felt trapped and helpless, as she had when Gadrath first spoke to her in the marketplace; when he named her Bride of Chaldon in the inn; when he visited her in the House of Correction. Her head swam, and her shoulder throbbed painfully as she tried to think of some way out. Her shoulder . . . ?

''But the Bride of Chaldon must have an unmarred body. You told me that yourself. I am no longer unmarred,'' she said, indicating her injured shoulder.

Gadrath's face twisted in frustrated rage. Ranira went weak with relief. She had not been sure Gadrath would accept her reasoning; he might have gone through with the ritual in spite of her wounded shoulder. Her relief, though, was short-lived. Gadrath's eyes narrowed. "For yourself, you are correct, my dear. These others, however, will make a suitable enough sacrifice to Chaldon, and with his aid I can easily learn what I wish to know. Yes, that will be much easier."

The High Priest turned and began giving orders to the Templemen. Several of them bowed and left the clearing. Gadrath turned back to the prisoners. "The preparations will take some time, I fear. Make yourselves comfortable for what little time remains to you."

Shandy whimpered. Gadrath turned away, still smiling coldly. Arelnath and Jaren exchanged glances, then sat down on the ground. After a moment, Ranira joined them. In silence, they watched the Templemen make ready for the sacrifice.

The guards who had left the clearing returned carrying armloads of wood. Under Gadrath's direction, they built a large mound at one side of the clearing. When he was satisfied with their work, he sent them off again in search of more wood. Soon a second mound was growing beside the first. The work went more slowly as the afternoon wore on and the guards had to go farther from the clearing in search of wood. Some of them started a small fire of their own for warmth and as a source for the larger fires to come. Daylight was fading when Gadrath at last strolled over to the small, silent group of prisoners. "You have very little time left," he said. "But perhaps you have reconsidered?"

Ranira looked at Arelnath. She did not think she could stand to see those she cared for burned alive—not again. But Arelnath and Jaren were shaking their heads. "Our oath is given," Jaren said.

Gadrath's lip curled. He looked at Ranira. Reluctantly, she too shook her head. If Arelnath and Jaren were willing to go to the flames rather than tell Gadrath what he wished to know, she could not betray them. At least Mist was not here to die with them.

"Such short-sightedness!" Gadrath said mockingly. "But

perhaps you do not realize what you are facing. An example might do you good. We shall take the boy first, as soon as the fire has begun to burn well. Think on it.''

He turned abruptly away. Ranira stared after him in horror. Not Shandy! She could feel him trembling behind her. This must be far worse than his worst nightmares of capture by the Templemen. It was certainly worse than anything Ranira had anticipated. Another thought struck her—Shandy had the moonstone! And he had no love for the foreigners. If he gave Gadrath the moonstone in exchange for his life . . .

The guards were crowded around the first mound of wood. One of them plucked a burning branch from the smaller fire and thrust it into the center of the unlit pile. The wood caught quickly, and two of the Templemen started back toward the prisoners. Ranira's stomach knotted, but before the guards reached them Gadrath raised a hand. ''Wait.''

For an instant, Ranira thought that this was one more of Gadrath's tricks. Then she heard the sounds of someone approaching. A moment later, two Templemen appeared, dragging Mist between them. A third guard followed. The Templemen around Ranira grinned and called noisy congratulations as their fellows joined them around the fire. For the moment, the sacrifice was forgotten. Ranira was stunned. Despite Gadrath's confidence, she had not really expected Mist to be caught. Now her last hope was gone.

The Temple guards fell silent as Gadrath came forward. ''Well done!'' the High Priest said to Mist's captors. ''You had no difficulty, I see.''

''None, Highest Born,'' the chief of the guards replied. ''She did not even see us until we took hold of her.''

''Excellent.'' Gadrath smiled. ''And did you discover where she was going?''

''She would not tell us, Highest Born,'' the guard said. ''However, there are not many possibilities. There is a woodcutter's hut not far from where we found her, and Cirraq's troop stopped a Trader caravan in that part of the forest yesterday.''

Gadrath considered the Templeman's words. The High Priest turned to one of the guards. ''Go to Cirraq at once. Tell him to burn the caravan. Arrest the Traders and take them to

Drinn. Do the same for the woodcutter, just in case."

"At once, Highest Born." The guard bowed and left.

The High Priest turned back to Mist. "I do not believe we have met. I am Gadrath, High Priest of Chaldon."

A slight nod was Mist's only response. Gadrath eyed her narrowly for a moment. "You have been very clever, but as you see, your plan has failed," he said. "You will now explain to me why you are trying to destroy Drinn."

"I am not attempting to destroy Drinn," Mist said in a low, steady voice. "You have an exaggerated idea of my abilities if you believe I could."

"I have explained to you that your plans are known," Gadrath said. "If you do not tell me how you are casting your spells, I will have to take other action. I have heard that when a witch dies, her spells die too. We can test the tale easily if you continue in your obstinacy."

"I have told you the truth," Mist replied. "I do not know what spells you refer to, but they are not of my making."

"You take me for a fool!" Gadrath said. "Or you do not understand. A painful death is the least of what I can do." His hand rose slowly and deliberately toward the crystal pendant, but stopped just short of touching it. The crystal was almost dead-black in the dying light. Ranira shuddered.

Mist whitened, but her voice was steady. "Do not deceive yourself. You have no power over me."

"You lie." Gadrath's eyes burned. "I have more power than any High Priest of Drinn has ever had, for I dare to use it. Do not think I am hampered by the stupid customs my predecessor was too afraid to break; my very presence here should tell you that. No other High Priest in the history of Drinn has sent men out of the city during Midwinter Festival, much less left the city himself. I sent guardsmen after you as soon as I was confirmed as High Priest, and I am here to deal with you myself. Stop your pretense and tell me: What have you done that so disturbs Chaldon's rest?"

Mist's eyes went wide. She straightened and seemed to grow taller. The guards beside her shifted, and their hands went to their swordhilts. Even Gadrath fell back a step. Mist ignored them all, except Gadrath. "You fool," she said in a flat voice. "You utter, incompetent fool."

Gadrath's eyes widened. Obviously, no one had ever dared to call the High Priest a fool. He opened his mouth to reply, but Mist cut him off. "Do you know what you have done, with your pride in your power and daring?" she demanded. "You have all but released one of the most deadly plagues of Lyra!"

"I?" Gadrath seemed to have forgotten that Mist was his prisoner; he spoke as to an equal. "But your spells are . . ."

"You know nothing of magic," Mist said with angry scorn. "Your 'god' is not at rest. He is bound—bound by the power of the traditions you so despise. Your Temple has repeated the same rites for hundreds of years, and they have become part of the pattern of Chaldon's binding. You are right to fear. You yourself have weakened the spell. It cannot hold for much longer."

"If I know nothing of magic, you know nothing of Drinn!" Gadrath sneered, but his voice held a note of uncertainty. "How could you know what purpose our rituals serve?"

"I have felt the spells that hold Chaldon," Mist said. "And Ranira has told me of your customs and rituals. I have studied magic for years, and I know how such things work. It does not matter whether you believe me or not; you will learn the truth soon enough when Chaldon frees himself."

"Your ignorance betrays you," Gadrath said with more confidence. "The rituals of the Temple are not broken. I have left a substitute to conduct the rites in my place."

"Do you think there is no reason why people are forbidden to leave Drinn during your festival?" Mist replied. "You sent guards to search for us, and you, the High Priest of the Temple, have left Drinn willingly. That is the flaw in the pattern. Do not think Chaldon cannot find it."

Gadrath's face was ashen. "You left the city before ever I did. If anyone broke this pattern, it was you."

"We left in spite of all you could do to hold us," Mist said. "But Chaldon's binding could not be seriously weakened by that. It was you who opened the gates and more—as the official representative of the Temple, you ordered men out of Drinn, deliberately breaking the tradition you should have been striving to maintain. Even that might not have been enough, but you left the city yourself, and that has shattered the pattern beyond anything you can do to repair it.''

Gadrath stared at Mist. His lips tightened briefly. His eyes glittered. ''We shall see. Chaldon has always responded well to sacrifice, particularly a powerful sacrifice. How will he receive a foreign witch, I wonder?''

Gadrath raised his right hand and closed it deliberately over the pendant. A shadow crossed his face as he held out his left hand, palm downward. Blackness began to form below it, swirling and thickening rapidly into a long, flat slab like the lid of a coffin. He stared at it for a moment, then lowered his left hand. At the same time, the fingers of his right hand opened. But the hand did not fall to his side. It hung at his breast, as if stuck to the pendant. Gadrath's mouth twitched; he jerked his hand downward. Ranira thought she saw blood on his palm as he turned toward Mist and gestured.

''Bind her to the stone,'' he said to the Templemen beside her.

CHAPTER TWENTY-THREE

Ranira saw Arelnath tense as the Templemen started forward. Before the Cilhar woman could move, the guards stopped. With their first step the last daylight had vanished with the abruptness of a shutter closing. The flickering red fire and the bright points of the stars above the clearing were the only sources of light left. The entire clearing was plunged into darkness. Except around Mist. Daylight seemed to linger about her, intensifying the impression of power that her regal bearing gave. The Templemen did not retreat before her, but neither did they continue advancing.

"Bind her!" Gadrath's voice rose above the startled murmurs of his guards. "Her spells cannot harm you while I am here. Bind . . ."

The priest's voice choked, trailing off in a bubbling gurgle. Ranira's head turned, and she gasped in horror. Gadrath stood frozen, the crystal pendant on his breast pulsing with darkness. His face writhed. Around his body swirled a blackness so intense that it hurt the mind to look at it. It was rising up from the black slab he had conjured.

The Temple guards retreated. "Witchcraft!" one of them cried, pointing at Mist. "Kill her," said another. One of the guards started forward again, sword in hand. Before he reached Mist, a dark figure leaped onto his back, throwing him to the ground. Simultaneously, one of the other Templemen fell backwards, choking and clawing at a short chain that had dropped over his head and pulled tight. The Temple guards had forgotten their other prisoners in their anxiety to be rid of Mist, and Jaren and Arelnath had taken advantage of their lapse.

The other Templemen wavered and fell back. A loud shriek from Gadrath completed their confusion. Templemen began running in all directions, some with drawn swords, looking for enemies, others without weapons, looking for a place to flee. Ranira tripped one and kicked another; there was little else she could do with her hands tied. Suddenly, the area in front of her was free of guards and she found herself with an unobstructed view of Mist and Gadrath once more.

Mist stood as if unaware of the chaos about her, her lips moving in a low chant that seemed somehow familiar to Ranira. In front of her, Gadrath still stumbled and shook, moving blindly first in one direction, then in another, mumbling to himself as he went. He strained as if he were fighting with something only he could see. The black slab was completely gone, melted into the air around him. Gadrath stumbled closer, and Ranira backed away. Then he looked directly at her. Ranira screamed.

They were not eyes that looked out of Gadrath's face at Ranira; two ovals of solid blackness glared blankly from under the High Priest's eyebrows. The words he muttered became clearer: " . . . eat you. I will. Down, slave! You thought to use me. Now you will learn." The voice was far deeper than Gadrath's own.

A convulsive shudder passed through Gadrath, and a pair of ordinary grey eyes stared into Ranira's for an instant. Then the priest cried, "Not me. The girl, your Bride—take her! Not me!"

A second convulsion shook Gadrath. He made a motion, as if throwing something with both arms, and blackness flowed toward Ranira. She had time to scream only once.

Then darkness swallowed her, cutting her off from all sensation. For a moment, she was aware of something reaching for her. Then even that faded. She could not see or hear; she could not even feel her own body. In utter panic, she struggled against the blackness that was crushing her. She did not move, could not move, but something in the very attempt made the blackness give way a little. She tried again to push the blackness away. The darkness retreated—she was learning how to resist the cold weight in her mind. It was a matter of determination, and six years as Lykken's bond servant had fully developed Ranira's stubbornness. Once more she tried to break free. She felt something snap, and suddenly she could see. She tried to move, but discovered that she was not completely free. She had no control over her arms or legs; she was a passenger in her own body.

Gadrath lay crumpled on the ground before her. Mist still stood apart, chanting. Ranira heard a distorted version of her own voice saying, "Struggle as you will. You are not strong enough to escape me." Her arms moved without her willing it. The ropes about her wrists parted under a strain far greater than Ranira alone could ever have exerted. *You see? I can do far more with even this feeble body than you. But struggle on; it only makes the victory more enjoyable.* She saw her arm rise and point toward Mist. She tried to scream a warning through the scornful laughter that poured from her own mouth. She could not do it.

Desperately, Ranira lashed out. She felt the pain of her wounded shoulder and saw her arm waver. The bolt of blackness that shot from her fingertips went past Mist's shoulder, missing by inches. The healer's chanting never faltered, but the shadow in Ranira's mind howled in rage and turned on her.

Sight vanished. Hearing stopped. She felt herself growing weaker as the darkness pressed closer, eating at the edges of her mind. She fought back, and the shadow withdrew for a moment. She had a glimpse of Shandy running toward her, arm raised, and then the darkness closed in again. With all her strength, Ranira struck again. Something was flying toward her, glittering in the firelight. Her vision failed before the object reached her. She was forced back, swallowed into darkness.

Without warning, white fire engulfed her. She felt no pain, but the darkness cringed and suddenly was gone, leaving her in control of herself once more. She looked down. Clenched tightly in her hands, the chain twining about her fingers, was Mist's necklace and the moonstone.

Shandy was beside her. "Renra, did it work? Are you all

right? I know it's magic, but I couldn't think of anything else!''

Ranira had no time to reassure him. Just as she looked up, light flared through the clearing. She squinted an instant too late; her eyes were blinded by a dazzling brightness that seemed crowded with faces. As her eyes adjusted, her fingers tightened involuntarily on the moonstone.

In front of her, barely three paces away, a black smudge stood outlined against the brightness. It was hardly recognizable as Gadrath. Darkness swirled around it, making it impossible for her to see the details of his form. She sucked her breath in and shoved Shandy behind her, holding out the moonstone.

Light shifted and flowed in front of her. Mist stood at the center of the glow, her garments whipping about her as if she stood in a strong wind. The healer raised her hands, and figures began to form around her, faint outlines sketched in white flame. They wavered and grew brighter as Ranira watched, and the light intensified until Mist stood at the center of a ring of white fire, forcing the shadow backward. Ranira's eyes met Mist's, and suddenly she understood: Mist had reached the Island of the Moon at last; the flaming shapes could only be images of the people Mist had been trying to contact for so long.

The shadowy horror that was Gadrath gestured, and a wall of blackness swept toward Mist. Lightning flared from Mist's outstretched hand. The blackness dissolved into a whirling mass of shadow shot with light and webbed with power, hovering in the air between the healer and the priest. Ranira's skin began to tingle. She backed up a pace.

A pale green light washed over the clearing: Elewyth had risen. The shadow withdrew into itself, forming a tall, dense pillar of darkness. Mist moved toward it, almost reluctantly, and Ranira remembered the healer's aversion to killing.

More lightning flashed around the shadow, without apparent effect. It seemed to be waiting, content to resist without striking back. Ranira stared in puzzlement as Mist struck again. Why should the shade wait? Abruptly, Gadrath's voice came back to her, and her eyes widened in horror.

The Temple of Chaldon! Gadrath had left someone behind

to conduct the rituals, and one of the rituals was designed to join the power of all of the people of Drinn and channel it through the Shadow-born to destroy the Island of the Moon. That was what the shadow waited for. Ranira had no doubt that it was already too strong for the Temple priests to control; whatever power it could draw from Drinn it would use for its own purposes.

Ranira opened her mouth to shout, but it was already too late. Red light bloomed in the clearing as Kaldarin rose, and she remembered that Mist had said Kaldarin strengthened the Shadow-born. The shadow swelled under the crimson glow; even Ranira could feel the surge of power. Mist fell back. The flaming shapes around her vanished. Darkness flowed out from the shadow, engulfing Ranira once more.

Cruel laughter echoed around her. Her eyes strained against the darkness. She put out a hand, but there was nothing to touch or see. An odor of decay reached her, something foul brushed her hand, and she recoiled from its touch. Something sucked at her mind. Terrified, Ranira pulled away. The suction grew stronger.

In desperation, she called on the magic she knew she possessed. She felt new strength rise within her and the warmth that heralded the beginning of the flames. Better to burn than be eaten, she thought fleetingly, and concentrated harder.

"That won't save you, little fool," a deep voice hissed near her ear. "You will come to me in the end, like the rest of Drinn, and your friends as well. Indeed, you are already half mine. Tell me, should I take the boy first, or the black-haired witch?"

Anger exploded in Ranira. Flames roared around her, but she did not care. She struck at the darkness with all the power she possessed. The only response was scornful laughter as the darkness pressed closer. In utter fury, she grasped at the flames around her and threw them at the shadow. She felt the thing draw back. With a surge of triumph, she seized more of the magic fire and threw it, drawing recklessly on her power.

For what seemed an eternity, Ranira hurled her fire into darkness. In her desire to hurt the shadow, she ignored her own pain. She was too angry to be afraid.

Then the flames began to die. Soon they were a mere flickering around her. The darkness began to close in on her again.

She tried desperately to call up her power again, to bring back the flames that were her only weapon, but nothing happened; her strength and her resources were all but exhausted. Then, as the shadow came closer, she remembered that she still held the moonstone, and she extended it like a shield between herself and the darkness.

Power coiled within the stone. Thanks to her new sensitivity to magic, Ranira could feel it. She reached for it as she had reached for the flames, but it eluded her. The last of her own fire died. She clenched her fingers around the stone, willing it to do something—anything. Sudden power flowed into her, and with a gasp of relief she struck out at the shadows once more.

The darkness drew back, but even as she struck, Ranira knew that she still did not have enough strength to seriously harm the dark thing. She lacked the skill and the knowledge necessary to use the power of the moonstone effectively. She could hold the shadow back for a little, that was all.

Abruptly, the shadow struck back. The blow drove her to her knees. It took all her power to keep from being swallowed at once. The pressure increased. Ranira was forced back, into herself, fighting all the while to maintain her precarious link to the power of the moonstone. She felt, rather than heard, the shadow's laughter, and she strained to draw more power from the moonstone. The bond between her and the stone was not strong enough to carry the power she needed. Desperately, she tried to widen the channel, to use all of the power of the moonstone.

There was a moment of swift disorientation, then Ranira's head cleared. Power ran through her like a high wind, clean and strong. It was too much for her to hold or control. It spilled out of her, blowing away the last traces of her fear of magic and driving the shadow back. She was briefly conscious of a large, pillared room, and an immense white stone that shimmered with power, and a damp smell of salt. Then she was back in the clearing, the darkness retreating in front of her.

Ranira began shaping her power for another blow at the shadow, then paused. She could see Mist standing at the edge of the darkness. The flaming outlines of the island witches were forming around the healer once more. Ranira felt more power spilling out of herself, and still she hesitated.

The shadow ceased its retreat. It hung in the air, growing darker and denser as Ranira watched. Light pulsed around it as Mist renewed her attack, but nothing seemed to harm it. Ranira's skin began to tingle again. She felt something pulling at her weakly and unpleasantly, groping for power. The sensation was vaguely familiar. Suddenly she realized what was happening: The Temple rites were still in progress in Drinn, and the shadow was drawing on them to replenish its power. Mist and the fiery shapes around her could barely hold it now; they would be utterly unable to contain it once its strength was renewed. Ranira thought of trying to join them, but even as she did, Arelnath's voice echoed in her mind. "That much power would burn out whoever was the focus." With no knowledge of magic, how could she guess what effect her impulse might have on Mist? And if Mist were destroyed, who could fight the shadow?

Ranira felt the tugging again, and recoiled in disgust. Somehow, she was still open to the command of the rituals, even though Mist had removed the Temple bindings from her mind. She could sense the power feeding the shadow in front of her, and knew that soon it would be ready to attack again. If she wished, she knew she could join the people of Drinn. The idea shamed her, but it would not go away. Her eyesight blurred, and once again she saw the room and the white stone, and felt the shadow draw back from the barest touch of the power she held.

The vision faded. Her eyes came back into focus just as the shadow began to move again. Ranira had an instant to wonder if her idea would work; then she took a deep breath, shuddered, and gave in to the insistent tugging of the mass of power that was the union of the people of Drinn.

Greedy fingers twisted into her mind, searching. The power that flowed around her was blotted up and whirled away. The fingers probed more deeply, seeking more power for the insatiable darkness behind them. Ranira felt as if she

were being pulled apart. A confused jumble of images
flashed before her: the Temple of Chaldon towering in smoky
torchlight; Mist and seven white-robed strangers facing a
shadowy form; the white stone shining with a blinding silver
light.

The image of the stone grew and brightened, absorbing the
other pictures. Power howled through Ranira, clean and
silver-bright and fresh as sea wind. It flooded the channel that
fed the shadow. She saw a brief picture of a thousand faces
looking at each other in wonder, the Temple rituals forgotten.
In the same breath, she heard an unearthly scream of agony,
and the fusion was smashed into a thousand pieces.

Something huge and dark rushed past Ranira, pursued
by shining forms. One of them reached out to her, and once
again power swept through her. An image of darkness surrounded by a web of pale blue light rose before her. She saw
the shadow withdraw into the heart of it. She heard a shout of
triumph from the pursuers and felt power run through her,
feeding the web of light until it shone bright silver instead of
blue. Then the vision faded, and the shining forms vanished,
and the power itself died, and the darkness around her was
only night.

CHAPTER TWENTY-FOUR

Ranira heaved a shaky sigh and looked around. Gadrath's body lay in front of her, crumpled and shrunken. She could see no trace of the crystal pendant the High Priest had worn. Beside the body stood Mist; the light and the flaming figures had vanished from around her, and she stood with her head bowed, one hand groping for the necklace she was not wearing. Ranira stepped forward and held out the moonstone.

The healer did not look up. "Mist?"

Finally Mist's head turned. The expression of sadness and regret on her face lightened as she saw the white stone. "Thank you," she said as she hung it around her neck once more. Her eyes returned to Gadrath's body.

"Stop thinking about him, Mist." Arelnath's voice came out of the darkness behind Ranira. "His death was necessary, and from what I saw of him, he isn't worth your grief."

"I know," Mist said quietly. "He was corrupt, and he would have spread his corruption like a disease. Even without the Shadow-born to consider, he is better dead. But no one deserves such a death as that."

"Such a death as what?" Arelnath asked. She stepped forward and stooped to examine the body as she spoke. "Didn't you kill him in the fight?"

Mist shook her head. "The Shadow-born took him. To be possessed by a Shadow-born is to dwindle into nothingness. I think the shadow has been eating at him for years, or he would not look so shrunken."

"As long as the Shadow-born is dead as well, it does not

worry me," Arelnath said. She looked up when Mist did not reply, then rose abruptly to her feet. "The Shadow-born *is* dead, isn't he?"

"How can something die that has no body? But be content; it is safely bound once more. Even if the Temple of Chaldon continues its rituals, I do not think Chaldon will be powerful enough to work any harm for a long time."

"Why not?" Arelnath asked skeptically.

"It has been too badly hurt," Mist replied. "Even if it can still draw strength from the Temple rituals, the Shadow-born will take a long time to regain its strength. Also, we were able to strengthen the old binding-spell when the Shadow-born fled back to it. It was still partly bound, you see, so the only way it could escape was to retreat into the spell to hide."

"If that was a partly bound Shadow-born, I hope I never meet one that's free," Jaren said from the darkness behind Arelnath. He limped forward. "Is there any reason why you are standing here in the cold, when there is a perfectly good fire a few steps away?"

Mist gave him a bewildered look. Arelnath laughed. "You're right. Come, Mist. It will do you good."

"But aren't there still Templemen around?" Ranira asked.

Jaren grinned. "Do you think we were idle while Mist was busy with her spells? They will not be back, or else they will never leave." He waved a hand toward five crumpled lumps near the edge of the clearing, barely visible in the firelight.

Ranira looked from Jaren to Arelnath in awe. "You killed five Temple guards? You didn't even have weapons!"

Arelnath shrugged. "We are trained for such things. And two of them were already wounded."

"Besides, they were more afraid of the sorcery behind them than they were of us," Jaren said. He smiled. "It is a common mistake, but it ruined their concentration. We were finished with them long before you were done with the priest." He gestured toward Gadrath's body. "Now, shall we get warm?" He started toward the fire; Mist and Arelnath followed. Shandy appeared out of the night and seated himself next to them, but Ranira stayed where she was, looking down at Gadrath's body.

Suddenly, she felt exhausted, though a moment before she

had not been tired at all. The battle had driven home the truths she had been trying not to face. She *was* a witch. Her power had helped to bring down the Shadow-born, and she could not be sorry. Her fear of magic was gone, but it had left only emptiness behind . . . What was she going to do now?

Ranira turned away and walked slowly to the fire. Arelnath motioned her to an open place across from Mist. Ranira collapsed gratefully to the ground. Jaren smiled and stretched his legs toward the fire.

"Now, Mist," he said. "What exactly were you doing while Arelnath and I were killing Templemen?"

Mist winced. "Must you be so casual about it?"

"They were trying to kill me. Don't expect me to grieve for them." After a moment, the healer nodded and Jaren went on, "Now, about this Shadow-born. How did you manage to kill it or bind it or whatever you did to it?"

Mist shook her head. "It is difficult to explain," she said. "The power of the Third Moon is so opposed to the power of a Shadow-born that even in small amounts it is painful for a Shadow-born to come in contact with it. My necklace was not large, but when Shandy threw it at Ranira, the shock made the Shadow-born lose its hold on her—and on the barrier around the Empire of Chaldreth. Once the barrier was down, I was able to reach the Temple of the Third Moon." Mist smiled at Shandy. "I think that throw saved more than Ranira from Chaldon."

Shandy shifted uncomfortably, but did not speak. Arelnath frowned. "Ranira used the moonstone against the Shadow-born? I thought that required training. Ranira must have even more ability than we had suspected."

Ranira looked up from the fire. "I was desperate," she said. "If Chaldon hadn't pushed me so hard, I would never even have tried to use the moonstone. I was too scared to worry about whether I was doing the right thing or not."

Mist smiled. "The Shadow-born knew that you come from Drinn. It did not expect you to be able to do anything with the moonstone. It was more afraid that you would throw it to me so the rest of the Temple of the Third Moon could work through it. It was a shock to Chaldon when you began to use the stone."

"But Ranira has used the moonstone before, I think," Arelnath put in. She turned toward Ranira. "You found it in your hand after the Temple of Chaldon attacked the second time, when the High Priest died. Remember?"

Mist looked at Arelnath in surprise. "I had not thought of that, but you may be right." She glanced thoughtfully at Ranira. "We must discuss this more later on."

Ranira nodded without much enthusiasm. She was trying to accept the implications of Mist's words. "You mean I could have given you the moonstone, and you could have used it against Chaldon?" she said finally. "I didn't even think of that!"

"It is as well that you did not," Mist said. "I could have used the power of the moonstone, but not as you did. The stone would have been an advantage, but the battle would have been long and the outcome uncertain."

"Why?" asked Ranira. "You know more about magic than I do."

"No one on the Island of the Moon could have touched the Shadow-born directly; he was guarding too closely against us. You are of Drinn; there is still a bond between you and the Temple of Chaldon. You fed the power of the Third Moon into the Temple rituals, and the Shadow-born was drawing so heavily on them for power that it took in the full power of the Third Moon before it even realized what was happening. The Shadow-born had to break its link with Drinn to avoid being hurt even more, and it was weakened enough that we could force it back into the binding."

"I don't want the Temple of Chaldon to be able to do things to me!" Ranira said. "I don't want to be a part of their rituals, even if it turned out well this time."

"Understandable," Jaren said dryly. He looked at Mist. "Is it likely to be a problem?"

Mist shook her head. "No. The Temple of Chaldon will be in no condition to perform rituals for days, possibly longer. By that time, we should be out of the Empire of Chaldreth and beyond the reach of any magic they can cast now that Chaldon is bound once more."

"What do you mean, the Temple is in no condition for rituals?" Arelnath demanded.

"When the power of the Third Moon hit the Shadow-born, the priests in the Temple felt its pain as much as it did. I would be surprised if any of them will be well enough to return to their rituals for several days."

"And the Temple guards . . . ?" Jaren asked in an odd voice.

". . . will be in the same condition, I think," Mist said. "The more involved they were with the Temple of Chaldon, the more heavily they would feel its collapse."

"And Gadrath probably brought the guards he trusted most to Karadreme Forest," Jaren said absently. Tension left him, obvious only in its passing.

Arelnath looked at him in puzzlement.

"Venran's caravan," Jaren explained. "Gadrath ordered his men to burn it. However, if Mist is right, the Templemen will be in no shape to burn anything. We should know soon enough; Venran should be here in a little while if he still has his wagons."

Mist sat with her head tilted to one side, as if she were listening to something far away. "There is no need to worry," she said after a moment. "Venran will be here soon."

"Then we can wait by the fire until he arrives," Jaren said with satisfaction. Arelnath shook her head, but did not say anything. Jaren leaned back with a sigh. "And what are *your* plans, Ranira?" he asked. "It seems you are free of your Temple at last."

"I don't know," she replied. She felt confused, and a little depressed, and she did not know why. "I don't know anything about places outside of Drinn, and all I can do is kitchen work. Do you think Venran will need a kitchen girl?"

"You need not work for Venran unless you choose," Mist said. "If you wish to travel with the caravan, it is your choice. But I hope you will come to the Island of the Moon for training. After the help you have given us, we owe you that. You already know that you have ability, and we would welcome you."

Ranira's head spun. She started to answer Mist, then her eye fell on Shandy. The boy was curled into a miserable ball, watching her. When their eyes met his flinched away.

"Shandy!" Ranira said, surprised. "What is the matter?"

"You really are a . . . witch," he said uncertainly. "There was fire and light and everything, *all over you!* I didn't know that rock would do that. I wouldn't have thrown it at you if I knew."

"But it kept Chaldon from eating me," Ranira said, considerably taken aback by Shandy's words. "Weren't you listening? And Mist has been saying I'm a witch—for days! Why should it only bother you now?"

"You don't act like a witch," Shandy said. "And you never did anything like that before. But now you're going off with Mist and take *lessons!*"

"Is it so bad to be a witch?" Mist asked gently. "Ranira has not changed, after all."

"But I don't *like* magic!" Shandy wailed.

"Neither do I," Jaren said cheerfully. "What has that got to do with it?"

"You don't like magic?" Shandy was startled out of his distress. "Then how come you go around with witches?"

"Mist is my friend," Jaren said. Shandy looked at him, considering.

Ranira turned back to Mist. "What is Shandy going to do if I come to your island?" she asked. "He doesn't know any more about the world outside Drinn than I do."

"He will be welcome too, as my friend and yours," Mist said. "He does not have to learn magic; we teach many other things on the island."

"Shandy would not be happy among so many sorcerers," Jaren said firmly. He looked at Arelnath, who nodded once. "His talents lie in other areas. I think he would make an excellent mercenary, if he cares to work that hard. Would you be willing to come with me and Arelnath as an apprentice?"

Shandy's face brightened, then clouded. He looked at Ranira uncertainly. "Will I still get to see Renra?"

"If Ranira goes with Mist, there is no doubt of it," Arelnath said. "We are oath-bound to the Island of the Moon. Therefore we spend a great deal of time there."

Ranira and Shandy looked at each other. "I guess so," Shandy muttered after a moment, but his eyes were shining.

Ranira breathed a sigh of relief; she had not realized how worried she had been about Shandy's future. Now there was only her own to consider. She looked at Mist.

"I will come," Ranira said after a moment. "How will I ever know whether I really don't want to be a witch if I don't try?"

Mist smiled and started to reply, but she was interrupted by a shout from the forest. Startled, Ranira turned. A string of glowing lights was winding through the trees toward the clearing. She could almost make out the square shapes of the wagons.

"The caravan!" Arelnath exclaimed. She jumped up and sent an answering shout into the woods, then turned. "Come on. We'll probably have to argue prices with Venran before he gives us dinner. And I'm hungry."

"You and Mist can make the arrangements," Jaren said, climbing to his feet. "I'm sure he'll allow the rest of us to eat in the meantime."

"You aren't getting out of it that easily," Arelnath said. They started toward the lights, arguing amicably, with Shandy in their wake. Mist rose and looked at Ranira. "Coming?"

Ranira nodded and stood up. There was a sudden commotion ahead; Shandy had evidently decided to join Jaren's side of the argument, as noisily as possible. Mist shook her head and started toward them. Smiling, Ranira followed.

ABOUT THE AUTHOR . . . .

Patricia C. Wrede was born on March 27, 1953. Her parents were sufficiently pleased with the results that she soon (taking the grand view; taking a cosmological one, better than instantly) had three sisters and a brother. Then she went to Carleton College (so we skip a few details; big deal) and, while ever intending to become a writer of fantasy, pursued a B.A. in biology, obtained it, and snatched an M.A. in business administration from the University of Minnesota.

Now she lives in Minneapolis with a husband acquired about the time of the B.A., and works as a financial analyst. When she is not writing or involved in the daily affairs of life, she plays guitar, sews and embroiders, and makes desultory attempts at gardening. Though she is one of the few writers of fantasy who has no cat, she likes other people's pets, and they like her—without even knowing that she's a vegetarian.

CAUGHT IN CRYSTAL

A Lyra Novel

Patricia C. Wrede

The Crystal holds a secret, a forgotten tale of dark magic . . .

After the Wars of Binding ended, the four races of Lyra – the catlike Wyrds, the shimmering, sea-dwelling Neira, the proud, pale Shee and the humans – went their separate ways. A millennium has passed since then, but the Wars have filled most humans with a deep mistrust of sorcery, and the Elders have banished its practice from their lands.

But in the Windhome Mountains an ancient evil is stirring, as the Wizards' spells which hold it there, locked into a perfect Crystal, are weakening. And so the Sorceresses of the Sisterhood of Stars have to find a warrior from their kind who can fight the evil in the Twisted Tower. Thus Kayl, whose sword has remained hidden beneath the hearth at her inn for many years, finds a Sorceress and Wizard on her doorstep, demanding she returns to the deadly trade of her youth. And, knowing that past debts have to be repaid, she cannot refuse them.

FUTURA PUBLICATIONS
AN ORBIT BOOK
FANTASY
0 7088 8313 3